LITTLE THINGS

A NOVEL

AMY FILLION

D1453059

ALSO BY AMY FILLION

Adult Novels

Grace and Ally

Secrets of Spaulding Lane: Nancy

Secrets of Spaulding Lane: Marni

Secrets of Spaulding Lane: Rose

Broken and Breaking Free

Children's Books

Fairville: Room of Reveries Book 1

FenneGig: Room of Reveries Book 2

Esmerelda and the Courageous Knight: Room of Reveries Book 3

Wonderwell: Room of Reveries Book 4

SkyTopia: Room of Reveries Book 5

The Ancient Curse: Room of Reveries Book 6

A Magical Farewell: Room of Reveries Book 7

CHAPTER ONE

Sam

Sam groggily rolled onto his back in bed, having just woken on a crisp Saturday morning in October. He reached for Annie, but she wasn't there. Odd. Annie almost always slept in on the weekends.

He sat up, rubbed the sleep from his eyes. Nine-year-old Hannah was sure to be awake, probably toasting some waffles for breakfast that she'd have with immense amounts of syrup that would dribble onto the kitchen table and that she'd fail to clean before it began to solidify. Ben was probably still sleeping. He did this more often on the weekends now that he was thirteen.

Sam pushed the blankets over his legs, touched his bare feet to the wooden floor, and brought his arms into the air for a morning stretch. The smell of coffee permeated the air.

Yawning, he trudged down the hall and worked his way downstairs. He found his daughter at the kitchen table as suspected and saw that his wife was at the counter making a packed lunch as the coffeepot was brewing. She was dressed in a deep orange corduroy skirt with brown tights and a tight brown sweater. Work clothes.

"Babe," Sam said as he approached Annie. "What are you doing?"

"Getting ready for work." Annie placed spinach in a large circular Tupperware bowl and added feta cheese. "You should probably wake Ben. He'll be late for school. And why aren't you dressed? This isn't your day off." Annie looked up at her husband with a frown.

"Annie," Sam said with a smirk, "it's Saturday. No kindergarten kids for you. No work for me. No school for the kids." He chuckled at the situation presented before him. "Today's the Halloween party. I'm surprised you'd forget about that. One of your favorite times of the year."

"No," Annie insisted. "I've got to get to work."

"Babe, look at me." Sam touched his wife's shoulders and turned her around to face him. "It's Saturday."

Annie shook her head. "No."

Sam took the container of cheese out of his wife's hand and laid it on the counter. Gently grasping her wrist, he led her to the basement door, where their dry-erase board was situated at its center, the days filled to the brim with work, school, kids' extracurricular activities, and appointments.

"See?" he said as he pointed the day out. "Yesterday was Friday. You said your kindergarten kids were 'unruly.' Your word. You said they were too excited for Halloween next week and were getting antsy." He looked at his wife with a smile. "It's Saturday."

"Oh." Annie scrunched her nose as she looked at the blue and black, red and orange markings on their family calendar. "Hmm."

"Little confused today, are we?" Sam teased.

"Well," Annie said, "I suppose I am." She looked into the green eyes of her husband, smiled, then walked back to the kitchen counter. "I guess I don't need this anymore, do I?" She placed the lid on her Tupperware and brought it to the refrigerator, where it would rest until Monday morning when she left to work at the local elementary school.

"I'm going to change," she announced after she cleaned up after herself. "I don't need to be in these tights. I might as well put my pj's back on and plop my butt on the couch with my coffee now that I can. Ben can sleep in, and then we'll get ready for the party. I need to do some baking. Funny that I got my days all mixed up."

"I'll pour you a cup."

"Thanks," Annie said as she turned the corner to ascend the stairs.

"Grammie's here!" Sam heard Annie call to their children in the living room from the front door. "Want to go meet her outside, see if she needs any help with the food she's bringing along?"

"Sure." Hannah appeared by her side, vampire teeth touching her bottom lip, her bridal gown smeared with fake blood. Sam smiled to himself from the kitchen. Many other nine-year-old girls would be princesses, Disney characters, cats, and witches this year for Halloween, but not his Hannah. Hannah beat to her own rhythm, and he desperately hoped it would remain as such as she hit her preteen years. All too often he saw children succumb to social conformity, but he and Annie were attempting to raise their children to embrace themselves for all their differences. She certainly did make a very compelling vampire bride.

Sam watched the sunlight seep through the entryway as Annie opened the front door, stared as its rays illuminated her dark blond bob tucked neatly behind her ears. He watched, too, as his daughter—very much her mother's miniature—

turned the knob on the glass storm door to exit and meet her grandmother outside.

"Ben," Sam called to the living room beyond the kitchen, "are you going to offer your grandmother some help?"

Ben begrudgingly made his way to the front door, but as he approached, Hannah and Caroline were already trudging in, the crisp autumn breeze caressing Sam from the door left ajar. Hannah carried a platter of baked goods in her arms as Caroline hefted a large reusable bag. Annie took the bag from her mother's hand and walked to the kitchen, where she deposited it on the countertop and began to empty it of its contents.

"Ma, thanks so much for bringing all this stuff. You're always such a big help."

"Not a problem," Caroline said. "I rather like to bake, and now that I'm retired I find I have more time on my hands."

"Well," Annie returned, "thanks all the same." She turned to her mother, kissed her cheek with a large grin.

"I'm guessing you're in costume, Ben," Caroline said to her grandson, "as I'm sure you don't wear a yellow rain jacket and green rain boots every day in the house, but I've no clue what in the world you are."

"Georgie," Ben replied.

"Georgie?"

"Yeah, you know," Annie said, "Georgie from that Stephen King movie *It*. The little boy who gets his arm eaten off."

"You're kidding!" Caroline exclaimed. "Ben, you like that kind of stuff?"

"Yep," Ben said. "Just saw the second movie."

"Annie, you've let him watch that?"

"We did," Annie said. "It was a tough decision for me to let him watch the first one, I'll admit, but Ben knew that I'd be turning it off if I felt it was too much. We watched it together, Ben, Sam, and I. I didn't end up turning it off, but it did have some adult themes that we needed to revisit after the movie finished."

"But all the blood!" Caroline declared.

"Yeah," countered Ben. "It's sick!"

"Darn right it's sick," Caroline said.

"'Sick' in Ben's language means it's super cool," Annie interpreted for her mother, who simply gave her grandson a frown. When Ben's left lip lifted in a smirk, Caroline couldn't help but laugh.

"Well, I certainly see a pattern here, don't I?" Caroline asked. "Georgie who gets his arm bitten off, and a gory vampire bride." She sighed. "Gone are the days of cute, fuzzy dinosaurs and tutus, I suppose." She grasped Hannah's shoulder with the palm of her hand and forcefully brought her to her bosom in an embrace. Hannah giggled through the vampire's teeth.

"All right," Annie announced, "time to get the food outside." She handed off a platter of cookies to Hannah and a large bowl of fruit salad to Ben. She followed them out the back screen door and onto the deck, with her husband and mother following behind.

Food was placed on tables, and decorations were already situated around the backyard. Sam watched his wife place her hands on her hips and survey the work she had accomplished with a satisfied, though exhausted, smirk. She impressed him year after year, all the effort exuded, all the love in each whisk of a spoon as she made Ben's favorite pumpkin whoopie pies. In the years prior to having children, Annie hadn't embraced Halloween beyond handing out candy to children who had come to their front door, but once Ben had reached preschool, she thought she'd throw a small party for his class along with a couple of other neighborhood families, and she had had such a wonderful time. They had kissed Ben good night when the party was through, the decorations taken down, and the dishes washed. The cold of the afternoon left a rosy tint to their son's cheeks. They had watched him laughing and playing, eating entirely too much sugar that particular afternoon. Hannah had only been three months old and was wearing her first Halloween costume, a warm and fluffy pumpkin. To keep her bald head from the crisp fall air, she donned an orange hat with black polka dots. He and Annie had rested upon the couch that evening while the children were sound asleep, and he remembered very vividly the spark in his wife's brown eyes as she turned her body to him, sat crisscross-applesauce on the leather, her feet with their black Halloween toenail polish resting under her thighs.

"That was awesome," she said. "Exhausting but awesome."

"You really liked it, didn't you?"

"You know, I really did, Sam. I wasn't sure how I'd feel. You know I get a bit nervous in large crowds of people, especially if I don't know someone well. But everyone was so nice. And did you see Ben?"

Sam nodded and grinned. "He was thrilled."

"He was!" Annie's white teeth shone through the enormity of her smile. "We've got to do this every year, Sam, we've just got to! Ben's only going to become more social. He's only going to make more friends each year by year. And this is something we can do for him, something I think he'll continue to love. And Hannah. It's kind of crazy, but next year she might even be walking. I mean, she won't really be social, but she can go on the tractor ride you did. Sam, thanks so much for that. I can't believe you put the little trailer on the back of the lawn mower and rode the kids around the yard. I think they all really liked it. Oh, my gosh! And our bounce house. Did you see those little princess costumes flying up? And Ben's Superman cape? This is it, Sam. We do this, and we've made a family tradition that we can have for so many years to come. And our kids will remember these days. I mean, *we'll* remember these days."

Sam wasn't a man of many words. He often allowed his actions to showcase his emotions. Sitting on the couch with Annie that Halloween night nine years ago, he had simply smiled and taken her hand in his.

"I'm beat, but . . ." Annie let the sentence linger in the air and nodded her head toward the stairwell. Sam bolted from the couch and pulled his wife along. All the way up the stairs, down the hall, and to their bedroom, Annie was giggling.

He thought upon this first Halloween party of theirs as he watched the satisfaction of a job well done play upon his wife's countenance now. To hold a full-time job, to be the one responsible for after-school activities (Sam worked until about six or six thirty most nights), and to still have the motivation to plan and prepare this party each year was a feat of determination and an area of his wife's personality that he admired greatly.

Soon the Halloween music was playing on portable speakers on the deck. Hannah and her friends were at the craft table; Ben and his friends were kicking a soccer ball around.

Sam opened the screen door of the deck from inside the house. The sun's rays were reflected upon the water of the lake in the near distance. Their small motorboat sat idle next to some trees near the water's edge, winterized now while it waited patiently for another summer to dawn. For a moment he stood and appreciated the slight autumn breeze before descending the deck's stairs into the backyard. He spotted Annie standing comfortably in a circle of conversation. He happily approached, placed the palm of his hand on his wife's lower back.

"Hi." Annie smiled up at him.

"Hi, yourself. What have you ladies been talking about?"

"Bitsy was telling us that she got a call from the school yesterday about Jonathan," Annie provided. Bitsy was a woman whom Annie had met when she and Sam first moved to their southern New Hampshire town, a woman who had a son the same age as Ben and two younger boys as well. Jonathan was only seven years old.

"Is that right?" Sam asked, eyebrows lifting.

"Mmm," Bitsy mumbled, "yeah. When I saw it was the school calling, I answered straightaway. I was totally nervous that something had happened, but as soon as I started speaking, I was assured that everything was okay. It was Jonathan's teacher. She began by saying that Jonathan was a sweet, very kind boy, and was easily liked by the other children in the classroom. Then she went on to say that through his enthusiasm he was a little too 'touchy' was her word. He liked to hug and to tug on arms. She said he even played with the girls' long hair during rug time. I can't say I was surprised by any of this. We've struggled with his being handsy since he was a toddler. She said she wanted to bring it to our attention as it was a bit over-the-top for the school environment. Though she didn't say so, I know she wants us to talk to Jonathan about it. I get it. Honestly, it even drives me crazy sometimes, so I can just imagine him being all touchy with the other kids, and I bet there's so much more for his teacher to worry about without my son being overly friendly. I really, really hope this stops before he gets a bit older and it can be misconstrued as harassment!"

"Ahh," Sam replied. "I see. Well, I like it when the little man gives me a hug. Annie and I both wish Ben would do the same, but according to him, he's 'too old for that.'"

"Yeah," Bitsy said, "I love my son's hugs. Tyler, being the same age as Ben, thinks it's beneath him to hug his mother as well. I love that our boys have so much in common and are such good friends, but this is one trait that I completely understand but totally hate."

The circle of friends chuckled and nodded their heads in agreement. Sam did appreciate the fact that Ben and Tyler were such good friends, and he loved, too, that Annie had found such a great companion in Bitsy. With his work hours, Sam hadn't met many men around town, just the husbands of the friends that Annie had made. He supposed he was happy with this, though. It was enough.

Audrey, another mother conversing in the circle spoke up. "I suppose I should be happy that Sophia is still young and loves hugs and cuddles at six. Though Grace does, too, and she's the same age as Hannah. Annie, Hannah likes hugs, too, right?"

Annie had been smiling brightly throughout this conversation with her husband by her side and her friends surrounding her. But now, as Sam looked down at his wife, he found she was devoid of emotion, her eyes trained on the ground. She lifted her head, gazed at Audrey.

"Breakfast isn't settling and I had coffee this morning. I need to take a shit." She made this abrupt statement rather monotonously, turned on the heel of her foot, and walked toward the screen door of the deck.

Sam watched her back as she went, then looked around the circle of Annie's girlfriends. "Holy shit," he joked. "Pun intended."

The women chuckled in response, but the mood within the circle had altered considerably. This was very unlike Annie. When excusing herself from a conversation, even with her closest friends, she was always polite. And his wife wouldn't typically say she had to take a shit in front of these women. To him, to her mother, yes. To Bitsy, yes. But to all these women? He thought again how unlike Annie that statement was.

"I'm gonna go check on Hannah," Sam said to the women. He saw the facade of comfort they displayed, knew Annie's comment had rattled them as well.

"Hey, Hannah Banana," he said when he approached the craft table. Her grandmother was sitting at Hannah's left. Grace, Audrey's nine-year-old daughter, was on Hannah's right. She and Hannah had developed quite a close friendship throughout the last few years. Hannah had been thrilled when she learned that Grace and she would be in the same fourth grade classroom this school year.

"Hi, Dad." Hannah had abandoned her vampire's teeth.

"Can I see what you're making?"

Hannah lifted an orange cardstock cutout of a pumpkin where she had glued black triangle eyes and a crooked black mouth. She had begun to decorate the pumpkin with marker designs.

"Great job," Sam told his daughter.

"Thanks."

Sam chatted with Caroline for a few minutes, then looked up when he heard the squeaking of the screen door. Annie exited. She surveyed the backyard, saw that the circle of friends had dispersed. When she spotted Bitsy, Sam watched as her mouth curved into a smile and she walked toward her best friend.

Sam slightly shook his head at his wife's behavior just minutes before, then looked down at his daughter as Hannah requested his attention be placed on her finished craft.

"Great job, Hannah Banana. But what's up with the blood dripping from your pumpkin's mouth?" He chuckled and tousled his daughter's hair.

⁓

"Come to the party tonight."

Sam looked at his roommate from across the bedroom they shared in the apartment complex just off the college campus. "Nah, man," he said, "I'm not feeling it."

"You can't have that much work to do," Brooks countered.

"I don't," Sam agreed, "but I still don't want to go."

"Why?"

"Don't know, really," Sam answered.

"Then come."

Sam merely shook his head, though his resolve was waning.

Brooks smirked. He knew he'd be able to convince his friend. He always did. *"Come for a bit,"* he said. *"If you're not having fun, then leave."* He stood from his bed and walked toward the door. *"Anyway,"* he continued, *"I think that girl from class is supposed to be there. What's her name again? The one with crazy red hair and big boobs?"*

"Melanie," Sam answered.

"Yeah, yeah," Brooks said, *"Melanie."* He raised his eyebrows as he stood in the doorway. *"She likes you, man,"* he said. *"You gotta come to the party. You've been working too hard, anyway. You need to relax."*

"I know I do," Sam said, *"but graduation's almost here and I'm just swamped. I don't have a whole lot I need to do tonight, but I'm beat anyway."*

"You're coming," Brooks said. It wasn't a question, though his smirk remained.

Sam sighed audibly from his bed. *"Yeah,"* he agreed hesitantly, *"I'm coming."*

Brooks smiled and walked out of the bedroom and into the kitchen of the apartment he and Sam shared with two others to make himself some dinner.

Sam remained seated. He looked out the second-story bedroom window at the setting sun. He really didn't want to go to this party. It would all just be more of the same: kids drinking; stinky, sticky beer-laden floors; loud music, crowded rooms . . . But he was also aware that when Brooks convinced him to attend these parties, he often found he enjoyed himself despite the obvious downsides.

And he really did need to relax. This five-year engineering program was killing him!

Sam stood from the bed and made his way to the kitchen to prepare dinner for himself alongside his friend. He'd give the party a try. Like Brooks had said, if he wasn't enjoying himself, he'd just come back home.

The bass was booming when they arrived at the party just off campus. Sam was ready to go home before the night had even begun, but he followed Brooks into the dingy basement. Maybe his friend was right and he'd spot Melanie. That was sure to put a smile on his face.

He poured some frothy amber beer into a red plastic cup from the keg at the back of the room. Boys were playing beer pong behind him; boys and girls both were dancing to the beat of the music. Cup in hand, he surveyed the room and walked toward a group of young men he spotted in a corner, acquaintances of his. They began conversing over the music, voices raised to be heard.

One beer. He'd drink this one beer and head back home. He'd rather put his feet up on the coffee table and watch TV.

Sam looked around the room a bit more. Brooks was off with some buddies of his from the football team. Next to him stood a kid from a class of his talking with another group of boys. He had no desire to go over and say hello.

He sipped his beer. At least he could admit that he did like the taste of beer, and now that he was over the legal drinking age he didn't have to attempt to hide it in a coffee mug as he walked around campus late at night as he had done when he was younger.

A parting of kids on the dance floor.

And there she was.

It wasn't Melanie whom he saw gyrating to the bass. No, this girl was a blonde, not a redhead. She wore a tight-fitting white T-shirt and a pair of blue jeans with a braided belt. Her skin was pale, but her cheeks were flushed from exertion. She didn't hold a cup in her hand; instead she was waving her arms in the air as she danced.

Sam was captivated.

He excused himself from the young men he was conversing with and slowly made his way through the crowd and onto the makeshift dance floor in this large, damp, basement room, the lights hanging down from the ceiling and eerily illuminating its inhabitants.

A few more steps and he was there.

Beside her.

He was quite a bit taller than she was, so he had to look down to catch her eye. She stopped her dancing and looked up into his face. Her eyebrows rose imploringly as he stood there with a goofy grin.

"Can I help you?" she asked him. Her girlfriends were still dancing, though they had slowed their movements down considerably to watch the scene unfolding before them.

"I'm Sam." Sam transferred the red cup to his left hand and held out his right. She looked down at it but didn't shake. Sam was nonplussed. "I haven't seen you around," he said.

"Nope," she replied, voice raised to be heard over the music. Her friends watched on, evidently amused.

"Are you a student here?" he asked.

She shook her head in reply.

"Visiting then?"

She nodded. By this point, she had crossed her arms over her chest and was staring him down.

Sam continued to smile. His green eyes crinkled at the corners. His brown hair was a disheveled mess as he hadn't bothered to style it before arriving at the party that night. "Want to dance?" he asked.

"I was dancing."

"Then, can I dance with you?" Sam asked. His smile never wavered.

"Sure!" It wasn't the girl he was speaking to but one of her friends. Sam deemed this a minor victory.

The girl began dancing again, slower this time, more hesitant. Sam joined in. Her friends went right back to it, hips swaying, arms in the air. Sam couldn't take his eyes off this girl, though. Man, she was beautiful. He forced himself to look at her friends, to avert his eyes a bit so she didn't think he was entirely too intense and wander off, but he found himself drawn right back to her. He respectfully watched her body move, watched a slow smile re-form on her pink lips. He watched as her eyes lifted slowly to meet his, and he reacted with an extremely large and genuine grin.

They continued to dance, Sam and the girls, until he felt an arm around his shoulder and turned to see Brooks at his side.

"Who are your new friends?" Brooks smirked that crooked smirk of his.

Sam merely shook his head.

"Didn't get names?" Brooks asked with contrived credulity. "I'm Brooks." He held out his hand, and the mystery girl's friends took the bait. Girls often did with Brooks. When he turned to the blonde beside Sam, she nodded her head slightly in acknowledgment, but her hands remained where they had been since Brooks arrived: in her back pockets.

Brooks began to flirt with the girls. Sam's smile wavered uncomfortably as he looked at the young woman by his side. At least she hadn't left.

She met his eyes and his smile returned. It grew considerably when she formed a slight grin herself.

He took a chance. "I'd love to talk to you. Want to maybe head outside for a bit?"

She stood there, hands still stuffed into the back pockets of her jeans. She looked into his eyes, considering, searching. Eventually, she nodded her head and leaned in to speak with her friends momentarily. Sam breathed in sharply with pleasure. When she looked his way once again, he dared place the palm of his hand on her shoulder. When she didn't resist, he gently led her outside.

Her name, he'd soon learn, was Annie.

CHAPTER TWO

Sam

Sam was sitting in his office cubicle the week before Christmas when his cell buzzed in his back pocket. He reached behind, grasped it. He looked at the screen before him. Annie's school? Why was Annie's school calling? Perhaps Annie's cell had died and she was using the main line to contact him.

"Hello?" Sam answered uncertainly.

"Sam, hi. It's Lucinda Daily." Sam knew Lucinda well. The principal of Annie's elementary school was a kind middle-aged woman, one who embraced every aspect of her job. Heading a tight-knit community of workers, Lucinda had often coordinated luncheons and family outings for her employees to elicit camaraderie outside the work environment.

"Hi, Lucinda."

"I imagine you're wondering why I'm calling."

"The thought did cross my mind," Sam said.

"I'm not exactly sure how to tiptoe around this conversation, Sam, so I'm going to jump right in. I'm worried about Annie."

"Annie? Why?"

"Honestly, Annie has always been such a fantastic teacher. She's amazing with her kindergarten children. She's always come to work with a smile on her face and seems to genuinely love her job here at the school. But recently we've been noticing some changes in her behaviors."

"Okay," Sam supplied warily.

"She seems to switch from happy and energetic to apathetic at times. I admit she has made some inappropriate comments to the other employees here, speaking off topic even. And Sam? I've gotten a few phone calls from concerned parents. One call was placed just today. Apparently, Annie spoke to one of her children yesterday in a manner that was very unlike her. She used the word 'puberty' to this five-year-old, and that child asked her mother to clarify once she arrived home. We can't have teachers speaking such terms to young children. And Sam?"

"Yeah?" Sam was attempting to let this information settle.

"Just this morning Annie left her classroom."

"Left her classroom?"

"Yes. But not just to the hallway. She left the building. She left her children alone, and a passing employee took over and used the intercom system to page me to the room. Sam, she left the building for forty-five minutes, and when I approached her upon her return and inquired as to why she would leave the building, she informed me that she simply wanted to go for a walk."

"Lucinda, you have to be joking."

"I most certainly am not. Sam, I'm extremely concerned. These are not typical behaviors for Annie, but we, as a team at the school, have noticed them from time to time these past months. I find it necessary to speak with you so that we can collaborate. I have spoken to Annie several times, and she seems unaffected by our conversations. It appears to me that she either believes her behaviors to be appropriate or simply does not care that they are not."

"Lucinda, I'll admit that there have been several times that Annie has seemed a little off at home, but this is still coming as a shock to me right now and I'm not even really sure what to say."

"I understand. It's a lot to take in, I'm sure. But Sam?"

"Yeah?"

"She can't continue like this. It's Friday. This means that when the school day is over, it's Christmas vacation. When Annie returns to school in January, I expect her to check herself here at school. These incidents have got to change. And I have told her so."

"Yes."

"And if they don't . . . well, then we will have to let her go."

"Let her go?"

"Yes. These behaviors simply cannot be tolerated here."

"Of course. Yes, of course." Sam was flustered. He sat, cell phone to his ear, unsure of what else to say.

"I'm so sorry, Sam, but perhaps something is going on with Annie?"

"Yeah, maybe."

"Again, I'm terribly sorry to be making this call to you. Especially so close to Christmas. But I need for you to be aware. Especially as Annie seems not to fully grasp the severity of the situation."

"Yes. I appreciate the call, Lucinda. Thank you."

"You are welcome. Take care, Sam. And I'm available at any time if you need to get in touch. But I do need to reiterate that she has been given many a warning and if she continues down this path come January, she will be asked to leave."

"I'm clear on the matter, though I admit I'm shocked. I'll speak with Annie tonight. Thanks again, Lucinda."

"You are welcome. Goodbye."

"Bye."

Sam hung up the phone, let it drop from his palm. He placed his elbows on the desk, hands on his cheeks, fingers splayed through the short silvery strands at the temples of his dark brown hair. He tightly closed his eyes.

What the hell was going on with his wife?

"Welcome home, handsome." Sam was greeted by his wife's smile as she stood over the stove stirring aromatic pasta sauce. He surmised Ben was in his room as indoor soccer practice ended around five thirty. Hannah could be seen beyond the kitchen, reading on the living room couch. No soccer for her on Fridays, and violin lessons were on Tuesdays and Thursdays. A busy winter schedule indeed.

"Thanks." He kissed his wife on the cheek, and she grinned in response. She certainly was in a good mood. This was more the Annie he was accustomed to. Could Lucinda have been overexaggerating the severity of the situation at school?

He looked into Annie's deep brown eyes, searched their depths, and saw nothing beyond the contentment she felt at this very moment. He pushed his thoughts aside. The conversation required could wait until after the kids had gone to bed. For now, he was going to enjoy time with his family.

"I'm going to go change," he told Annie. "Be right back."

When Sam returned to the kitchen, Annie had already placed a large bowl of spaghetti on the wooden kitchen table atop a pot holder. Beside it lay a steaming pot of sauce and meatballs. Ben was dispersing plates and silverware as Hannah placed napkins at each place setting.

"Annie, it smells delicious. I'm really hungry," Sam announced.

"Busy day at work today?"

Sam sat in his chair. "It was. And I didn't take much of a lunch break. They've got me working another project right now in addition to the one I've been working on the last year. I'm swamped."

"Sounds it." Annie sat and looked around the table. "Dig in!"

Conversation flowed freely at the dinner table. Sam asked Ben about his day, and though not entirely forthcoming (typical thirteen-year-old, Sam thought to himself), Ben did offer some information about gym class and the lack of recess time. Hannah, quite the opposite personality, spoke readily about her time with Grace and the science project they'd done in class. Apparently constructing a DNA model out of mini marshmallows was "wicked."

Dinner done, Annie and the kids cleared the table as Sam started on the dishes. When through, the family sat back down at the table to a game of Uno Attack. Friday nights were family game night, at least as long as Sam and Annie were able to keep up the tradition with a teenager in the house. They knew that soon Ben would rather spend time out of the house with his friends, and they'd foster those relationships, but they both felt the need and desire to hold on to family nights as long as they were able. Annie, especially, savored these moments with her husband and children.

"Yellow or two," Annie said to herself as she looked at the cards fanned in her hands. "Nope. I can't go."

"Ohh," Hannah crooned. "Here you go, Mom!" She pressed the small black button at the top of the game console. Sam heard the slight *ding* of the mechanism and watched as several Uno cards shot out the front to land before his wife.

"Thanks a bunch, Hannah Scrumptious," Annie said with a chuckle. Sam smiled at the pet name for his daughter he knew his wife to use when she was in a particularly pleasant mood. When Hannah was about five years old, Annie had used the word "scrumdiddlyumptious," and Hannah had giggled uncontrollably. This had made both Sam and Annie laugh in return, and to egg her daughter on, Annie had used the word again while tickling Hannah to the ground. For months afterward Annie had called her daughter Hannah Scrumdiddlyumptious when they were fooling around together. In time, the pet name had somehow shortened to Hannah Scrumptious and had stuck.

"You're welcome," Hannah laughed.

"Your turn, Ben," Sam supplied. At times Ben was into family game nights; other times Sam could tell he was antsy to get his time on *Fortnite* or *FIFA* with his friends, shutting the door to his bedroom and situating himself in his gaming chair before his computer.

Ben played a yellow four before Sam took his turn and placed a wild card down. "This is the one where I can get anyone at the table," Sam said sinisterly. "Hmm . . . who am I going to attack?" He looked at Ben, then Hannah. Lastly, he rested on Annie.

"Don't you dare!" Annie squeaked.

"Oh, I dare!" Sam chuckled. "Anyway, I need to get another giggle out of Hannah."

Hannah laughed as her father clicked the button at the top of the device and cards shot out toward her mother once again. Ben rolled his eyes.

"There's no way I'm gonna win this game," Annie said. "Not with all these darn cards I've got now. Thanks a lot, Hannah. And Sam," she said with a mock frown and scorn in her voice.

"No problem," Sam said, making his daughter giggle once again.

The game continued with lots of laughter and friendly bantering. Sam placed a card down on the large discard pile and yelled "Uno!" On his next turn, he rid himself of his last card to win the game.

"Well, I'm not even sure I want to add up all these darn cards," Annie said. "I got my butt kicked this time around."

"You sure did," Sam laughed.

"Hannah, how'd you do?" Annie asked.

Hannah laid a card on the table, then another. She added the two together, eyes rolling to the top of her head as she did the math. She continued adding cards until there were none left in her hands. "Thirty-four," she announced.

"Not too shabby," Annie said. "Ben?"

"Seventeen."

"Even better." She looked at her son, saw his eyebrows rise slightly. A question, she knew.

"All right, all right," Annie conceded. "Thanks for playing with us, Ben. You know how much I love my time with you all." She started lifting the cards from the table, gathering them to clean up. "Go ahead."

Ben didn't need any further urging. He scooted his chair backward, stood quickly, then ran upstairs to his bedroom and his waiting computer and any friend or friends who would be available to play with him electronically for a while.

Annie looked at Sam and shrugged her shoulders, slightly defeated. Sam knew that his wife wished Ben were more into family time than he actually was, though they both understood fully that he was now a teenager. It was typical for him to want his video games, his privacy. Where once he couldn't wait to pick a book from the extensive offerings of the bookshelf in the living room, sit with his mother on the couch, and cuddle against her bosom as she read to him; where once he was eager to go apple picking in the fall, and pumpkin picking, to carve that pumpkin he had chosen and roast the seeds, now this was all done because it was requested of him by his parents and not done because it was a cause of pleasure for himself. Though he never complained, Sam could tell he wasn't entertained by these once beloved activities by the slight slump of his shoulders, by his lack of conversational offerings, and by his flat affect.

Hannah went off to play while Annie finished clearing the game from the table. When she was through, she and Sam sat on the couch and talked a bit before heading upstairs to help Hannah brush her teeth. When Hannah went to her room to dress into her pajamas, Annie and Sam followed to tuck her into bed and wish her a good night. When through, Sam followed Annie back down the stairs. He paused and watched as she walked toward the living room. He knew he needed to broach the subject of work and the behaviors Lucinda had spoken of earlier that day, but if he were being honest with himself, he was dreading the conversation.

He knew Annie hadn't entirely been herself these past few months.

He watched as Annie headed off to grab her phone and knew he needed to intercede if he had any chance of grasping her attention. Now that the day was almost through, he guessed she was probably tired, and her phone was how she relaxed. But it also stole her attention. She wouldn't want to converse with him if she sat on the couch and started playing her games. She'd ask to talk later.

"Annie?" Sam touched her arm before she reached her phone on the charger against the windowsill.

"Yeah?"

"Can we talk?"

"I'm kind of tired, Sam. We talked for a bit after the game. Want to talk tomorrow? I just need to relax. Be by myself."

"I understand," Sam said. "But we really need to talk."

"Why didn't you say whatever you have to say when we talked before putting Hannah to bed?"

"I wanted to talk to you once Hannah was tucked in. It's kind of important. I didn't want her interrupting."

Annie sighed. "Okay."

Sam led his wife to the couch, where they both sat down to face each other.

Annie raised her eyebrows, inviting Sam to begin.

"I got a call from Lucinda Daily today," Sam said.

Annie grimaced. "Why'd Lucinda call *you*?"

"She's concerned for you."

"Why?" Annie's frown was still evident.

Sam looked into his wife's eyes. "She said you haven't been acting yourself recently, said you've been saying some things to the kids and even to your coworkers that you really shouldn't. She even said you walked out of the school the other day without telling anyone. Annie, did you really do that?" he asked gently, concern evident in his voice.

"I suppose."

"You suppose? What in the world does that mean?"

"I wanted to walk."

"You wanted to walk?" Sam was becoming exasperated, and the conversation had just begun. He closed his eyes tightly and took a deep breath in, exhaled. When his eyes opened he saw his wife looking at him with an expressionless countenance. The grimace was gone, but so was any sign of Annie's having been affected by his words.

"Annie, babe." Sam reached for her hands, held them firmly within his own. "I have to say that I'm concerned for you as well. The past couple of months you've been acting differently. You have nights like tonight where you're entirely yourself. You smile. You're happy. Then you have nights where you don't seem to care much about anything at all. I admit those nights haven't happened much at all, and I know how busy you are, so I'm guessing you're just stressed. Maybe with work?" Sam paused, but Annie made no indication that she'd answer his question. "Annie, she said you talked about puberty to a five-year-old. What's going on?"

Annie broke his grasp, flung her hands into the air. "Don't talk to me like this, Sam. I'm not a little kid. I don't need to be ber–ber— I don't need you to talk to me like I'm a little kid."

"I'm not trying to talk to you like a little kid, but I shouldn't get phone calls from the principal of your school, Annie. You walked out of your room and went for a walk! In the middle of the workday! I'm just really confused here. How could you have thought that was okay to do?"

"I wanted to walk."

Sam shook his head, closed his eyes again.

"You have sauce on your shirt," Annie offered. "Makes you look like a slob." She stood up to leave.

"See?" Sam said. "This, too. You've been saying things like this these past couple of months. They come out of nowhere, Annie. We're not talking about my shirt right now."

Annie continued to walk away from her husband. Sam stood up and hastened his steps toward his wife, took another deep breath to calm himself.

"Annie, she said she'd let you go."

"Hmm?"

"Lucinda. She said she'd let you go. As in fire you. You can't be doing this stuff at work. She said she's talked to you already, lots of times, in fact. She said that if you continue down this path, then she couldn't keep you on at the school."

Annie shrugged.

"Annie, help me. Please help me to understand what's going on with you right now. What are you thinking?"

"I want coffee."

"What!?"

"Want some coffee."

"Annie, you can't have coffee right now. You know your body can't take it after the morning. And Jesus! We're trying to talk about you losing your job and you want coffee? Please look at me, Annie," he implored. He waited for her eyes to meet his. "Please, please tell me what's going on."

Annie shrugged once again.

Sam knew he needed to walk away; he wasn't going to get anywhere with his wife tonight. He was frustrated, yes, and bewildered, but concern for his wife was the emotion in the forefront of his mind as he climbed up the stairs.

A few minutes later he could smell the coffee brewing.

CHAPTER THREE

Sam and Caroline

"Hello, hello!" Caroline opened the front door of her daughter's home on Christmas morning. Three years prior, she had lost her husband. With Annie being her only child and Caroline having a close relationship with not only her daughter but the entire Carson family as well, she was at their home often. Annie had invited her to join them Christmas mornings after her husband had passed, and she was extremely pleased to accept the offer. She loved nothing more than watching the joy on the faces of the ones she loved most in the world.

"Come on in," Sam called from the kitchen.

Caroline stepped into the home from the cold, snowy outdoors, and made her way to the kitchen area with a bag full of gifts.

"Oh," Sam said. "I'm so sorry, Caroline. I should have offered to help. Let me grab those."

Caroline handed him the bag and Sam brought it into the living room. He lifted the gifts from the bag and placed them with the others already under the Christmas tree in the corner of the room.

"Grammie!" Hannah bounded into the kitchen and embraced her grandmother heartily.

"Hannah," Caroline said. "I'm so happy to see you. Merry Christmas."

"Merry Christmas."

"Where's your brother?"

"In his room." Hannah rolled her eyes. "He's always in his room."

"Well, yes," Caroline said, "but on Christmas morning?"

"Yeah. Dad said we had to wait for Mom to get up before we opened gifts or had our pancake breakfast, so he went back upstairs. We usually stay upstairs until she gets up, but she was taking too long, so Dad said we could come down."

"Your mom is still sleeping?" Caroline was astonished.

"Yeah," Hannah answered. "She's been sleeping more."

Caroline looked at Sam, who was returning to the kitchen from the living room. He raised his eyebrows at her and mouthed the word "later." Caroline knew an intense conversation was in the near future. She also knew not to prod any further while Hannah was in the room.

"Daddy, can't we just wake her up now that Grammie's here? She's always been awake on Christmas morning. We do presents once Grammie gets here."

"I know, Hannah Banana." Sam sighed. "I tried earlier, but I think maybe she's just tired today. Think maybe you and Grammie would like to start some Christmas music and I'll make some hot chocolate? Then maybe your mom will come down."

"With whipped cream and sprinkles?"

"With whipped cream and sprinkles," Sam agreed with a wink and a facade of joy. He felt fortunate at this moment that his daughter was often easy to appease.

He began to heat a pot of milk on the stove, then told his

mother-in-law that he was going to get Ben from his room. Now that Caroline was in his home, his son should certainly come down and greet her.

"Knock, knock," Sam said as he opened the door to his son's room. Ben was lying on his bed, Marshmello's music seeping through the speakers on his computer desk. "Whatcha doin'?" Sam asked as he walked forward and sat on the edge of his son's bed.

"Just listening," Ben said.

"Your grandmother's here. You should really come on down now and say hello."

"Okay."

"You look bothered, Ben. Like you're somewhere else right now." He paused, gave his son the time he needed to reply.

Ben looked out his large bedroom window. Sam followed his gaze, saw the sun glistening off the snow in the backyard, the ice on the small lake.

Ben's gaze didn't waver from the window, but he began to speak. "It's Mom," he admitted. No further words were offered.

"Mom," Sam said in acknowledgment. "Ben look at me." He waited for his son's eyes to reach him. "I know something's going on. Really, I do. I'm kind of at a loss right now, I'm not gonna lie. But we'll figure this out. We will," he insisted when he saw the doubt on his son's face, the face of a young man now, cheeks thinner, jaw more pronounced, a little boy no longer. "I'm going to talk to Grammie. She's a rock, you know." He paused, contemplated. "Together we'll figure this out. Please know that, Ben. I'm not ignoring this. I'm not in denial that your mother has been acting differently."

Ben's face was expressionless, but his eyes were watering. "Last night I tried to say good night. She's always given me crap when I don't say good night. She always wants a hug. She even swats me if I don't. I mean, like, in a good way. But last night I went to say good night and she ignored me. When I went to give her a hug, she moved away and told me to leave her alone."

Sam's stomach lurched. "Ben, I didn't know."

Ben merely shook his head and returned his gaze to his bedroom window.

"That probably felt like shit, huh?" Sam didn't often swear in front of his kids, but this was one time that he felt the pronouncement was needed. Ben shrugged his shoulders as a tear found its way from the corner of his eye, dribbling down his cheek and landing on his pillowcase.

"Okay," Sam said, attempting to make light of the situation, "it's Christmas Day! We need to be happy today, gosh darn it!" He playfully bumped his son's arm. "Let's go. The milk I've got on the stove for hot chocolate is probably burning by now."

Together they made their way downstairs. Caroline had taken the milk off the burner, and five cups of hot chocolate were now on the countertop.

"Ah!" Caroline announced joyously. "Decided to come down to be with us, did you?"

"Hi, Gram." Ben smiled sheepishly, the few tears he had shed now gone.

"Come here and give your grandmother a hug, will you?" Caroline said with extended arms. Ben walked into her embrace.

"Benjamin, stop growing," Caroline joked. "You're almost taller than me now. Pretty soon I'm going to have to look up to see you." Her smile was warm, her love all-encompassing. Ben grinned in response. "And that blond hair," she added as she brushed the strands from his forehead. "I bet you're driving the girls crazy at school."

"Gram," Ben mumbled in embarrassed protest. Caroline chuckled. She loved teasing her grandson. It was entirely too easy to do!

"Thanks for making the hot chocolate, Caroline. I appreciate that," Sam said.

Caroline turned from her grandson to her son-in-law. "Not a problem at all," she said, "but Hannah, we need to get you that whipped cream. And you'll have to show me where the sprinkles are, although I still think it's funny to put sprinkles on hot chocolate."

"Try it, Grammie," Hannah suggested. "It's delicious!"

The foursome were at the kitchen table with their mugs when Annie lethargically walked down the stairs.

"Well," Caroline said, "look who decided to join us on this Christmas morning. Are you feeling all right, Annie?"

Annie merely nodded her head and walked to the kitchen. Caroline and Sam exchanged looks of bewilderment and watched as she ground some coffee beans and poured them into the top of the machine, adding water and turning it on. She rummaged through the refrigerator while the coffee was brewing, then walked out of the room.

"Where's Mom going?" Hannah asked through a slurp of whipped cream. Sprinkles stuck to the top of her lip.

"I'm not sure, Hannah Banana, but she'll be back. Then we'll open gifts." Sam forced himself to sound chipper, unaffected. Ben hid his face behind his mug.

The coffee machine beeped to tell the room it had finished. Annie didn't return.

"I'll be right back," Sam announced as he scooted his chair out from under him. He walked down the hallway. No Annie. Upstairs. No Annie. He was baffled. Where could she have gone to? He would have seen if she was in the living room as she would have passed him at the kitchen table. The basement, too.

He descended the stairwell, and as he began to turn the corner, he saw a slight movement through the window of the front door. He turned the knob, opened the door. Annie was sitting on the front steps in the cold. No shoes, no jacket.

"Annie, it's freezing out here. What are you doing?"

"Wanted to look at the snow."

He walked forward and crouched to be at level with his wife. "And you couldn't look at the snow from a window inside?" His voice was soft.

Annie made no response. Her face was expressionless as she looked out into the front yard.

"Come on, babe," Sam urged, "let's head back inside. Your mom is here, and the kids are eager to open their gifts. We're all just waiting on you now." He extended his hand, and when Annie didn't take it, he lightly grasped her arm and guided her to a standing position. She didn't protest, simply followed him back indoors and to the kitchen table, where hot chocolates were being finished.

"Did you want your coffee?" Sam asked. "You can take it to the couch."

Annie nodded and worked her way to the kitchen, where she pulled down a mug and poured herself a cup of coffee. She added cream and took a sip.

"Ugh! This tastes like shit!" she spurted.

Hannah snorted from the kitchen table at her mother's choice of language, hot chocolate dribbling down her chin. Caroline's eyes widened, though she said nothing.

Sam watched as Annie dumped the contents of her mug down the kitchen sink and poured herself a fresh cup. Watched also as she added the cream and took another sip.

"What the hell!?" Annie grimaced as she plunked the mug down on the countertop, hot liquid spraying out the top to make a light brown mess.

Sam rushed to his wife's side. "Annie, Annie, stop," he pleaded before she could pour another cup of coffee down the drain. "You just forgot the sugar. You don't like coffee without sugar. Here," he said as he walked to the pantry and took a small canister of sugar out, "we'll grab it now." He took a spoon from the silverware drawer and added Annie's typical desired amount, then stirred. "Try it now."

"Oh," she said after swallowing.

"Better?"

"Yep," she declared happily, then giggled as she took her mug to the couch.

Sam watched her walk away, perplexed at the change in temperament.

Caroline broke the silence. "Okay," she announced loudly, "shall we open gifts, then?"

"Yay!" Hannah exclaimed.

Gifts were slowly distributed to the enjoyment of all. Hannah was beyond thrilled as she tore into her packages. Still believing in Santa Claus allowed for even further delight and merriment for her on this Christmas morning.

"Annie," Sam said, "this one's for you." He handed his wife a gift wrapped in shiny red and gold polka-dotted paper. "It's kind of silly, but I saw it and immediately thought of you."

Annie had been rather animated throughout the gift opening thus far, her coffee mug long ago abandoned on the end table. "Ooh." She anxiously accepted the present from Sam's hands and tore into it unabashedly.

"Awe," she sighed. "He's so cute!" She had opened the package to find a small stuffed elephant. She sat on the couch stroking its short, soft gray fur, running her fingers down its trunk before bringing the animal to rest upon her bosom and rocking side to side.

"He's so cute!" she repeated with a large grin.

Sam was pleased to see his wife acting more like herself, though he had to admit, her demeanor was a bit more child-like than it typically was. "I'm glad you like it," he said.

"Sweet!" Ben had just opened a copy of the movie *It* as well as a poster he had told his parents a while ago that he wanted to hang on the front of his bedroom door. This had elicited playful protestations from Annie, who claimed she didn't want to "look at that creepy clown's face" every time she ascended the stairs.

"Thanks so much, Mom and Dad!" Sam laughed at his son's exuberant reaction while Annie continued to cuddle her stuffed elephant, though she did acknowledge her son's gratitude.

"Well, looks like that's it," Sam announced when all gifts had been revealed. "Annie, you usually like making the Christmas pancakes. Want me to cook this time?"

"I can make them," Annie answered. She stood from the couch with her stuffed elephant and walked to the kitchen. She propped the elephant on the countertop and announced he would watch as she made brunch. This made Hannah giggle as she toyed with her new witch-hunter's crossbow. Annie had often joked with Sam that their daughter was going to be the next Kate Beckinsale. A couple of years into their relationship together, the two had watched the actress play a werewolf-hunting vampire in *Underworld* and the sequels that followed.

The aroma of chocolate chip pancakes soon filled the air. Sam and Caroline tidied the living room as Ben and Hannah explored their new gifts.

Pancakes were eaten merrily, and as the last bite was taken, Sam turned to Caroline at the kitchen table. "Hey, Caroline," he said, "I'd love your opinion on something. Maybe we can bundle up and go sit on the chairs at the lake? I've cleared a path."

"Brr," Caroline shivered at the thought. "It's cold out there, but sure. Let me just grab my jacket."

"Ben and Hannah, clear the table for your mom?" Sam asked.

"Yep."

"Thanks." Sam grabbed his coat from the mudroom and slipped his winter boots on. He and Caroline exited onto the back deck and made their way down to the edge of the lake, where two Adirondack chairs awaited them. They were devoid of snow, as Sam was down here often and maintained a path and an open area.

"I'm so sorry I took you outside," he said to his mother-in-law. "I just wasn't sure where we could talk without either Annie or the kids overhearing."

"Not a problem. I understand," Caroline said. "I'm listening."

"She's scaring me," Sam admitted. "You've seen some of the things she's been doing. Like this morning with the coffee? She's forgotten simple things like that before. Dates? She gets all messed up sometimes, doesn't know what day it is. I've had to wake her up a few times so she's not late for work and she tells me she thought it was the weekend. And the kicker? She doesn't seem to care, or if she does, she doesn't show it. Sometimes I really think she just has no idea that what she's doing isn't typical, you know? At times she's so happy; she's my Annie. And then there are times she just lacks any sort of emotion. And the kids notice. The kids are affected. Ben told me this morning when I went up to go get him from his room that Annie had brushed him aside last night when he went to say good night to her. For Ben to actually tell me something like this really means it hurt him. He doesn't often talk to me if something's going on." He paused, drew a breath. He looked out onto the snow and ice of the lake as he held his jacket tighter around his torso and watched his breath billowing in the air.

Caroline continued to look at him, allowing him time to speak further. "I got a call from her boss," Sam said. "She told me Annie left her classroom the other day to go for a walk. She left her damn room of kindergarten kids alone because she wanted to go for a walk. I can't make this shit up, Caroline. I was told that when Annie got back to school at the beginning of the new year, she had to smarten up or she'd be fired." Sam removed his gaze from the lake and trained his eyes on Caroline, the woman whom Annie resembled, just as Hannah resembled Annie. The woman who had birthed the woman he loved dearly, the wife who was unraveling before him.

"What the hell is going on?" Sam asked.

"I don't know," Caroline admitted. "But Sam? This is really disturbing. Maybe it's time we see the doctor?"

"Yeah, you're probably right."

"I don't live far away, I'm retired. I have time on my hands, and you know how dear Annie is to me. Let me help in any way I can, Sam."

Sam looked at Caroline, nodded his head, attempted to stop his eyes from watering. "I feel like there are little things here and there. But the little things add up. And when I look at the whole picture, this is big. Really big." He paused, shoulders slumping. "I think my wife's gonna lose her job."

Caroline sighed audibly.

"When I'm by myself and I think about this all, I always come back to the day we had the Halloween party. She got up that morning thinking it was a workday. Even though it was a day she's always looking forward to. Even though she'd been preparing all that week. She still got dressed in her work clothes and was starting her day. But you know, if I'm being honest with myself, there were little things even before then. I remember I had a dentist appointment back sometime in the spring. I got home early that day. Annie was at the table helping Hannah with some math homework. Some simple triple-digit addition. Annie was adding some of the numbers wrong, and she was acting as if everything was totally fine, as if she didn't realize she was adding these really simple numbers incorrectly. I stood there and just watched. There were a couple of times that Hannah caught on and laughed at her mother. As if Annie were doing it all purposefully as a joke to trip her up. But she's had trouble with numbers since.

"I can't even pin when any of this started, I just know a lot has happened—and for long enough—to make me know that something is going on, that something's wrong."

Caroline reached for her son-in-law's hand, squeezed. Her brown eyes bore into his, the green accentuated by the water pooling within. "Again, Sam, maybe it's time to see a doctor? Maybe they can shed light on what's going on with Annie?"

Sam nodded his assent. "I'll call tomorrow."

CHAPTER FOUR

Ben

*H*e didn't want his mother there.

Ben stretched with his teammates on the turf field of an indoor sports facility before the soccer game. Soccer was his thing. His passion. He was good at it. School? Sure, he did well in school, got good grades, made the honor roll. But he always turned to soccer. It's where he wanted to be, and his parents continuously supported him year-round. So here he was, just days after Christmas, about to play another game. And though he wanted to be nowhere else at this moment—typically he could immerse himself in the game, kick the ball to stave off anger or frustration, destress, aware of nothing but the ball, the field, and the goal—today he thought of his mother on the sideline.

His mother.

She had always been his biggest supporter, and he supposed she still was, though her support had morphed. In years past he had always known she was there among the other parents and grandparents who came to watch the boys play, but his focus was always trained on the game itself. If she yelled, he was never aware. But his mother was the type who would yell words of encouragement if she yelled anything at all. His mother was one to clap her hands when applause was warranted. His mother had never been one of those obnoxious parents on the sidelines opening their mouths to holler at the refs when they were incensed by a call; she wasn't one to shout obscenities, to snap at other parents. She wasn't one to get kicked out of a game.

But today he was fearful.

His mother had been acting strangely. Had been acting strangely for a while. His mother hadn't really been, well . . . his mother. Sure, she looked the same, sounded the same. And there were days when she was her typical self, joking, playful, smiling, staring at him and telling him he was "so incredibly handsome," but not today. Today Dad had to wake her up. Today Dad had to remind her that Ben had a game.

Today she had been snapping at her family, and he didn't want her to bring that to the sidelines.

The whistle blew and the game began. He focused on the ball.

The opposing team had possession. A teammate of Ben's won the ball, looked around, kicked it to Ben. He saw nothing else, heard nothing around him as his eyes tracked the ball's fast movements. He extended his chest, and the ball hit hard, ricocheting off and to the ground, where his foot immediately made contact. He sprinted up the side of the field, turf hard on his cleats. The player defending his position was fast. Too fast. He caught up to Ben, forced him farther to the side of the field. Still Ben ran, teeth clenching down on his mouth guard. The defender cut in front of him, kicked the ball beyond the boundary line.

The whistle blew. Ben's team had a throw-in and a chance to obtain possession once again.

Ben got the ball, began to run. He made it past the first

defender just to lose ownership of the ball to another. Damn, this team was good.

He continued to play and he played hard.

The halftime whistle blew, and Ben ran off the field to reconvene with his coach and team. When the whistle blew once again, indicating to the boys that it was time to start the second half of the game, Ben was eager to get back on the field and play. His team had a fighting chance here and he was going to work it.

A lull before the whistle blew. Ben was in position next to the parents on the sidelines. His concentration was on the ball at the center of the field.

"Go, Benny!"

It was loud. Loud because there was nobody else talking. Loud because they were indoors and the acoustics amplified her voice.

Loud because she hadn't called him Benny since he had asked her to stop when he was six years old.

He turned his head and found his mother. There she was, standing between his father and Hannah. Her hands were in the air, and she was gyrating to apparent music in her own head. She began to giggle and then began bobbing up and down while clapping her hands.

"Go, Benny Boo!"

Oh, Jesus Christ! She had not just called him Benny Boo in front of his entire team, had she?

The whistle blew, but he was still watching his mother clap, was still watching her ridiculous behavior.

"Ben!" A yell from behind. "Wake up!"

The ball was next to him, but he missed it. The other team won possession, and he had to scramble to orient himself on the field, to run after the ball. But he was too late. The ball was passed beautifully to an opposing team member, and with a high kick to the upper left-hand corner of the net, they scored.

Because of him.

Because he hadn't been paying attention.

Because he had, instead, been watching his mother dance and clap her hands like an idiot.

He ground his teeth tightly into his mouth guard, clenched his jaw.

"Ben, what the hell?" It was Mike DaSilva, a team member he didn't much appreciate in the first place, but it pissed him off nonetheless. "You gotta pay attention, man." Mike had been nagging Ben since they were in the second grade together.

Ben tried to ignore him. He knew Mike had the tendency to act like a jerk, and not just toward Ben. In past games, his mother had even commented on the car ride home that she had heard inappropriate language from Mike or that Mike had said something to a team member that made him a "poor sport." She had urged him to ignore Mike if he ever said something to Ben, and oftentimes he could. Oftentimes he'd just smile or shake his head, get back into the game. But today he just couldn't. His concentration was lost. He was pissed. He wanted the damn ball, wanted to plow through that defensive line and score a freakin' goal. But he couldn't shake the image of his mother from the back of his mind.

A pass to him. He missed, and the opposing team took control.

He ran, kicked at the ball, and sent it careening to the side of the field, where he was able to sprint and command the ball once again. He ran, passed to a team member at the center of the turf. A beautiful cross.

"Whoop! Way to go, Benny Boo!"

He clenched his fists, willed his attention to remain on the game. Pleaded with himself not to look over his shoulder at his mother.

His teammate passed to another. That boy kicked and sent the ball flying past the goalie and into the net.

Score!

Ben leaped up in the air, raised his arms. They had got one, tied the score!

Cheers erupted from his teammates, and screams were pulled forth from the spectators on the sideline. Luckily, with the projection of excited voices surrounding him, Ben couldn't decipher which yell was from his mother or even if she was yelling at all. This facilitated his reabsorption into the game.

He continued to play, immersed himself in this sport he loved so much. He wasn't bothered by his mother again, and for this, he was immensely thankful.

When the last whistle blew, indicating the end of the game, Ben's team had won 2–1. When he had slapped hands with the opposing team and said goodbye to his teammates and coach, he walked to meet his family at the sidelines, grinning broadly.

"Hey, great game," his dad said when Ben approached.

"Thanks."

"It was so much fun to watch you play, Ben," his mother said. She leaned in and gave him a fierce hug. Ben had grown considerably this past year and was now at a height with his mother's five feet, five inches.

"Ugh," his mother exclaimed when she pulled back, "you're so sweaty!"

"Uh," Ben remarked, "yeah. Usually am, Mom." He watched as his mother rubbed the palms of her hands down her jeans.

"All set?" his father asked.

Ben nodded, and they began to walk toward the exit of the indoor sports facility. They approached the car, and his mother popped the trunk of the minivan. Ben shoved his gear in and climbed into the middle row of the vehicle next to Hannah. His mother took the wheel, and his father sat in the passenger seat in front of his sister. His mother started the car and backed out of the parking spot.

"Let's get ice cream!" His mom jubilantly bounced in her seat.

"Ice cream!" Hannah exclaimed. Ice cream was Hannah's favorite food, and she'd never turn it down. She hadn't really found a flavor yet that she didn't enjoy.

"Nah." Ben didn't really feel like ice cream right now. He just wanted to get home.

"What do you mean, 'nah'?"

"Just don't want ice cream."

"How can you not want ice cream?" his mother asked, obviously flummoxed.

"I just don't."

"I do," Hannah remarked. "Daddy, do you want ice cream?"

"I don't really care one way or the other," he answered.

"Well, Hannah Scrumptious and I want ice cream, so here we go!" Ben smirked at his mother's enthusiasm. She might have annoyed the hell out of him at the game, but she hadn't used her pet name for Hannah in a while and it sounded comforting to him right now. Normal, really.

They chatted on the car ride over to get their ice cream, his mother and Hannah mostly. Ben had his earphones on and was listening to Train on his phone. His mother didn't always love it when his earphones went on, especially when the family was all together. She often wanted to converse, spend time together as a cohesive unit. He knew to have the music low enough where he could still hear everyone else in the car.

They continued to drive. Five minutes, ten.

His father was on his phone. Ben guessed he was checking a work email, as he knew they had him on a deadline. His father was often on his laptop at the kitchen table after Hannah went to bed at night. Ben nodded his head ever so slightly to the music as he watched his dad look up, then turn to gaze at the surroundings outside.

"Annie, where in the world are we going?"

"To get ice cream. You know that." His mother's eyebrows creased as she frowned.

"What place?"

"You know . . . that indoor place. Ah, that place, Sam." She sounded flustered as she looked out the window, attempting to retrieve the correct name. Ben felt the car slow down, saw his mother look left, then right before staring forward once more.

BEEP!

Ben bounced in his seat, paused his music, and took his headphones off. A car passed them on the right, the male driver flipping his mother the finger as he sped past.

"Annie, babe . . ." His father's voice was soft, though pleading. "Why don't you take a left here. We'll figure out where to go after we're stopped."

"I know where to go, Sam!" The car slowed even further. Cars passed, horns blared.

"Annie, for Christ's sake! Pull the damn car over!" His dad sounded terrified.

His mom put her foot on the gas and swerved into the left lane, stopping at a street light. When it was green, she pulled into the parking lot of a Wendy's, parked, and turned the key in the ignition to off.

His dad took a deep breath, sighed audibly. He turned to look at his wife.

"Babe, you okay?"

"Mmm-hmm."

"You don't sound convincing. Do you know where we are?" His mom shook her head slowly from side to side.

"Jesus." It was just a breath, but Ben heard it all the same. He turned to look at Hannah beside him. Her bottom lip was trembling, and her eyes were wide in her round face.

"Okay . . . okay." His dad opened his door. "Well," he said, his voice more chipper, though Ben knew it was a pretense of bravery, "I still want that ice cream. I don't mind driving, Annie. Why don't you come take my place?"

His mother hesitated in the driver's seat, but Ben looked on as she slowly pulled the latch on the door and it popped open. His dad had made his way over to her side by then and grasped the handle, pulling it farther open. His mother ploddingly stepped out.

They were soon back on the road, his father driving as Ben stared at the back of his mother's blond bob, her gaze trained out the window as she tapped the thumb and middle fingers of her left hand together vigorously for the remainder of the car ride.

"All right, Benny Boo, are you ready?" Annie had finished packing the beach bag and a large cooler with lunch, snacks, and drinks surrounded by cooler packs and ice. She scooped Hannah, who had newly turned two years old, from the living room floor, where she had been playing with blocks, and carried her to the mudroom to help her with her sandals.

"Mom, I told you to stop calling me that!" Ben protested noisily with exasperation.

"Yeah," Annie confirmed, *"I suppose you did. It's just hard for me to think of my little boy getting to be so big."*

"I'm not little. I'm six."

Annie paused after velcroing a sandal to his sister's foot and looked at her son with a knowing smirk. *"No,"* she said, *"I suppose you're not little."*

"There you go, Hannah," Annie said, then leaned over and kissed the chubby cheeks of her daughter over and over, pulling forth squeals of laughter as Hannah scrunched her nose and grasped her mother's T-shirt.

The threesome piled into the minivan (Ben's dad was working, but his mom had summers off) and exited the garage. Ten minutes down the road, his mom pulled into a Dunkin' Donuts, a maneuver that had become ritualistic on beach days, and to which Ben certainly would never complain about.

"Munchkins?" his mom asked as she looked at Ben through the rearview mirror.

"Yes!"

Hannah clapped her chubby toddler's hands. "Yes, yes, yes!"

His mom laughed as she idled the minivan behind a large pickup truck in the drive-through line.

When it was their turn, she ordered a box of twenty-five assorted Munchkins. "But can you be sure to put some extra jellies in there, please?" she asked. She knew Ben loved the jelly Munchkins.

She pulled forward after ordering, and it was soon their turn to pay at the window and retrieve their box.

"Here you go, Benny Boo," she teased as she handed the box to her son behind her.

"Mom!" Ben protested.

Annie laughed as she faced forward again and slowly pulled out of the drive-through lane. It was entirely too easy to get a rise out of her son.

They had hit the highway and been driving for another ten minutes when Ben and Hannah had their fill of Munchkins, a few left over in the cardboard box. White sugar outlined Hannah's lips, and dollops of red jelly were smeared on Ben's cheeks. His mom took a sip of a smoothie she had made for herself at home, placed it back in the cup holder, and swallowed.

"All right," she announced enthusiastically, "we've still got a way to go. How about some Wiggles?"

Hannah clapped her hands again, and Ben smiled. He watched his mom's fingers fiddle with some buttons on the van's dashboard, and then she bopped in her seat as "Hot Potato" came through the speakers. She turned the volume up and looked at Ben in the rearview mirror.

"'Hot Potato'!" she exclaimed. "Let's do it, kids." Her hands momentarily left the steering wheel as her gaze drifted back to the road before her. She placed one fist on top of the other and then switched so her top fist was now the bottom. She began singing the song loudly.

"Tato!" Hannah giggled.

Ben mimicked the hand motions with a grin, looked at his sister beside him as she bopped in her car seat.

"Cold spaghetti now!" His mom's left hand rested on the steering wheel, and her right arm was raised in the air, the fingers of her hand splayed and moving up and down like a wave.

"Sketti!" Hannah exclaimed, still bopping in her seat the best she could with the belt tight against her shoulders and chest.

Ben knew the motions well as this was one of his favorite songs. His arms rose, his sticky fingers wiggled as he sang along to the music.

When "Hot Potato" finished, his mom hit a button on the dashboard a few times, and "Fruit Salad" poured from the speakers, another of Ben's favorite songs. He began rubbing his belly, the predominant motion the Wiggles performed when singing this particular track.

They sang and moved to the music for a while, and when his mom turned the Wiggles off, Ben gazed out the window until he saw the sun's rays glisten off the water of the ocean. He watched the seagulls flying above, looked at the people walking and running along the side of the road as the minivan veered closer to its destination. He could smell the salt in the air, and when his mother turned the air-conditioning off and opened the windows, he could hear the wind, feel the dampness on his cheeks.

She pulled into a parking lot and paid an attendant standing next to a small wooden hut, then pulled forth and found a parking spot in the large lot. At this time of the day, there were plenty of spots available. His mom liked to leave the house extra early. She always said they were able to get a great spot on the beach when they did.

His mom exited the car and helped Hannah out of her car seat. Ben was in a booster and perfectly capable of undoing his own seat belt, thank you very much. He hopped to the floor and jumped to the concrete as his mom had already opened the door automatically from the driver's seat. He met his mom and sister at the back of the van.

"Here, Ben," his mom said. "Can you hold your sister's hand while I get our stuff?"

Ben didn't so much want to hold Hannah's hand, but he did as he was told. He watched his mom open the beach buggy and load it with belongings: a bag of towels and sunscreen, the umbrella, a large beach blanket, Hannah's diaper bag, some beach toys, and a chair.

"Here we go," his mom said. "Ben, stay close to me and don't let go of your sister's hand. We're in a parking lot." She pushed the beach buggy along and dragged the cooler on its wheels behind her. She struggled quite a bit when they hit the fine tan sand, but she eventually halted and announced they had found a great spot. She laid the large, thin blue blanket on the sand before unpacking anything else, and Ben and Hannah sat down and took off their sandals. His mom soon had the beach umbrella erect, her chair resting underneath. She had towels splayed out on the blanket, and the cooler resting to the side. She dumped the sand toys in front of the blanket.

"What would you like to do first?" she asked her children once sunscreen had been applied. "Toys? Water? A snack?"

Hannah stood from the blanket and toddled over to the beach toys. She picked up a shovel and started filling a bucket with sand. Annie joined her. "Come on over, Ben," she said. "I can even bury you in the sand!" This captured Ben's attention as he loved it when his mother did this.

"Help me dig your hole," Annie said. Together, Ben and his mom dug their shovels into the cool sand and scooped until there was a large area for Ben to lie in. He climbed inside and rested his head above the hole. He felt his legs become heavy as sand was shoveled onto them. His sister soon joined their mom and clumsily poured sand over his stomach. Her next scoop landed on his chin, some sand accumulating on his lower lip.

"Hannah!" Ben exclaimed as he attempted to spit the sand off. "Watch it!"

"Ah," his mother countered, "it was just an accident. No harm done. Here," she continued as she lifted a towel from the blanket and used the edge to wipe the sand from his lip. "All set. Hannah, can you help me over here? Ben's feet need to be buried." He watched as his sister toddled farther away from his mouth and began scooping sand onto his feet.

Minutes later, Annie patted the sand around Ben's body firmly and announced he was good and buried. He felt completely weighted down from the tips of his toes all the way up to his chin. He began wiggling his fingers, and the sand sprinkled downward to reveal his white fingertips and nails. He forced his little muscles to work in his favor and broke free of the sand with his arms, then his legs, mounds of sand falling to the sides. He used his elbows to help prop himself into a sitting position and then stood. He brushed sand off his naked torso, though much of it remained sticking to the sunscreen on his skin. "Again?" he asked.

"Maybe your sister would like a turn?" his mother suggested.

"Hannah, you want to go, or you want me to go again?" Ben asked. He rather hoped she'd let him go again.

"Annah," she said. She still couldn't pronounce her entire name correctly.

Ben grimaced, but the grimace didn't linger. His sister didn't typically remain lying down for long at all. They couldn't even really bury her before she stood up triumphantly and moved on. She'd be quick and he could go again.

When they tired of sand play, they ventured into the freezing water. Ben ran in the waves as his mother stood by Hannah at the shoreline. His sister enjoyed bringing her palms forcefully down upon the water and splashing droplets onto her face. She'd squint and laugh, her short but growing hair wet and sticking to her cheeks. His mom often tried to put a sun hat on his sister, but she always managed to yank it right off. Mom had since given up.

His back was turned to his family when he felt hands stealthily slip around his waist and lift him up in the air, spinning him around and around, his feet dangling and skimming the water. "Whoo!" He knew it was his mom who had him, so he began to laugh as his eyes tried to focus. Eventually, he just closed his lids and squealed through the momentum of the swing.

His mom put him down. "Oh, goodness," she said. "Now I'm super dizzy. But I can still do this!" She bent down, placed the pinkies of her hands together, and scooped some water into her palms. When she splashed Ben, he closed his eyes and tried to cover his face with his arms.

"Hey!" Ben protested happily.

"Hey yourself," his mom replied as she splashed him again, a bit more gently this time. She walked over to Hannah and lifted her onto her hip. She brought her farther into the ocean so she could also join in the fun.

His mom bent down, and Hannah used the splayed fingers of her chubby right hand to splash in the water. His mom then lifted Hannah under her armpits high into the sky and then zoomed her back down until she was waist-deep in the biting cold water. His sister giggled her delight.

The morning progressed quickly, merrily. When Ben's skin prickled in goose bumps and his teeth began to chatter, they made their way back to the blanket, where his mother wrapped him and Hannah tightly into their towels to dry off and warm up in the hot, ascending sun. They played in the sand some more, went for a walk along the shoreline, explored the rocks, and ate their lunch. His mother made Hannah comfortable under the beach umbrella, and she soon fell asleep for an early-afternoon nap. Ben played with some sticker books on his towel as his mother read from her novel.

The afternoon sun soon began to wane in the sky. The ice cream truck had come, and Ben and Hannah both got to enjoy a treat, Ben a SpongeBob SquarePants popsicle that left his mouth yellow, and Hannah a snow cone that dribbled red and purple down her chin and onto her frilly bathing suit. Even his mom got a fudge pop.

They were drying off on the blanket once again after another dip in the water when Ben yawned. His mother chuckled. "It's been a long day, hasn't it? Long but good."

"Yep."

"How about we stop for some pizza on the way home?"

"Yeah!"

"You, too, Hannah? Would you like some pizza?"

"Yay!"

They packed up their belongings and slowly made their way back to the car. When the trunk was full and Ben and Hannah were both buckled in their seats, they were off. The pizza place was only ten minutes away, a wonderful ending to a perfect beach day. When they pulled into a parking spot and his mom shut the ignition off, she turned around in her seat and looked at Hannah first, and then at Ben. She found his blue eyes and smiled. "I love you guys so much," she said. "I wouldn't want to be with anyone else right now. What a wonderful day we had."

Ben smiled brightly, for yes, a wonderful day it had been!

CHAPTER FIVE

Sam

*C*hristmas vacation ended, and Sam went back to work.
Annie did, too.

Sam had called Annie's primary care physician the day
after Christmas and made an appointment for Annie to see
her the first week in January. So here they were on a Friday,
sitting on hard brown chairs in the waiting room.

Sam had taken the day off, something that wasn't so easy
to do these days with the demands of his job, but he *needed* to
be here with his wife. He didn't fully trust that she'd relay all
relevant information to him if she did this alone. Caroline had
offered to take Annie, but Sam wanted to be here in person.
He had so many pressing questions and was hoping that Dr.
Dorsinger could provide answers.

"Annie." Both Sam and Annie looked up. A middle-aged
nurse with short brown hair called to the waiting area from
the doorway over a brown clipboard resting on her large
bosom. An immense number of small, vibrant dogs adorned
her nursing scrubs.

Annie leaped up from her seat and hop-skipped toward her. Sam followed behind.

"Oh!" Annie exclaimed. "Just look at your puppies! Oh, I love puppies!" Annie clasped her hands together and bounced on the balls of her feet in the doorway.

The nurse raised her eyebrows and looked at Sam, who simply shrugged his shoulders in response.

"Well, I'm Belinda. Follow me." Annie followed behind, beaming, with Sam at her side.

"Right in here." Belinda motioned for Sam and Annie to enter a small room. Annie sat on the examination chair, white paper crinkling with her movements, feet dangling down the end.

Belinda closed the door behind her. "Annie, I'll just need to take your weight first, if you don't mind."

Annie hopped back down to the floor and walked the few steps to the scale in the corner of the room. She stepped on.

"You can take your boots off if you'd like," Belinda suggested.

"Oh," Annie said, "okay." She stepped off and removed her winter boots, then stood back on the scale.

"Okay," Belinda announced, "all set. You can have a seat."

Annie sat back on the crinkled paper of the examination chair, where Belinda proceeded to take her blood pressure.

"Looks good," she announced when through. "The doctor will be in to see you soon." She opened the door and walked through. Sam heard a slight click as the door shut once more.

"Now we wait," Sam said.

"Yep."

"Want a magazine?" Sam asked. He began to reach for the small bundle on the countertop but stopped when Annie shook her head. Instead, he sat down on a black chair between the scale and his wife.

Silence. Sam could hear the ticking of the circular clock

upon the white wall. Minutes passed and Sam was finding it difficult to endure the stillness in the room.

"Thanks for coming today, Annie."

His wife nodded. "Sure." A smile formed.

"I just . . . I just really want to figure some things out. I know you don't think we need to be here, but it means a lot that you're doing this."

"Of course."

More silence.

Apparently, the doctor was running late because it was another twenty-five minutes before there was a light knock on the door.

"Come in," Sam said.

Dr. Dorsinger was a slight woman in her early sixties with short curly brown hair and glasses. She entered with a laptop in hand.

"Good morning to you both," she said in a cheerful manner.

"Good morning," both Sam and Annie returned.

"So, Annie," Dr. Dorsinger said as she placed the laptop on the counter and opened it, "how can I help you today."

"Your boobs are bigger. Did you get work done?"

Dr. Dorsinger looked at Annie through the lens of her glasses. Sam gasped, and his eyes widened considerably.

"I did not get work done," Dr. Dorsinger said, "no." She stole a quick glance at a blushing Sam, who returned an embarrassed look. "Perhaps it's just my shirt today."

"The nurse had the cutest puppies on her clothes. I love puppies," Annie announced, changing the subject. "I was hoping you'd have puppies, too. Or maybe kittens. Kittens are cute, too."

"No puppies or kittens for me today. Just my ordinary clothes." Dr. Dorsinger sat on a black swiveling chair beside the counter and began to type on her laptop.

"So, how can I help you today?"

As Annie said nothing in response, Sam began: "Thanks so much for seeing us. I'm really concerned about Annie. She doesn't seem to be concerned herself, but I am. And her mother is, too."

"What concerns you?"

Sam looked at his wife. "Annie's been acting very differently lately. She's just not herself."

"How so?" Dr. Dorsinger continued to type while looking over at Sam intermittently.

Sam proceeded to convey Annie's forgetfulness and the call he had received from Lucinda Daily at the elementary school. He told her about Annie's sleeping habits. Sam paused, thought. "Sometimes she says things that just don't make sense, or maybe they do make sense, but it's so far off the topic we're talking about. She has days where she's just really not happy and she'll snap at me and the kids, but then she'll have days where she's incredibly happy and is acting almost childlike. Happy, yes, but not happy like Annie happy. I'm not even sure that makes sense." Sam paused.

"Go on."

Sam looked at Annie, who was toying with the white paper of the examination chair. "She got a little lost recently while driving to get ice cream. That was really strange. And concerning."

"How did you react to that, Annie?"

Annie shrugged her shoulders, so Dr. Dorsinger looked at Sam.

"She didn't have much of a reaction, really. I had her pull over and she sat there for a while. I took over driving and she didn't say anything for the rest of the ride, just looked out the window. No expression."

Dr. Dorsinger continued to type.

"She's just not herself."

Dr. Dorsinger continued to ask questions, and Sam answered. Finally: "Annie how do you feel about all of this?"

Annie shrugged. "Don't really know. Sam says all these things and I guess I can understand but . . ." She trailed off.

"Do you think you're acting any differently?"

"Not really."

"Do you feel sad sometimes?"

"Sure."

"Sleeping more?"

"I don't think so."

"Do you feel really happy sometimes?"

"Yeah," Annie said.

"Do you feel anxious sometimes?"

"Sure."

"Annie, has anything changed in your life for you to be feeling differently?"

"No."

"Have you lost pleasure in doing normal things, things that used to make you happy?"

Annie contemplated this, then: "I don't know."

Dr. Dorsinger continued to type, asked a few more questions of both Annie and Sam. "Annie," she said, "I think you may be suffering from a bit of mild depression."

"Depression?" Sam was surprised.

"Yes, I think so. The symptoms are there. I think she has depression with manic tendencies."

"Manic?"

"Yes," Dr. Dorsinger confirmed. "That may explain why she has some days where she's very happy, maybe even over-the-top as you've described, though I don't believe we're looking at bipolar disorder here."

"What does this mean?" Sam asked. Annie just watched her husband and Dr. Dorsinger converse.

"I think we should consider some medications for Annie in conjunction with weekly visits to a psychiatrist. I'm happy to provide you with recommendations in this area. As far as medications, if you're willing to go that route"—here she turned her attention to Annie—"my suggestion would be to start you on something called a selective serotonin reuptake inhibitor, or SSRI. SSRIs tend to be a bit safer than other medications and have fewer side effects. I'd start you with a low dose to be taken in the morning, and we can see how you're doing after about a month. How does that sound?"

Annie shrugged. "Okay, I guess. But I don't like to take medications."

"I can understand that, but I do think this may help."

"What are the side effects?" Sam asked. "Annie's always been healthy, she's never been on any medications beyond something for strep throat or the occasional Advil tablet, as far as I know."

"Insomnia, maybe feeling tired. Upset stomach, dry mouth, maybe changes in weight or appetite, possible flu symptoms, possible feelings of anxiety. And a decreased sex drive. Though," Dr. Dorsinger said, "depression itself can cause this. Have you had less of a drive for sex, Annie?"

"I don't know."

When Dr. Dorsinger looked at Sam, he nodded affirmatively.

"I do highly recommend seeing a psychiatrist. Would you like me to get you that list of psychiatrists in the area that specialize in depression?"

Sam swallowed, nodded again. "Yes, please."

"I would also like to do some bloodwork to rule out any other possibilities, specifically hypothyroidism. Are you familiar with this?"

"I've heard of it, but I don't know much about it," Sam admitted.

"Our thyroid gland is here." She pointed to the lower front of her neck. "It makes thyroid hormones that are carried throughout our bodies. When the levels are too low, the body slows down. You may feel tired, forgetful, or depressed. All symptoms that Annie is portraying."

This was just all too much.

They spoke a bit longer, and then Dr. Dorsinger left the room to obtain the paperwork.

Sam stood and walked to Annie, taking her hand in his own.

"How do you feel, babe?"

"Fine."

"I mean, depression. Annie, I didn't even know. Why didn't you tell me you were feeling like this?" His countenance fully displayed his concern for his wife.

"I don't really."

"You don't feel like this?"

"I don't think so."

"But Annie, you haven't been yourself. Surely you know that."

Annie merely shrugged her shoulders again.

Dr. Dorsinger reentered the room. "I just called the prescription into the pharmacy listed on your profile, Annie. You can pick that up once we get the bloodwork results in. Obviously, we won't need the medication if you have a thyroid issue." She handed Sam a sheet of paper. "The list of psychiatrists in the area," she confirmed. "Feel free to make some calls after the bloodwork results.

"Annie, have you got any questions for me?" Dr. Dorsinger readjusted her glasses.

"No."

"Sam?"

"I don't think so. Not right now, anyway. I'm trying to let it all sink in."

"Of course. Call if you need to, and I'd like to see you again, Annie, in a month. I'll call you once the bloodwork results are in and we'll go from there."

Sam nodded. "Okay." He sighed.

Dr. Dorsinger gifted him with a sympathetic grin before leaving the room.

"Let's get out of here," Annie said as she bounced off the examination chair and walked toward the door. "I want pizza!"

CHAPTER SIX

Ben

They were just sitting down to dinner when his father arrived home from work. It was Friday evening and now officially February vacation. Ben was stoked! His dad said they might be able to get to the slopes on a weekend since he couldn't take any time off of work. Ben loved to ski, was good at it, too. Loved the speed, the jumps. He loved the thrill. He loved skiing almost as much as he loved soccer. And it was his fourteenth birthday on Wednesday. Last year he'd had a couple of friends join him for a game of laser tag and then back at his house for pizza and a movie and a sleepover. This year he preferred to stay at home, have Tyler over. His mother had met Tyler's mom, Bitsy, way back when they first moved to town, and they had hit it off. He was too young to remember this time himself, but apparently, he and Tyler had also become fast friends immediately. As much as toddlers could, anyway. His parents had promised Ben that he could have Tyler over on Wednesday, his actual birthday, along with their mutual friend Cole, who also played soccer. *Fortnite,* games of *FIFA*, pizza and a movie as well as a sleepover sounded good to Ben!

"Hi, Dad!" Hannah's long blond hair whipped around her face as she turned to look behind her shoulder. His father often joked that he didn't have much to do genetically with his children's appearance, as they both had blond hair like their mom instead of his darker brown.

"Hi, Hannah Banana." His father had already kicked off his winter boots, hung his jacket up on the hook. He placed his laptop bag on the counter and looked at Ben's mom, dejected.

"Annie," he said, "anything happen today that I should know about?"

"Nope."

"No!?" His father sounded incredulous. "Excuse us, kids. Your mother and I need to talk. Go ahead and start dinner without us. Annie, join me upstairs?"

His mom stood from the kitchen table and walked behind his father. He heard footsteps ascend the stairway, retreat down the hall. He heard an abrupt and hard closing of their bedroom door.

"He's not happy," Hannah observed.

Ben shook his head. "No. Something happened." His dad had said to eat, but he couldn't think about eating just now. He pushed his chair out from under him and slowly walked to the bottom of the stairs. He didn't dare go any farther in fear that his parents' bedroom door would open and they'd see him standing there eavesdropping.

Hannah sidled up next to him as he trained his ear on his parents' muffled voices. He couldn't hear much just now, them being so far away and with their door closed, but he desperately tried nonetheless.

"No!?" His dad. *That* word he heard. "Damn it, Annie!" A few moments later: "You have to be kidding me!"

For minutes he listened in and for minutes he heard

nothing from his mother. Then, just when he was about to give up and head back to the kitchen table, this: "You are such a fucking asshole, Sam!"

Hannah gasped beside Ben. She had obviously heard their mother, too.

"She's never yelled at Daddy like that," Hannah protested. "What's going on, Ben?"

"I don't know." He looked at his sister, saw her terrified expression.

"Lucinda told me that you had to have a helper in your class since you returned from Christmas vacation and you just can't cut it anymore! You were fired today! What the hell are we going to do now?"

"Oh, my God," Hannah breathed disbelievingly, "Mom got fired?"

"Come on," Ben began walking back to the kitchen, "we shouldn't be here." Hannah hesitated. "Come on!" Ben raised his voice, which set Hannah's bottom lip to tremble and tears to pool in her brown eyes. He sped back to his sister, yanked on her arm to get her moving.

"Ow!" Hannah protested.

"Then move it!"

They were at the table for just a couple of minutes when their father reemerged. He was visibly incensed. Ben looked at his plate of chicken nuggets as if they enthralled him. His mother didn't return, and there was no amicable dinner conversation to be had. When his father finished his meal, he simply stood back from the table and brought his plate to the sink. He turned the hot water on, let it pour from the faucet as he braced himself on the palms of his hands against the counter and closed his eyes.

Ben looked at his sister across the table. She met his gaze, then looked back at her empty plate.

~

Ben stepped out of the shower and dried himself off. Only a few hours had passed since dinner, but his mother was still in her bedroom. Hannah would be sound asleep by now.

He opened the bathroom door, and hot steam wafted out into the hallway. He had forgotten to turn the fan on again. His mother hated it when he forgot the fan; she was incessantly nagging him when he did so. Something about mold or whatever.

He was pretty sure she wouldn't care to nag him now.

"I know, Caroline." His father's voice carried up the stairs.

Ben crept lightly on the balls of his feet to sit on a middle stair, towel around his waist, and listen in.

"No . . . no, I don't think so." His father paused for a moment. "Now that she's not working, our entire dynamic is going to change. I'm not sure what I'm going to do. Hannah always just went to work with her. She's got another year at the elementary school, so it was just an easy thing for Annie to do. I suppose she'll just have to take the bus now, which isn't a big deal in the grand scheme of things. But we've relied on the money Annie's brought in. I've got a great job and it pays well, but we overstepped when we bought this house. Annie fell in love with it, especially the fact that it was right on the water. I love it, too, but it was Annie. Her face, Caroline. I couldn't say no. She was so happy. But now it's on me if she doesn't find another job, and honestly, I'm not sure she will with the way she's been acting. And the doctor even upped her meds and we're already seeing a psychiatrist once a week. I got names from her primary care. I basically had to go through the list and see if anyone was in our insurance network. I mean, a psychiatrist? We've never been here before. I didn't know where to begin."

Another pause from his father and then, "No, she didn't cry, didn't even seem to care very much about losing the job. What she seemed to care about was the fact that I was so pissed off. We yelled at each other, Caroline. We never yell at each other. Sure, we get upset. Show me a couple that doesn't. But she called me a fucking asshole. No . . . no, I'm not joking. We've been married for sixteen years and she has never once called me an asshole. Not seriously, anyway. It's always come with a smile and a playful shove.

"Tomorrow? Yeah, tomorrow would be great. I could use the support right about now. I really appreciate it. We can talk more then. Thanks, Caroline . . . Yeah . . . Okay . . . See you tomorrow." His father had stopped talking and Ben heard footsteps. He scrambled back up the stairs and ran into his bedroom, clutching the towel tightly to his waist. He closed the door softly behind him. He turned his Spotify playlist on. Nico & Vinz filled the stifling air around him. He had a few more minutes before he had to head to bed. At least it would give him time to compose himself.

Ben sat at his desk, placed his forehead on his folded forearms resting on the smooth wooden surface, and inhaled.

Ben knocked on the door to his parents' bedroom. No answer. He slowly turned the knob and poked his head inside.

"Mom?"

"What?" She didn't sound angry, but neither did she sound pleased.

Ben walked farther into the room and saw his mother propped up in bed, her back resting on several pillows against the headboard. She had her phone in her hands.

"Good night," Ben said. He walked to the side of the bed.

"Good night," his mother replied. Her expression was flat.

Ben leaned in and gave his mother an awkward hug. She allowed him to do so but didn't return the affection. He let go and began walking away. Hesitating, he stopped his steps and looked behind his shoulder. His mother's attention was back on the small screen of her phone.

Ben feigned disinterest, tried to convince himself that he was unaffected.

He was lying.

If Ben had tried to head to bed in months past without saying good night to his mother, she would have knocked on the door to his bedroom and pounced on his bed, showering him with kisses as a punishment. Man, he hated those kisses. He was almost fourteen, after all. Way too old for her damn kisses.

Then why was this bothering him so much?

He lumbered down the hallway, opened the door to his bedroom, and walked in. He climbed under the blankets of his unkempt bed and pulled them up to his chin, looking at the white ceiling.

He waited eagerly for a knock on his door, for his mother to walk in, sit on the edge of his bed, and talk to him like she so often did when she felt something was bothering her son.

It was silence that finally lulled him to sleep.

CHAPTER SEVEN

Caroline

S am had called her last night and told her that Annie had lost her job. Annie, the daughter who had always been so responsible, the woman who loved her work with the kindergarten children of her community, had been fired.

Could depression rip one's life apart so wholly, so viciously?

She needed to see Annie, wanted to talk more with Sam, and so she found herself tying the laces of her walking shoes, exiting her garage, and turning the key in the ignition of her Honda Accord.

Twenty minutes later she was knocking on the front door of her daughter's home.

It was Annie who answered. "Hi, Mom." Her voice was soft, though Caroline was pleased to see she had a slight smile on her face. Perhaps this was a good day for a visit?

"Hi, honey. I'm happy to see you." Caroline walked over the threshold.

"Okay." Annie's answer wasn't what Caroline had

expected. More often than not, Annie would reply that she was happy to see her mother as well. And always, always, with a large smile on her face and a ready hug.

Not today.

"Hi, Caroline." It was Sam who leaned in and embraced her. As hugs were almost always instigated by Caroline, she knew Sam appreciated her presence in his home this day.

"Sam," she acknowledged, looking intently into his green eyes when he released her.

"Come on in." Sam moved aside, and Caroline took her boots off in the doorway, laid them in the corner of the entryway rug. She hung her coat on the coatrack beside the door.

"Grammie!" Hannah bounded over, hugged her merrily. "Dad told us you were coming today. He said maybe we could go to the movies or maybe we could walk around the mall. Ben needs new pants because his don't fit him anymore."

"Well, either of those plans sound good to me," Caroline said, happy to see the genuine smile on her granddaughter's face.

"Hi, Gram." Ben approached from the living room.

"Ah, come here and give your grandmother a hug." Caroline reached out and Ben, slightly abashed, moved in to allow her arms access to encircle his shoulders. "You're taller than me now, Ben, and I feel like I just saw you the other day. I've told you already that you need to stop growing," she teased.

This brought a grin to Ben's lips as his eyes found the floor. Caroline gently touched his chin, and when Ben looked up, she said, "I love you, you know," softly, passionately.

Ben made no verbal response, but the blue of his eyes and his intent gaze on her was all she needed in reply.

"Okay," Sam announced. "Hot cocoa. We have to have our hot chocolate when your grandmother is over. Let's get that ready and then we can decide on how we'd like to spend our day." Caroline observed Sam look at Annie, a silent prompt to elicit agreement, maybe? Annie made no response, simply walked away from her family. Sam stepped to the kitchen, extracted a pot, and placed it on the stove, pouring a generous amount of milk inside and turning the knob to medium heat.

Minutes later they were seated at the kitchen table, hot mugs in hand. Sam brought over a canister of whipped cream and a cylindrical plastic tube of rainbow sprinkles. Caroline grinned as Hannah squirted the whipped cream on top of her hot chocolate, brown liquid speckles spraying onto the table from the force of the white substance she adored so much.

"Okay," Sam began as he took a sip of his hot cocoa. "We've got a couple of options. What should we do today?"

"Movies," Hannah said.

"Whatever," was Ben's response.

"Caroline?" asked Sam.

"I'm indifferent. I'm just glad to be with you all. I'll go wherever you want."

"Annie?" Sam turned to his wife. She looked up from her mug at the sound of her name, but her expression was blank. "Annie, babe, what do you want to do today? We were thinking of either going to the movies or heading to the mall to walk around and get Ben some new pants, maybe stop at that frozen yogurt place the kids like so much, too. Maybe get you a latte. I know how much you like them."

"Oh," Annie said in response. "I don't know." She paused for a moment, looked down at her hot drink. She stood abruptly from the table, picked a wedgie, and walked to the living room. Caroline watched Sam's concerned expression as Annie sat upon the couch, feet tucked under her thighs.

"That one right there," Annie said, pointing to a vase of artificial flowers on the fireplace mantel. "That one . . ."

"What?" asked Sam.

"That one," Annie said more forcefully. "That thing."

"The flowers?"

"Yeah, the flowers," Annie said. "I don't like them."

"You don't like them?"

"That's what I said," Annie whipped her head to look at Sam behind her, still sitting at the kitchen table.

"Annie," Sam said gently, "you bought those just last year. I put them out before Christmastime because Hannah was asking to decorate for Christmas and winter. Usually, you like to decorate, but I assumed you were busy or didn't feel much like decorating this year. I thought you loved those flowers. You were so proud that you had made the arrangement yourself."

Annie stood from the couch and approached the mantel. She reached above, took down the large vase, and plopped it on the couch. She grasped the flowers by their hard, artificial green stems and pulled them out.

"I'll put these away." She began to walk back into the kitchen. Sam assumed she was heading to the basement door as the basement was where they stored all their out-of-season decorations. Annie stood there in the middle of the kitchen, almost transfixed; her family looking on, their cups of hot chocolate forgotten before them. Eventually, Annie walked forward, opened a large kitchen cabinet, and shoved the flowers inside. When done, she walked back to the living room and turned the television on.

They decided to head to the mall. Sam convinced Hannah with the enticement of frozen yogurt.

Annie sat behind the wheel of their minivan and Caroline was opening the back door when Sam interrupted.

"No, no," he said. "Have the front," he told her, gloved hands lightly touching the large puffed sleeve of her winter jacket, his breath billowing in the cold air. The car was parked in the driveway and not the garage.

"I don't mind sitting in the back with the kids," Caroline countered.

"I know, but the front's more comfortable. I'll get out back."

"Well, okay, then," Caroline said. "Thank you." She hoisted herself inside—this vehicle was a bit of a jump compared to her Accord—and buckled herself in. Sam climbed into the seat behind his mother-in-law, pushing Hannah over to sit in the middle. Ben was in back of his mother.

"And we're off," Annie announced, "like a dress on prom night."

"Annie!" Caroline admonished. "Really?"

Annie turned to her mother, gave her a quizzical look. Ben snorted from the back seat. Hannah stared blankly at the scene unfolding before her.

"It's okay," Sam announced, leaning forward. "It's okay. Let's just get going."

Annie backed out of the driveway and onto the street. It had snowed two days ago, but the roads were luckily devoid of ice.

"Annie, you know where we're headed?" Sam asked.

"Of course I do, Sam," she replied. "I'm not stupid!"

Sam chose not to reply to this retort.

Annie drove down the back roads of their neighborhood and then onto the busier route where shops and restaurants were situated before she was to take the on-ramp and merge onto the highway.

"Look at all this traffic," Caroline observed. "You'd think everyone and their mother was out today." She chuckled at her own joke.

Annie turned the radio on, nodded to the beat. She looked out the window, left, then right, before training her eyes back on the road before her. Caroline steadily watched her daughter.

"Let's get lasagna," Annie announced. "We can go to that place . . . What's the one called, Sam?" She lifted her voice slightly to be heard in the back seat.

"What's what called?"

"That place," Annie said, "that lasagna place."

"Annie," Sam replied, "we're going to the mall."

Annie sneered, looked over her shoulder. "I know that, Sam!"

"Annie, watch the road!" Caroline cried.

Annie pushed forcefully down on the brakes and stopped the car behind others waiting at a red light. Caroline found her knuckles whitening with the force of her grasp on the side of the seat.

"Hey, Annie," Sam said wearily. "Want me to drive?"

"I can drive the damn car, Sam," Annie said.

The traffic began to move, and Annie with it. Her head continued to bounce with the beat of the music. Caroline watched her daughter remove her left hand from the steering wheel and furiously tap her middle finger to her thumb. Over and over. Annie was looking forward, but her eyes didn't waver. It seemed that she was transfixed.

Caroline whipped her head around, looked in front her.

Taillights glowed red.

"Annie," she said, "slow down. There's a red light."

Annie made no move to slow down, didn't even seem to acknowledge that her mother had spoken.

"Annie, for Christ's sake!" Sam yelled from the back. "Stop!"

Annie shook her head, came out of her trance. She seemed to see now that the cars were piling up before her at the red light, but instead of lifting her foot off the gas and hitting the brakes, she pushed down even farther on the gas pedal.

Caroline saw them advance, saw the butt of the car in front of them loom ever nearer. Her entire body tensed, her jaw clenched. She breathed deeply between her teeth, braced herself for what was inevitably to transpire.

She heard an ear-piercing scream from the back seat: Hannah.

Then . . . *CRASH!*

The sound of metal on metal, an airbag deploying and smashing into her face. For a second, blackness all around.

It took her several moments to reorient herself.

"Is . . . is everyone okay?" It was Sam from the back seat of the car.

Caroline's nose throbbed; her jaw ached. Liquid dribbled down her cheeks, her chin. She lifted her fingers to swipe at the trickles, and as she lowered her hand, she saw blood, the vibrant color a stark contrast upon the paleness of her skin. Tears seeped from her eyes, stinging.

Hannah sobbed from the back seat. Caroline knew instinctively that if Hannah was sobbing, then she was at least conscious. She didn't believe they had hit entirely too hard, despite the fact that Annie had pushed on the gas. She threw up a silent prayer of thanksgiving that they weren't on the highway.

"I'm okay." Her voice didn't sound like her own.

"Yeah, yeah . . ." Ben sounded weary.

Caroline turned to look behind her. Sam's face was contorted, his palm was on Hannah's arm.

"It hurts," Hannah sobbed.

"I know, Hannah Banana," Sam said. His voice trembled.

Ben looked shocked but otherwise unhurt.

Caroline turned to her daughter in the driver's seat.

"Annie, what were you thinking?"

"I stopped the car." She sounded a bit dazed and confused.

"You didn't stop the car. You sped up, Annie. You sped up. You could have seriously hurt someone." Then it dawned on her that at least one other car had been affected by the crash.

She steeled herself, painfully opened the door, and stepped outside.

The driver of the car Annie had hit was walking furiously toward Annie's door when he saw Caroline emerge.

"What the fuck was that, lady?" His face was red with rage, but Caroline didn't detect any blood or any altered movements.

"I'm . . . I'm so sorry," Caroline said, her voice was muffled, blood steadily dripping from her damaged nose.

"You're sorry?" He was infuriated.

"My daughter—" Her daughter what? What was she to tell this man? This man whose anger was so pronounced that nothing she could do or say would bring him down. She found herself stepping back toward the car when he advanced her way; then he changed his mind and stomped toward Annie's door instead.

"Sir—"

"Don't you 'sir' me, bitch! Your daughter just hit me!"

Annie's door opened and she stepped out. Caroline was relieved to see she appeared unhurt but was floored by the fact that she looked rather nonchalant. She herself was shaking profusely, blood staining the collar of her winter coat.

The man lunged, but Sam was there, stepping to shield his wife. The stranger's fists were clenched by his thighs. Two onlookers who had exited their vehicles surrounded them.

"Calm down, man," one said. "Police are on their way."

Hannah slowly exited where her father had left the door ajar. "Get back in the car!" Sam scolded. Hannah was still sobbing considerably, but she obeyed her father. Ben never left the back seat.

"What the fuck is wrong with your wife?" The man was seething.

"I don't know what happened, but it was an accident."

"An accident? Here I am, stopped at this red light here, and wham! Your fucking car hits me."

"I understand that."

"I'm gonna sue your ass, lady. You hear me? Fuckin' sue your ass!" He looked beyond Sam to Annie and spat on the ground before him.

"Seriously, man. Calm down." Caroline was incredibly thankful to the stranger whose mindset wasn't as addled as hers.

"You stay out of this. Ain't no business of yours."

The onlooker lifted his arms into the air, a sign of capitulation.

Caroline closed her eyes. This could not be happening.

In the distance, sirens blared.

～

A broken nose.

The airbag had broken her nose.

And her daughter had been carelessly driving the van.

Caroline sat on the hospital bed, the doctor having examined her nose along with the rest of her body. Her nose had since stopped bleeding, but the pain was acute.

Hannah hadn't broken her arm, thank goodness. She'd only banged it up. Her wrist, too. She'd be sore for a while but was otherwise unhurt physically.

And a broken nose? She'd survive. But as she sat upon the white sheet in the hospital examination room, her mind wandered to Annie. With all the research she had done since her daughter's depression diagnosis, she was left questioning if this was depression at all. Sure, some of the symptoms were certainly there. She seemed to lack emotion; she didn't derive pleasure out of things that had, in the past, been a cause of great happiness for her. She seemed sad. She had trouble concentrating. Sam had said her sleep patterns just weren't the same, and that she had been overeating. All symptoms that, less than a year ago, hadn't thrived in Annie at all.

But depression didn't explain the wandering. It didn't explain the inappropriate speech and behaviors. It didn't explain Annie's difficulty retrieving words that should have been very easy for her. It didn't explain her nastiness at times.

It didn't explain Annie's lack of physical and verbal affection toward her or Sam—or, most especially, her kids.

Did it?

She was determined to speak with Sam. They needed more definitive answers.

CHAPTER EIGHT

Ben

*T*he day had arrived!

It was just four days since the accident. Ben was fine. Hannah was coddling her arm, which annoyed the hell out of him. Yeah, she'd banged it, but even the doctor said she was okay. That was just Hannah for you, though.

Gram had broken her nose. Ben might have been tough on the soccer field, could plow through a defensive line, knew how to fall, but blood? Blood he couldn't take. Blood and needles. So when he saw all that blood pouring from his grandmother's nose and dripping into her mouth and onto her jacket, he had to look away. Thought he'd puke, really.

So yeah, he was fine. Physically. But he had to admit that it had really shaken him up. The way that man was yelling at his gram, at his dad, at his mom. The way Hannah had been screaming. The police sirens. All those people staring at them.

And his mom. What the hell was wrong with his mom? Even Hannah would have known how to slam down on the brakes instead of speeding up to hit the car in front of them. I mean, seriously? What the actual hell?

But today he wasn't going to think about the accident. Today he turned fourteen, and Tyler and Cole were coming over. All he wanted to do was kick some ass in *Fortnite* and *FIFA* (his favorite electronic soccer game), eat some pizza, and maybe watch *It*. If Mrs. Bower let Tyler watch the movie, that is. His mom's friend Bitsy was even more strict than his mother when it came to movies. His mom had a really hard time saying yes to Ben watching *It* for the first time. She said she was fine with all the "blood and gore," but it was the "adult themes" she was worried about. She interrupted all throughout the movie to talk about something that had just happened, or language he had just heard. This annoyed him. So much! He just wanted to watch the movie. He did hope Mrs. Bower let Tyler watch *It*. That would make his birthday just so much better. His dad was working since it was a Wednesday (he loved school vacations!), and he knew his mom wouldn't care.

"Hey, Ma," he called, "I'll be outside waiting."

"Okay." Ben didn't know why he had told his mother. She didn't even look up from her phone to acknowledge him. She was doing that more often. Not looking at him, yeah, but that had been going on for a while now. It was the phone. He knew she had always had her phone on her person. Or at least with her. She had always said it was because she'd been afraid of an emergency with either him or Hannah during the day when she wasn't with them. And he knew she liked playing her games, said they relaxed her at night after a long day at work. But now she wasn't working. And he hadn't caught her playing games, either. It was the pictures. She just sat there staring at her pictures.

Again, what the actual hell?

He walked out to the backyard while zipping his jacket to the neck and pulling his hat farther onto his ears. He had shoveled a small area of snow off the ground so he could reach his soccer net. He hated shoveling. Hated it. But he loved soccer more than he hated shoveling.

It was quiet on the lake today. No snowmobiles. His mother had always commented about how much she loved being on this lake. She often mentioned that she loved the size, said it was large enough for them to take a boat out but small enough that not a ton of people lived there and made noise. At the end of any given day, he'd often find his mother on one of the Adirondack chairs at the edge of the water, reading a book and relaxing.

Ben found a ball left in the net from yesterday's soccer play and began dribbling and juggling, aiming for the corner near the metal bar and kicking hard in his winter boots. All net.

He fooled around for a few minutes more, then heard the tires of a vehicle crunch up the driveway. Abandoning the ball in the hard, frozen net, he jogged over to the side of the house. It was Mrs. Bower driving with Tyler in the front seat.

Ben walked to the passenger-side door and smiled when Tyler stepped out onto the plowed but icy driveway.

"Hi." Tyler spoke first, then closed his door.

"Hey."

"Happy birthday," Tyler said.

"Thanks!"

Mrs. Bower exited the Pathfinder and walked to the back, opening the trunk. "Tyler, come grab your stuff."

Tyler obeyed, breath billowing into the cold February air. He wasn't wearing a jacket. Or a hat. Or gloves. At least he was wearing boots, Ben thought.

Ben followed his friend and offered to help. Tyler had brought a stuffed backpack as well as a pillow and sleeping bag for the night. Ben grabbed onto the backpack and slung it over his shoulder.

"Is your mom inside, Ben?" Mrs. Bower asked.

"Yeah."

"Mind if I come in and say hello? I'm surprised she's not

out here, actually. I'm so used to seeing her waving from the walkway with that big smile on her face."

Ben wasn't sure what to say in reply, so he said nothing, simply led the way through the garage and into the mudroom of the house, where he kicked off his snowy boots. Tyler and Mrs. Bower did the same before they all walked into the living room toward his mother.

"Hey, Annie." It was Mrs. Bower who spoke. "I'm used to seeing you all the time, and we haven't seen each other for a while. I miss you! I wanted to come in to say hello. Hope you don't mind."

"No," his mom replied. Ben was pleased to see a small smile on her face, though she didn't stand from the couch.

"What are you doing?" Mrs. Bower sat beside her friend.

"Looking at pictures. See? This is Pumpkin from next door. She's a . . . She's a . . . you know? That dog? That type of dog? She's little. So cute!"

For all the times his mom didn't seem to care, she certainly became more animated when talking about dogs. She had been walking the streets of their neighborhood taking photos of dogs on leashes, dogs behind invisible fences, and dogs that had escaped the confines of their homes to wander the streets. Pumpkin, Ben knew, was a Yorkshire terrier, and appeared to be his mom's current favorite. It was an obsession almost, these neighborhood dogs. And here she was, just sitting on the couch looking at the photos she had taken of them.

"Yeah," agreed Mrs. Bower, "she really is."

Ben didn't want to witness this conversation. He'd heard enough about dogs recently, and he really didn't care right now. "Let's go upstairs," he said to Tyler.

Tyler followed his friend up the stairwell and plopped his pillow and sleeping bag onto Ben's bed before jumping in the air and crashing down on the soft mattress.

"So, did you ask your mom?" Ben said.

"Ask my mom what?"

"About *It*."

"Oh. Yeah. She doesn't want me watching it," Tyler admitted.

Ben grimaced. "Darn."

"Yeah, I know," Tyler said, "but . . ." He trailed off, shrugging his shoulders.

The boys chatted a few more minutes in Ben's room, then came downstairs to open the front door when the bell rang out. Cole had arrived. He entered happily, bringing with him a gust of cold air. He turned back and waved goodbye to his father idling in the car before closing the front door behind him.

The boys began to walk back up the stairs, but Ben halted when he heard Mrs. Bower call to Tyler. She poked her head around the corner and looked up at her son.

"Ty, I'm gonna get going now," she said. "Have a wonderful time."

"Thanks, Mom."

Mrs. Bower smiled warmly. "Ben, may I speak to you for just a moment?"

"Sure," Ben agreed. He turned to his friends. "Meet you in my room."

Tyler led the way up the rest of the stairs, Cole following behind with a blanket and pillow in his arms, a cinch-bag on his shoulders.

Ben walked back down the stairs to Mrs. Bower's side.

"Any new news on your mother?" she asked.

"I don't think so," he replied. "I know Dad made some more appointments. I think maybe her medicine is different or they put her on more medicine or something. I'm not really sure."

Mrs. Bower nodded. "Okay. I'll touch base with your dad later on. I know he's busy and he's got a lot on his mind right now. But hey," she added, "you know you're welcome over to our house whenever you'd like, right?"

"Thanks." And he *was* thankful. He had always liked Mrs. Bower. He had met her before he could even remember having done so, and he felt comfortable around her.

"You're welcome." She smiled at the young man who was her son's best friend. "I'll leave you to it. Tyler has my number. Call if you need me at all."

"Okay."

"Happy birthday, Ben. You've officially joined the ranks of the fourteen-year-old boys."

Ben smirked. "Thanks, Mrs. Bower."

Ben stalled a moment. He watched as Mrs. Bower turned the corner, heard as she put her boots back on. He listened to the mudroom door close. He slowly walked to the living room. His mom sat in the same spot on the couch she had been sitting when Tyler had first arrived. She'd been sitting there for most of the morning, hadn't even stood to walk her best friend to the door and say goodbye.

"Hey, Ma?"

The day had progressed swimmingly thus far. Hannah had kept to her room or watched TV downstairs. The boys played *Fortnite* for quite some time behind Ben's closed door, then ventured out into the cold of the February day to kick the soccer ball around. Soccer was a large commonality and passion that the three boys shared with each other. Soccer, *Fortnite*, *FIFA*, and friends. At times, Ben felt he needed nothing else.

"Yeah?" His mother was peering into the open fridge, apparently deciding what she'd like to eat. Again.

"Hey," Ben said. "We're hungry. We talked about a pizza movie night. You think we can eat now?"

"Go ahead." His mom removed a square of cheese, some pepperoni, and a yogurt from the refrigerator and brought them to rest on the kitchen counter while she continued on to the cabinet to extract a plate.

"Okay," Ben said. "Um . . . well, were we gonna order, or just cook what we have?"

"Whatever." His mother began to cut the block of cheese on the plate that was now on the counter.

"Okay. Well, then can you call?"

"Sure." His mom continued to cut the cheese, and when through, she peeled off the foil from the top of the yogurt container.

"Okay," Ben continued, though hesitantly, "do you think we can call now?"

"Yeah," his mom said, though she made no movement toward her phone, simply continued preparing her snack. Ben had noticed his mom eating a whole lot more these days and eating weird things, too. I mean, pepperoni? She claimed she didn't like pepperoni. And pepperoni with yogurt. Kind of gross.

Ben looked back at his friends apologetically.

Tyler reached in his back pocket and offered his phone to Ben. "Want to call?"

"No," Ben said, "it's all right. I'm not sure where my mom's purse is. It's okay. I think we have pizzas in the freezer. You guys okay with that?"

"Sure," Cole said, "fine with me."

"Yeah, me, too," Tyler agreed.

"Okay." Ben walked to the stovetop, where he pushed the oven's preheat button. He lingered for just a moment longer than necessary, pondering the fact that his mother was directly in back of him eating her snack while ignoring his friends. During past sleepovers or even when Ben just had a friend over to hang out, his mother had been bubbly and accommodating. She had even been known to play *Fortnite* with them, her competitive side taking hold and talking smack to the computer. When through, she'd often happily bake cookies or pumpkin bread for the kids to eat. Always. That was his mom.

It was a stranger who stood behind him now.

Hannah had come down to eat with her brother and his friends. Because Tyler couldn't watch *It* and Hannah was in the room, they searched through Netflix and Amazon as well as Hulu, attempting to find a movie he and Hannah agreed upon. Cole and Tyler were good sports and didn't seem to care what they watched. "Hey, it's your birthday, man," was what Tyler had said just moments before.

"*Hocus Pocus!*" Hannah squealed. "Ben, we have *Hocus Pocus!*"

"No!" Ben exclaimed. "Hannah, we had to watch that stupid movie at Halloween. It's my birthday, so I choose."

"Come on, Ben, please?"

"Nope."

He continued to look through the movies that he could stream on the TV. Hannah stood from the couch and placed her plate of pizza down on the seat. "*Hocus Pocus,*" she chanted. "*Hocus Pocus.*"

"No way, Hannah."

"*Hocus Pocus!*" Hannah threw her arms into the air and turned around in circles. Cole and Tyler smirked at his sister's antics, and instead of getting upset with Hannah, Ben threw the remote onto the couch, leaped up, and gently tackled her to the hardwood floor, tickling her just under the ribs. Hannah giggled profusely, then screamed heartily.

Ben yelled over her:

"No *Hocus Pocus!*"

Tyler and Cole began to laugh. Ben continued to tickle.

An ear-piercing screech from the kitchen and pounding footsteps advancing their way.

"STOP!" It was their mother. She held the palms of her hands over her ears. Her eyes were closed and scrunched. "Shut the fuck up! Son of a motherfucking bitch! Shut the fuck up!"

Holy shit!

His friends immediately stopped laughing. His mother turned her back on the kids and walked out of the room on heavy feet. Ben peered down at a supine Hannah on the floor. Her eyes were watering, and her bottom lip quivered fiercely. "Ben?" she queried.

"I don't know, Hannah," he replied. "I just don't know."

CHAPTER NINE

Sam

The next two months were a stressful whirlwind of activity, with Annie exhibiting a plethora of behavioral changes with increased frequency and severity.

Sam had come home the night of his son's birthday sleepover with friends to find a shaken Hannah on the living room couch, eyes glazed over as her gaze was trained on the television. Her brother sat beside her; his friends occupied the love seat that formed the head of the L-shape orientation. Sam was surprised to see *Hocus Pocus* playing. This was Ben's night, after all, and *Hocus Pocus* was not something his son would have typically chosen.

"Why so sullen?" Sam asked as he walked into the room. Ben filled him in, and as he did so, Sam watched a tear find its way down his daughter's cheek, her eyes still vacantly pointed on the screen before her.

"Where's your mother?" Sam asked.

"Don't know," Ben replied, shrugging his shoulders.

Sam had searched the house but to no avail; he couldn't find Annie. It was dark outside now, and Sam began to worry.

He reentered the living room and turned to his son. "When was the last time you saw your mom?"

"I don't know," Ben replied. "Pretty much right after she yelled at us. Then I let Hannah watch what she wanted." Sam turned to the television set before him and recognized the movie was about halfway through. "Maybe forty-five minutes? I don't know."

Approximately forty-five minutes of not knowing where his wife had gone to. "I'm going to check the house again."

"Okay," Ben said. He looked at the worried expression on his father's face, and where he wasn't anxious before, he was now. He sat erect on the cushion of the brown couch. "Do you want me to help you?"

"No," Sam replied. "Not just yet. Stay with your friends." He turned on his heel and walked out of the living room and back into the kitchen calling his wife's name. "Annie!"

No reply.

He opened the basement door and turned the light on. "Annie," he called. When he heard no answer, he walked down the carpeted steps and descended until he hit the Pergo flooring below.

"Annie, are you down here?" He turned the corner. No Annie.

Sam walked back upstairs and explored the first floor of the house again. Annie wasn't anywhere to be found. He ascended the hardwood steps to the second floor calling his wife's name. Annie wasn't in Hannah's room. She wasn't in Ben's room. He walked through the doorway of the master bedroom. Annie wasn't there.

"Annie!"

No answer.

Sam rushed back downstairs and to the small mudroom by the door to the garage. He hurriedly placed his boots back on his feet, threw his coat on, and walked outdoors. He quickly stepped throughout the small front yard calling Annie's name but heard no answer in return. Instead, a silence greeted him, a slight breeze nipping at his nose and chin. His boots trudged through the untouched snow in the yard, but he still couldn't find his wife.

Sam continued to plow through the deep, thick snow, hugging his jacket closer to his body to stave off the biting cold. With trepidation his feet found their way to the paved path he had made that led from the side of the house to the snow-covered Adirondack chairs near the edge of the frozen lake, their small motor boat winterized and sitting idle just to the left by the trees near the water. He was farther away from the house, away from any artificial light to illuminate his steps. The moon was his guide now and he was relieved to see its soft glow reflected off the snow ahead of him.

He hastened his steps. If Annie wasn't down by the lake, then he wasn't sure where else he was going to look.

Panic took hold.

"Annie!" he yelled once more, though it hadn't helped in the least these past few minutes.

A slight movement before him.

Sam ran until he was standing by the side of a chair. In the chair sat his wife.

"Shit, Annie!" he exclaimed with irritation. "What the hell?" He released his jacket and breathed on his cold fingers.

"Hi."

"'Hi'?" Sam retorted incredulously. "Annie, I've been looking for you everywhere. I've been calling your name, but you didn't answer. How long have you been out here?" Though relieved to have found his wife unharmed, he was agitated that she hadn't answered his calls.

Annie shrugged her shoulders, looked out onto the snow-and-ice-covered lake. Had this occurred only months prior, Sam never would have panicked at not having seen his wife in the house upon his arrival. He would have simply brushed it off as Annie having gone to run an errand and would have texted her to be sure. But Annie didn't answer texts much anymore. And Annie wandered at the most inopportune times.

These days he worried. And often.

Sam looked from Annie's face to her body covered only in her jeans and sweatshirt. She wasn't wearing a hat or gloves. She wasn't even wearing a jacket. He looked farther down and noticed that his wife was only wearing her socks. She had traipsed outdoors in this freezing-cold February weather without shoes on her feet!

"Annie, why aren't you wearing a coat? Or shoes, for God's sake?"

He watched as Annie removed her eyes from the lake and gazed down at her feet. "I don't know."

Sam sniggered. "You don't know?"

"No."

"Aren't you cold?" he asked.

"No."

"You didn't think to put boots on? Or a coat?"

"No."

"Annie, you're really not cold?" Sam asked, feeling his anger lessen and concern for his wife returning.

"No."

"How long have you been out here?" He worried now that she had been outside for a full forty-five minutes. Jesus, she could get frostbite!

Annie looked at him again and said, "I don't know."

Sam was flabbergasted at his wife's claim that she wasn't cold, but as he looked at her, he noticed that while he was shivering and his chin was becoming numb, Annie didn't seem outwardly affected by the weather at all. Still, he felt apprehensive.

"Let's get you inside, yeah?" He extended his hand. Annie looked at it momentarily and then reached out and placed her palm in his. She stood from the icy chair and willingly let her husband lead her back to the welcoming warmth of their home.

~

The incident of Annie outside by the lake wasn't the only thing of concern for her family. She had forgotten extracurriculars for both her children often enough that Sam was obliged to find alternate methods of getting his children to and from these activities. After the car accident, he was extremely hesitant to have Annie behind the wheel but wasn't sure what else he was supposed to do. Nothing further had transpired in the way of accidents, thank God, but when Ben had been left stranded at soccer practice twice in a row, Bitsy Bower had taken it upon herself to bring her son's best friend back home, and Sam asked with embarrassment if she wouldn't mind doing so regularly from then on. And for that matter, would she mind taking him to practice also? He'd be happy to compensate her financially. She had fervently refused to take any of his money, claimed she was happy to help in any way she could. Sam felt angered, discomfited, and embarrassed that he had to ask his wife's friend to help him manage his family when his wife remained right there in their home.

Sam had procured a ride to and from soccer practice for Hannah as well. Sadly, she didn't have teammates for her Tuesday and Thursday violin lessons, and with Annie's forgetfulness, Hannah had been left to her own devices a few times when her lessons had finished. She had used the telephone at the music studio to call home. Ben was the one to answer and was able to convince his mother to pick Hannah up two of the three times she had been left past lesson time. On the third time, Annie had apparently been perseverating on something and refused to pick Hannah up, so Ben had called Sam at work. Sam had to leave work early to pick Hannah up from the studio, which led to an intense and heated argument with his wife once he was back home, Sam doing the majority of the yelling. Hannah had sobbed when Sam told her she could no longer take lessons at the studio and that they couldn't afford to hire a professional to travel to their home. Hannah had inevitably spoken to her grandmother about this debacle, after which Caroline had called Sam and told him she would take Hannah to and from her lessons. Sam refused out of pure, prideful humiliation, but Caroline had insisted it was not a problem. Sam capitulated and Hannah was appeased.

But to have to rely on your mother-in-law because your wife couldn't be trusted? What the fuck was going on?

In April, Hannah had a take-home school project that she tirelessly worked on. She had accosted Sam one day when he walked through the garage door and into the mudroom of their home. He hadn't even taken his boots off when his daughter had approached him. "Mom ruined my volcano!" she had passionately declared.

"What are you talking about, Hannah?" Sam finished with his boots and walked farther into the house.

"My volcano, Dad, don't you remember? I'm supposed to make a volcano for science to erupt at school. I put the plastic bottle in the middle, you helped me the other night with the duct tape and papier-mâché, and I had it all ready because it's due at school tomorrow. We put it on the counter, remember? I came downstairs from my room and Mom was tearing all the papier-mâché off! She ruined it! Why did she do that? How am I going to make another one?" Hannah's face was red, her eyes watery. Her fingers were fisted at her sides as she walked with her father to the kitchen, where he placed his lunch box on the countertop and looked at the ruined mess of his daughter's creation.

"Oh, Hannah," Sam breathed. "I'm so sorry."

"Why did she do this, Dad?" Hannah sniffled. "Why?"

"I don't really know," he admitted. "Something is wrong

with your mother. I think we both know that. But I can't seem to find answers."

"I tried to talk to her," Hannah said, "but she just looked at me and said it was something she wanted to do. She didn't even say she was sorry, and she didn't even look upset when I started to cry. Mom used to always give me hugs when I was sad, and now she never does." Hannah's eyes began to overflow with tears. "She didn't even care that she did this," she sobbed. "She didn't even care!"

"I'm so, so sorry Hannah," Sam said. He leaned over and held his daughter in a tight embrace. "So sorry." He smoothed her blond hair down as she wet his chest with her tears.

That night he had tried to talk to his wife. "Why did you do that, Annie?"

"Don't know," Annie said. She was giggling like a little girl. *Giggling!*

"Can't you see that this is something that has really affected her? For Christ's sake, Annie, this was for school. She worked really hard on this project and you've just destroyed it. Now I need to contact her teacher, and what the hell am I gonna say? 'Oh, sorry, Mrs. Andrews, but my wife decided it would be fun to rip her daughter's volcano to pieces. Bet you get that excuse all the time, don't you?'" Sam said mockingly.

Another giggle from Annie.

Sam shut his eyes tightly, took a deep breath. "Can't you understand that this has really upset Hannah?"

"Yeah, I guess that would really upset Hannah," Annie said with a smile.

Sam's eyes creased and his nose scrunched with disgust.

Again, *what the fuck?*

He had called the psychiatrist's office and left a message for Dr. Patel as soon as he left Annie's side. Sam had taken another day off of work to accompany Annie (with her permission) to the psychiatrist's office just two days after the volcano incident. Up until this point, transportation had worked out well. He was able to call Annie on Friday mornings from work to remind her that she needed to leave the house for her weekly appointment. Often she'd answer, and when she didn't, he'd call Bitsy, who had insisted on being his backup. There had been a few times that Bitsy had driven the five minutes to their home and taken Annie to her appointment. It was times like these that Sam was incredibly thankful for friends like Bitsy Bower and thankful, too, for the fact that Bitsy didn't work outside the home and had the ability to help her best friend.

It was a twenty-five-minute drive to Dr. Patel's office and they rode in silence, Sam behind the wheel of his car. As it was the end of April, most of the snow had melted, save a few stray dirty piles in the parking lot that had accumulated through many pushes of a plow truck. Sam parked the car, and he and Annie exited simultaneously, closing the doors behind them. A click of the button on his keychain, and the car announced with a loud beep that it had locked. Sam walked to the back of the car and extended his hand to Annie with a slight, weary smile on his face. She smiled back, giggled, and hopped to stand by his side, taking his proffered hand in her own. Sam smiled in return but shook his head slightly in confused wonderment. Didn't Annie realize that they had made an extra appointment to see her psychiatrist? One didn't often giggle and find pleasure in seeking the aid of a shrink, did they?

"Dr. Patel, here we come," Sam said.

"Yes," Annie replied with a smile and a hop to her gait. "Dr. Patel, here we come."

Sam opened the brick building's door and Annie walked over the threshold. Sam followed, and together they climbed the stairs to the second floor and headed into Dr. Patel's waiting room, which he shared with three other psychiatrists. Annie walked over to the woman sitting behind the counter and happily announced that she was here to see Dr. Patel.

When she turned on a heel and bounced over to a couch beneath a large window in the waiting area, Sam followed and sat beside her. Annie pulled out her phone and began swiping through her photos. Sam would normally have looked to see if there was a magazine he'd be interested in riffling through while he had to wait, but today he simply couldn't. It was strange to be here with Annie. It was strange to be in this office. Stifling, even with the April sun illuminating the small white space and the soft music playing from hidden speakers in the ceiling.

"Look at this one, Sam," Annie said as he leaned in, her head brushing his cheek. He looked at her then. Really looked. So many thoughts had been running through his mind that morning that he hadn't noticed Annie's blond bob was disheveled and a bit greasy. He reached his hand out, brushed her hair off her forehead, and tucked it behind her ear, slowly rubbed the palm of his hand down the back of her head, her neck, and then over the light blue T-shirt that rested upon her shoulders. He stared at Annie's profile, at her smile as she looked at a photo of a neighbor with their golden retriever. He looked at her pale white skin, at the tinge of pink seeping in her cheeks, at her chapped lips. He breathed her in and sighed.

And noticed that she smelled a bit of body odor.

He leaned back a bit, and his gaze wandered over her. She was wearing an ill-fitting pair of jeans and her son's Adidas sandals with mismatched socks. To her psychiatrist's office. If he were the one seeing this guy once a week, he'd be sure to make the best possible impression. The man was scrutinizing Annie, wasn't he? If it were Sam in that office, he'd want nothing more than Dr. Patel believing he was normal.

But Annie wasn't acting normally, was she?

"Hey, babe?" Sam said lightly.

"Hmm?" Annie mumbled in reply, still looking at the small screen of her iPhone.

"Did you shower this morning?"

"Don't know."

"I don't think you did, Annie. I can kind of smell you." He attempted to tread lightly but realized it didn't matter when Annie just shrugged the comment off and continued to swipe through her photos.

Sam sighed heavily.

Annie looked at the photos on her phone for another ten minutes, and then Dr. Patel appeared in the doorway that led from the waiting room into his office. "I'm ready for you, Annie," he said by way of greeting, a smile on his weathered face.

Annie didn't appear to hear the man.

"Hey, Annie," Sam said as he placed the palm of his hand on her shoulder. Annie looked up. "It's time to head in with Dr. Patel."

Annie's gaze turned from Sam to Dr. Patel, and she stood from the couch and pocketed her phone. "Dr. Patel," she said as she made her way over to him, "that's a really funny thing you're wearing." She giggled.

"What funny thing, Annie?" Dr. Patel asked, amusement evident on his face. Was Dr. Patel used to Annie's antics?

"That," Annie said, "you know . . . that thing." She pointed to Dr. Patel's chest as she approached him, and he looked down.

"Ah, yes," Dr. Patel said with a slow manner. "My tie. It is rather funny, I admit. My son gave that to me many years ago when he was a young boy. It's rather on the older side, like myself." The left corner of his mouth lifted in a grin, and Sam decided he liked this Dr. Patel. He had only met him once just a couple of months prior when they were searching through Dr. Dorsinger's list of recommended psychiatrists in the area. "Shall we go in?" He motioned to the other side of the door, and Annie walked over the threshold. Sam followed.

Annie situated herself on a love seat in the center of the

room facing her therapist's chair and the wall behind him that was burnt orange in color. A large window stood partially ajar to the left of Annie, and a slight breeze seeped through. Potted plants filled the corners of the room, and there was a large dark wooden desk behind the love seat. Before Sam situated himself next to his wife, he noticed a stack of files and papers littering the top of the desk as well as a closed laptop computer and a pile of hardcover books.

"I'm pleased that you are able to join us today, Sam," Dr. Patel said. Sam turned to look at him.

"Thank you for having me join in. I just really find we need to talk. Too much has been going on."

"Yes," Dr. Patel agreed, "as you mentioned over the phone. And your presence here will lend us the opportunity to speak freely, yes? I have my own observations I would like to impart. Is that all right with you, Annie?"

"Yep," Annie said, a large smile on her face.

"I see you are in a very good mood today, Annie," Dr. Patel observed.

"Sure am," Annie agreed.

"And why is it that you are feeling so blissful today, may I ask?"

"I don't know," Annie said jovially.

"Well, regardless of the reason, I am happy to see you so happy," Dr. Patel said. He turned to Sam.

"I would like to begin today's session with you, Sam," the therapist said kindly. "You are the one that made the telephone call, and you have expressed concern for your wife, yes? Please," he continued with the wave of a slight hand, "what is it about Annie that has you additionally troubled these days?"

"I don't even know where to start," Sam admitted.

"You may find that if you simply begin to speak, the words will find their way," Dr. Patel suggested.

Sam took a breath in and nodded. He looked at his wife beside him, who smiled in return. He returned his gaze to Dr.

Patel. Then he began. "It was just a couple of days ago," he said. "I came home and Annie had completely destroyed our daughter's science project, a volcano that she had made on her own and was supposed to bring to school the next day to explode in front of her class. I had to contact her teacher and explain what had happened, and it wasn't easy, I can assure you. I was embarrassed. I had to tell my daughter's fourth grade teacher that her mother had ruined her project. I didn't go into detail. How was I going to talk about the fact that Annie had taken the volcano and pulled it apart *deliberately*, that she had done this and made Hannah cry?" Sam shook his head again. "But that's not all," he continued. Dr. Patel had been right: it did help to just talk. He found his mind was flowing now, and the words were spurting out.

"Our entire schedule has changed. Annie lost her job a while ago, as you know. We're not pulling in her salary and it's a financial hardship for our family. I'm losing my mind here," Sam admitted, his voice beginning to rise in volume as his words became increasingly impassioned. "I try not to let her drive because I honestly don't know if I can trust her, but there are times where I just can't get around her not driving, so she gets behind the wheel. And I worry every minute she's in that van.

"She's forgetful. She can't remember dates or times and just seems to get confused about so much. Her best friend has to take our son to and from soccer practice, and my mother-in-law takes our daughter to and from violin lessons because I'm not home to do it after school. Annie was always the one to do everything for the kids, really. She was a schoolteacher, so it was easier on her schedule to take over all those things. Soccer, violin, school events, having friends over . . . all that stuff.

"Hannah's best friend isn't allowed to come over to our house any longer because Annie has a tendency to become frustrated with loud noises and sometimes the girls get silly, as you'd expect girls would, right? If Annie's had enough, she just yells. But not just yelling. She swears. And she's left the girls alone, too. Once, she decided she was hungry, so she took the van over to the grocery store to grab herself some sweets. Oh!" Sam exclaimed as he sat up straighter on the side of the couch, "that's another thing! Sweets. And greasy food. And meat! For as long as I've known Annie—and I've known her for, what, about nineteen years now—for as long as I've known Annie, she's been a healthy eater. She's always liked her pizza and she's liked her ice cream, but other than that, she's been health-conscious. But now? She doesn't seem to care. She eats anything and everything. She even tried to eat pure sugar the other day, so I don't even want to think about what she's eating when I'm not around.

"And the other day I had to head into work," Sam continued. "Had my clothes on, kissed everyone goodbye, and I go to the mudroom and I can't find my shoes. I looked everywhere. I always leave my shoes right by the door on a welcome mat we've got there. But my shoes weren't there. In fact, nobody's shoes were there! Not a single pair! I asked the kids where our shoes were and they had no clue, so I asked Annie and she said she didn't know. I knew our kids hadn't done anything to our shoes and with the way Annie's been acting, it could only have been her. But she looked at me with a completely blank expression like she really didn't have a clue as to where our damn shoes could have gone. Oh!" Sam stopped himself. "I'm sorry, I shouldn't have sworn."

"That is perfectly all right, Sam," Dr. Patel assured him. "Swearing is just fine. I can see that you are upset."

Sam gulped another deep inhalation and continued. "Anyway," he said, "we had no shoes. I looked everywhere, but I was running late by this time. I had to go. I had a meeting early that morning. Already I had been heading into work later than ever. Months ago I would have gotten up at five o'clock in the morning and left by six. I still get up at five o'clock, but I linger a bit until at least Ben has gone off to school. He catches the bus a bit before seven. Hannah doesn't walk to the bus stop until about seven forty-five. She used to head into work with Annie because Annie worked at the same school as our daughter, but . . . well . . . she doesn't work anymore."

Sam paused.

"So you had no shoes," Dr. Patel urged him on.

Sam nodded. "I didn't have any shoes. I had to search through the garage until I found an old pair of sneakers that were moldy and had a few holes near the toes. I'm lucky I didn't see my boss that day," Sam said. "When I got home that night, I found them."

"Ah, you did?" Dr. Patel said. "Where, may I ask, did you find your shoes?"

"They were in the bathtub." Sam sniggered with annoyance.

Dr. Patel's eyebrows rose. "In the bathtub?"

"Yeah," Sam confirmed. "I pulled back the shower curtain when I went to take a shower, and there they were. All of our shoes. In the frickin' bathtub." He shook his head and pursed his lips. "When I asked Annie about those shoes, she again claimed she had no idea how they had gotten there, but I knew the kids would never have thought to prank me like that. Not with all that's been going on. I'm glad they had old shoes in their closets they could wear that day."

"I see," Dr. Patel said with a slight nod of his head. "Would you like to continue?"

Sam looked into the kind brown eyes of the man who had been treating his wife, then quickly glanced at Annie beside him on the couch. He reached for her hand and she accepted his grasp. "Annie," he began, "I've noticed a bit lately that you don't seem to be bathing. Or maybe you are, but if you are, then you're not doing a thorough job because I smell some body odor." He smiled apologetically as if this statement would humiliate his wife. "Like, right now," he said. Then added, almost as an afterthought, "I'm sorry."

"It's okay." Annie smiled.

"Annie," Dr. Patel said, "is there anything you would like to say right now?"

"I don't think so."

"Is Sam correct? Have you forgone bathing lately?"

"Maybe?" She still presented a smile.

"Maybe?" Dr. Patel lingered for clarification.

"Maybe." Annie's word was produced with a high inflection as she shrugged her shoulders and bounced slightly in her seat.

"Okay," Dr. Patel said, "thank you, Annie." He turned to Sam beside her. "Sam, I would like to impart to you some of my observations, as I have seen Annie several times now. With Annie's permission, of course." He turned back to Annie for confirmation. She merely smiled in return, but he took this as permission to continue.

"I am pleased that she has continued with her medication. It is meant to treat not only depression in individuals but obsessive-compulsive tendencies as well. I assume you have noticed that Annie exhibits symptoms of OCD?"

"I'm not really sure," Sam admitted. "There's just been so much going on."

"I understand," Dr. Patel said soothingly. "Have you observed Annie tapping the middle finger and thumb of her left hand together in fast motion?"

Sam thought for a moment. "Well, yeah," he said. "Now that you mention it, I have."

"Annie," Dr. Patel said as he looked at her, "have you noticed this in yourself?"

"I don't know," Annie admitted. "Maybe?"

"I see," Dr. Patel replied. "Also," he continued, "SSRIs—or selective serotonin reuptake inhibitors, as they're called—are used to help treat individuals with anxiety, and from what you have told me, Sam, Annie seems to suffer from a bit of anxiety, yes?"

"I suppose maybe she does," Sam offered.

"You have expressed that she does not react to noise very well, that she will yell at the children if they are being too loud."

"She does that, yes," Sam agreed.

"Does she seem to hesitate when you ask for her to do something that in months past she would not have hesitated to do?"

Sam's eyes lifted to look at the ceiling as his brain worked to piece out the answer to the posed question. A moment later, he found Dr. Patel's eyes once again. "She does," he answered. "A lot, actually. I'll ask if she wants to head out with the kids to a particular place—the mall maybe, or to a friend's house with other families. She used to jump at the chance. Though she's always liked to make herself comfortable at home after a long day well spent, she's also always loved to get out of the house and do things with the kids and she's always loved spending time with her friends. Not anymore. I'll offer for us to do something like this and she's constantly refusing. I never really thought of it as anxiety, though, but I suppose I have to admit that it could be."

"I see," Dr. Patel said. "Yes. I do believe Annie may be struggling with a bit of anxiety. Annie"—he moved his gaze to look in her eyes—"how do you feel about this?"

"I don't know," she responded. "I guess you could be right." She still had a smile on her face.

"Annie, I would like for you to make an appointment to see a neurologist," Dr. Patel announced.

"A neurologist?" It was Sam who spoke.

"Yes," Dr. Patel confirmed. "Although I do believe Annie may be struggling with depression, as Dr. Dorsinger diag- nosed, and I do believe, also, that Annie has an anxiety disorder and obsessive-compulsive tendencies, I also find the need to admit that we should explore these diagnoses and open our minds to the possibility that Annie's struggles may be a byproduct, if you will, of a further, more serious issue. A neurologist will have the expertise and technical ability to conduct further testing, specifically testing of Annie's brain. Perhaps they may help us further understand your wife, yes?"

Sam sat mute. Dr. Patel crossed his legs and patiently waited. Eventually, Sam said, "Okay . . . yeah. That's probably a good idea. I really hadn't thought of seeing a neurologist. Do you have names of any particular doctors or even hospitals that we should look into?"

"I do, yes," Dr. Patel confirmed. "I recommend you call both Mass General and Brigham and Women's, both in Boston. You may certainly find a neurologist closer to home that you personally care for, but after my many, many years in practice, I tend to refer my patients to Boston. That is not to say that we do not have highly skilled neurologists here in southern NH. On the contrary, we have many. You may find with your scheduling difficulties that staying local is more conducive to your family's needs. I am happy to provide you with more detailed information to help you make an informed decision. I do warn you, though, that you may find a wait time of up to a month, maybe longer until Annie's scheduled appointment."

"At this point, I feel like we've been playing a waiting game for almost a year now," Sam admitted with a frown.

"I understand," Dr. Patel replied gently. "Let us hope that together, we will answer your questions."

Dr. Patel was right: it took a month to procure an appointment for Annie to see a neurologist—thirty-one days, to be exact.

Her appointment was set for a Thursday afternoon at the

very end of May. On the afternoon prior, Sam was sitting at his cubicle desk typing an email when he heard footsteps approach. He turned to find his boss hovering.

"Hi, Steve," Sam said as he removed his fingers from the keyboard and pivoted in his chair.

"Sam," Steve replied, voice deep and gravely. He was a large man, both in height and girth, which elicited a sense of unease within Sam. The man was looming.

Sam paused, looking up at Steve. He stood from his chair. Though they weren't looking at each other eye to eye, it at least brought Sam closer to his boss and made him slightly less threatening. He had never disliked Steve, but neither was his boss an easily approachable man. When Steve failed to speak further, Sam said, "Is there something I can do for you?"

Steve looked from Sam to the laptop on his desk and back to Sam once more. "I hear you're taking the day off tomorrow."

"That's right," Sam confirmed. "My wife has an appointment in Boston to see a neurologist."

"Been taking quite a lot of time off work, Sam, haven't you?" It was a rhetorical question; they both knew he had been missing work frequently these past months. Sam said nothing in return.

"Definitely don't want to appear insensitive here, Sam, but I've noticed the amount of time you've been gone, and your projects are piling up. You're not getting the work done."

Again, Sam said nothing in response.

"We need to see the effort pulled forth here, Sam. We need to see those numbers." He paused, crossed his arms over his chest. "I'm sure there are others out there that would be more than happy to take your place and more than capable of running this project and running it well."

Sam's mouth opened slightly in shock.

"Am I making myself clear?" Steve wasn't smiling. His eyes bore into Sam as he waited for confirmation.

"Yes, sir," Sam said, "loud and clear. My wife is sick. I need to be there for my family, but I can take work home. I'll be sure to make up any hours I miss and get this project done."

"That's what I like to hear," Steve responded. One last look into Sam's eyes and Steve turned on his heel and walked out of sight.

CHAPTER TEN

Sam and Caroline

She didn't bother knocking on the door. Sam was expecting her.

Caroline walked into her daughter's home on the morning of the neurology appointment. She would accompany Sam and Annie to Boston while the kids were in school. She took her shoes off in the mudroom and called out a hello. When Sam replied, Caroline walked into the kitchen, where she found Annie nursing a cup of coffee at the table and Sam loading the dishwasher. The kids had already left for school.

"Hi, Sam." She walked to him and placed the palm of her hand on his shoulder.

"I'm glad you're here, Caroline," Sam replied.

She made her way to Annie, leaned over, and embraced her. Annie smiled at her mother but didn't bother to embrace her back. Her hands remained around the steaming coffee cup.

"Good morning, Annie."

"Hi, Mom," Annie said.

"Big day today."

"Yeah, okay," Annie said. "I guess so."

Sam closed the dishwasher door, and it began to run, making a rather loud noise to announce its efforts.

"How are you feeling about your appointment?" Caroline asked her daughter.

Annie shrugged her shoulders. "Don't know," she replied. "Fine."

Caroline nodded and turned to Sam, who had approached the table and sat down empty-handed. With his elbows resting on the table, he ran his hands through his disheveled hair and then slightly startled when he looked at his mother-in-law. "Caroline, would you like a cup of coffee? I should have asked you already, I'm so sorry. I've got a few things on my mind this morning."

"Sam," she responded, "please don't apologize to me. You have nothing to be sorry for. If I want a cup of coffee, I'll make one myself. I understand that things have been rough, and I do hope you'll allow me to help in any way I can. That includes helping myself around your house."

Sam smiled thankfully. Caroline reached for him and placed her hand upon his, squeezing with her fingers. When Sam looked up and met her gaze, his green eyes were pooling with tears. He abruptly stood from the table sending his chair to scrape backward on the tiled floor. "We should go," he announced.

"Yes," Caroline said, "yes, of course."

Sam started the car with Caroline beside him and Annie in the back seat and pulled out of the garage and into their driveway. They had left themselves plenty of time to contend with traffic heading into Boston.

After approximately an hour and a quarter, the city loomed before them, large and imposing in its magnitude. Sam was in the middle lane of traffic, and vehicles were passing him left and right. Caroline's window was halfway down, and Sam could hear the sound of tires on concrete and engines revving. The air he breathed felt thick and stagnant.

"I'm glad you're driving," Caroline said as she turned to her son-in-law. "The city makes me nervous."

Sam grinned. "Does it?"

"It does," Caroline confirmed. "Cars everywhere, people everywhere. Noises everywhere! And if I miss a turn, I become all flummoxed, really. And those horns. People certainly do like to use them, don't they?"

"That they do," Sam replied.

"Annie"—Caroline turned to look in the back of the car— "how are you doing?"

"Fine," Annie said.

"Not getting sick at all? I know you tend to get ill if you're not driving."

"No." Annie smiled back. "I'm fine."

"Well," Caroline said, "that's good then."

Sam continued to drive, and they soon crossed the city line. Traffic slowed and became more condensed. Amidst buildings that reached toward the heavens and throngs of people crowding the sidewalks and crossing the congested city streets, Sam pulled into a parking garage. He stopped at a booth upon entrance and pushed a button that thrust a ticket his way. When he grasped it within his fingers, the gate opened and he crept forward. Sam was obliged to circle around several stories before finding a small open spot that he squeezed into.

"All right, Annie," he announced when he parked the car and turned off the ignition, "we're here." He turned to look behind him.

"I don't like it," Annie said.

"I understand," Sam cajoled, "but we've got to do it. I'm here. And your mom's here. And they say this Dr. Barnard is quite something—the best in his field."

In fact, Sam wasn't entirely sure this was the truth; he

had merely taken Dr. Patel's suggestion and the first available appointment offered to him over the telephone. After all his family had been through thus far, he hoped this Dr. Barnard was able to offer up more clarification as to why his wife seemed to be slipping out of his grasp. There simply had to be a reason why Annie was who she was these days, a reason beyond depression and hormones. If they could solidify this reason, then perhaps Annie's behavior had nothing do with *him*. The notion that his wife was distancing herself from him and from their kids, that she was cocooning herself with introversion and apathy because she was no longer happy with the life she led with him, had crossed his mind on several occasions. If she were truly still happy in this marriage, if she were truly still in love with her husband, then she couldn't possibly choose to act as such. *Would she?*

No. He was convinced of this. So, again, if they could pinpoint a reason beyond what they had been offered as to why Annie was who she was at this moment . . . well, then, perhaps he could attempt to push away the guilt and anger elicited from these horrific thoughts. For, though Annie might not appreciate him as she once did, he was still very much in love with her. Even through the frustration, vexation, and sorrow that her behavioral deteriorations had evoked within him, he still cared for his wife.

He couldn't endure the notion that this love was no longer reciprocated.

Sam opened his door and wedged himself between his car and the SUV beside him. He shimmied the few steps toward the back of the car and opened the door for Annie, who obliged him and stepped out onto the concrete. Caroline emerged and Sam heard her door close. A car passed behind them, the tires audible in the echoing confines of the garage. Sam watched it turn the corner before guiding Annie into the open. He reached for her hand and grasped onto her palm, but she jerked at his touch and took her hand back, allowing it to drift by her side.

Sam feigned nonchalance, though he was taken aback and slightly wounded by his wife's rejection, especially as she offered no explanation, no smile.

Caroline approached and her brown eyes expressed her sympathy. She had seen what her daughter did and the look of hurt on her son-in-law's face. Sam returned a slight, wounded grin, and together, the threesome walked toward the garage's elevator, riding it down to ground level and exiting from near silence into a horde of traffic. Caroline watched her daughter respond to her surroundings, saw her body become rigid, the corners of her eyes crease. She wanted to reach for her, to touch her elbow and lead her toward the white doors of the hospital's entrance and into the supposed safety of its embrace, but she dared not. She didn't want to feel the rejection Sam had surely felt when Annie had refused his assistance.

Eventually, they did make their way to the front doors and inside the lobby. After asking a receptionist where to find the department of neurology, they walked to the waiting room, where Annie was able to check herself in, although Sam was needed to help her find her insurance card. He found it stacked with her license, credit cards, and reward program cards in a bundle on the floor of her packed and disordered purse.

It was only the end of May, but already they had hit their deductible for the year with all of the appointments Annie had had with her primary care physician and psychiatrist. Add to that the cost of care for Hannah after the car accident and the fact that Annie was no longer working, and it was no wonder Sam was overly stressed about making ends meet financially.

Sam and Annie joined Caroline in the waiting area, sitting upon hard-cushioned chairs. Annie took her iPhone from the back pocket of her jeans and pushed the home button to illuminate the screen and the wallpaper of Ben and Hannah blueberry picking almost a year prior. She clicked on the camera icon and began to peruse her photos. Both Sam and Caroline watched her do so; neither felt their attention could be diverted elsewhere. A magazine simply wasn't an enticing enough means of distraction.

They waited quite a while, or at least Caroline assumed it had been a large amount of time. It seemed so when she was convinced she could hear every second tick from the circular clock on the white wall, but Annie's name was eventually called by a woman in a doorway to an adjoining hall. Caroline stood instantly. Annie necessitated a gentle coax to join her, but once she was convinced to pocket her phone, she walked forward willingly with a smile on her face and a bounce to her step. Caroline was transported back momentarily to a time many years ago, a time when her daughter was just a child. A happy, jaunty child. She had surprised Annie with tickets to see *The Nutcracker* at their local theater, and Annie had been so enthralled that she had bounced on the balls of her feet in the parking lot while holding Caroline's hand. Annie hummed "Dance of the Sugar Plum Fairy" while tapping the tip of her black dress shoe onto the icy concrete of the theater's parking lot, much to the enjoyment of her mother, whose love for her daughter permeated within.

The irony didn't elude Caroline now as she watched the bouncing gait of her adult daughter move toward the nurse in the doorway. The love that had burst through Caroline on that winter day many years ago was now joined with despondency.

The threesome were led into a small room where the nurse proceeded to take Annie's vitals. Though she had a merry disposition and attempted to lighten the spirits in the room, Caroline was entirely too fretful for this woman's attempts to succeed in assuaging her anxiety.

"Dr. Barnard should be in shortly," the nurse said before

walking out the door and leaving them alone with their thoughts.

Annie suddenly broke the silence. "I'm hungry," she announced.

"Annie," Sam said, "we ate right before your mom got to the house."

"Okay," Annie said. A pause and then, "I'm hungry."

Sam slowly nodded. "We'll get you something to eat as soon as we're out of here, okay?"

"Okay," Anne agreed. "I want pizza."

"I'm not sure your mom likes pizza much," Sam said gently. "There are tons of places around here that we can eat. Maybe we can find something that your mom likes, too?"

"Okay," Annie said again. Another pause as Annie looked around the room, and then a smile aimed at her husband and "I'm hungry, Sam. Let's get pizza."

Sam pursed his lips.

Caroline intervened. "It's all right," she told Sam. She looked at her daughter. "Pizza it is."

Annie's smile intensified.

They sat in silence for a while, Annie rubbing the nail of her pointer finger along her chair.

When there was a knock on the door, both Sam and Caroline started. "Come in," Sam said.

The door opened fully and a middle-aged man stepped in, closing the door behind him. He was rather tall and stocky, though not overweight by any means. He wore a plaid button-down shirt that was slightly in need of ironing. The uppermost button was left undone, and his shirt was tightly tucked into the waist of his blue jeans. The hair on his head was dark brown and extremely thick and disheveled. His olive complexion was smooth and unblemished, though Caroline noted that he was in need of a shave as dark stubble lined his chin and upper lip.

"I'm Dr. Barnard." He introduced himself in a deep voice

as he thrust his large hand forward first toward Sam, who was sitting in nearest proximity, then to Caroline, and lastly to Annie. The smile on his face was wide, displaying crooked yet extremely white teeth. His brown eyes shone. Caroline took an immediate liking to him.

"Now, Annie, I believe we're here for you," Dr. Barnard said. He looked directly at Annie in front of him as he took a seat upon a swivel chair next to the door.

"Yeah," Annie said. "Okay." She smiled.

"And how can I help you today?" Dr. Barnard's voice was pleasant, his demeanor approachable.

"Sam says I need to see you," Annie replied.

Dr. Barnard's bushy brown eyebrows rose with amusement, and his lips lifted into a slight smirk.

"So it's Sam that has asked you here today?" Dr. Barnard said.

"Yeah," Annie confirmed.

"And may I ask why it is that your husband would like for you to see me?"

"Sam thinks I'm not acting like myself."

"And you think?" Dr. Barnard probed.

"I don't know," Annie said.

Sam sat looking at his wife, thinking only that he had borne witness to this very scene entirely too many times now.

"Then Sam"—Dr. Barnard turned in his chair—"I'm listening."

For a while, both Sam and Caroline relayed their worries to the receptive neurologist. Sam repeated the statements, the symptoms he had imparted to both Dr. Dorsinger and Dr. Patel. He conveyed his misgivings about Annie's diagnosis and stressed upon the fact that he was convinced of an underlying reason beyond what he had been given that was causing his wife's behavior to transform so fully.

Dr. Barnard listened intently and asked several questions of Sam, Caroline, and Annie. Though Sam didn't fully understand the doctor's thought processes with some of the questions, he didn't argue. He merely answered as effectively as he could when asked about Annie's sleeping (no, Annie didn't snore; yes, she napped at times during the day; no, this hadn't always been typical) and eating habits (yes, she had a hearty appetite; in fact, she had been overeating).

Dr. Barnard asked all three onlookers about Annie's behaviors, obsessive-compulsive tendencies, mood swings, apathy, coordinated movements, memory (both short-term and long-), emotional reciprocation, and the results of any bloodwork that they'd like to make him aware of, though he stated that he'd thoroughly looked through Annie's file.

Caroline was pleased with the amount of time Dr. Barnard was allocating. She didn't feel rushed in the least and appreciated this immensely as she had personally seen other doctors who made her feel like she was an imposition. She found her body begin to relax and intuited the same from Sam beside her.

Annie continued to periodically flick the chair with her fingernail and tap the ball of her foot upon the hard white floor, yet her countenance remained relaxed. Though she had changed the subject several times and had interrupted to announce that she was ready to leave and get pizza, Dr. Barnard remained unaffected and was easily able to alter the course of conversation to steer Annie back to the task at hand.

Forty-five minutes passed in the small white room with Dr. Barnard before he offered up any indication he was ready to proceed with further testing or offer up any sort of prediction as to what was going on with Annie.

"Annie," he began, "here's what I'd like to do. Although you've had bloodwork taken with your primary care physician, I'd like to have your levels retaken. Just precautionary. I'll order a full metabolic panel and want your thyroid checked again. I expect nothing new to come of these. I don't want to overwhelm you all, but I do want you back in for some neuropsychological testing, more questions asked of you orally. This may take several hours, so we'll make a separate appointment for just this portion of your follow-up. After this testing, I'll want you to have an MRI. An MRI will indicate any abnormality in the brain, such as tumors or even atrophy." He turned to Annie. "Annie, how are you with enclosed spaces?"

"Okay." Annie's inflection was indicative of an unsure question rather than a statement.

"Have you ever had an MRI before?"

"No," Annie said, then turned to Sam. "I haven't, right?"

Sam shook his head. "She hasn't."

Dr. Barnard continued. "You'll be lying down on your back and placed in a tight machine that resembles a tunnel. It's painless, but the catch is, you'll have to remain completely still for about a half an hour if all goes well. How does this sound to you?"

"Fine," Annie said.

Dr. Barnard nodded, then turned to look at Caroline before resting on Sam. "We'll want to give this a try. It could tell us a great deal about the inner workings of Annie's brain and if there's anything signifying an issue that needs to be addressed. I may want to also do a PET scan. A PET can offer up even further insight, but I warn you that they are costly."

Sam frowned. "How much?"

"Typically around five thousand dollars, though I'm not sure what your insurance will cover. I can refer you to billing. They can look into your insurance and better help you financially through this process."

Sam sighed audibly. He had just barely been able to cover the mortgage for that month, and now he'd have even further medical bills to pay. He had already delved into the savings, nearly depleting it. Granted, their savings had always been meager, but it had been there in case of emergencies. What if the dryer broke, the roof leaked, or they were in need of a new car? Now he wasn't entirely sure what he'd do if a financial cushion was needed—

Annie was currently his emergency. Sam had recently decreased his contribution to his 401(k), allowing him extra leeway financially, but what impact would this have for his and Annie's future if he was forced to cease contributions entirely? He and Annie had always vehemently claimed they'd never do so; money allocated to the 401(k) was for their financial comfort after he retired. What would they do if they didn't have this money to fall back on?

With the behaviors Annie was exhibiting, would she even want to be with Sam that far into the future?

Sam ran his fingers through his dark brown hair and closed his eyes tightly.

Breathed.

When he opened his eyes, he looked directly at Dr. Barnard. "We'll do whatever we have to do for Annie," he said.

Sam had fallen for Annie after their initial meeting at the party in that dingy, stale basement. Annie readily admitted later that night that she had been initially hesitant to let Sam in. She explained that she had been in similar positions a few times prior when random men would approach her or one of her friends and always, always they wanted nothing more than a hookup and Annie wasn't looking for that. She admitted later in their relationship that she knew Sam wasn't like these other men because of the goofy grin he wore that entire night when he looked at her.

"I didn't have a goofy grin!" Sam laughed.

"Mmm-hmm," Annie mumbled a reply as she rested her head on his chest. "Sure."

"Well, okay," Sam relented, "maybe I did have a goofy grin. But you made me, you know."

"I made you?" Annie asked as she wrapped her arms around his waist and looked up into his eyes. "And how did I make you wear a goofy grin, huh?"

"Oh, I don't know," Sam replied. "Maybe it was just that tight white shirt you were wearing?" He chuckled at the surprised look on Annie's face.

"You're such a jerk," Annie teased as she swatted his arm.

He proposed at the top of Mount Jefferson, a two-hour drive north from where they had found a small apartment to share in southern New Hampshire after Sam graduated from college. Annie had always been health-conscious as far as Sam was aware. She began her days with a run and a protein smoothie before driving twenty minutes to school, where she was studying for her master's in elementary education. On the weekends she'd convince Sam to walk the neighborhood, bike the Nashua Rail Trail into Massachusetts, or, upon occasion, travel north to the White Mountains. He didn't begrudge her any of this; in fact, though he had never been an extremely active individual, he found he rather enjoyed his time outdoors with Annie. Yet even once he had a year's worth of practice, Annie could still kick his ass athletically, and that's exactly what she had been doing on Mount Jefferson.

When they had finally approached the peak of the mountain early that summer afternoon, Annie was exhilarated. Sweat gleaned from her forehead, and her cheeks were rosy. Sunlight illuminated her blond ponytail and the wisps of short hair that clung to the back of her neck. Her brown eyes watered as she stood with her hands on her hips, her backpack discarded to the ground beside her. This was one thing about Annie that Sam had always appreciated: the fact that she was constantly overcome with the natural beauty that surrounded her.

He was panting, and sweat dribbled down his temples as he stood beside her. He removed the pack's straps from his shoulders and let the mass fall to the ground, feeling instantaneously lighter and free. Sam gazed at Annie as she stared at the surrounding mountaintops, the earth so far below them, and the thick white clouds in the azure sky.

"Hey, Annie?"

"Mmm?" She didn't look his way, merely continued to stare out before her.

"Let's go over here." He motioned with a nod of his chin to the right *of where they stood, an area that appeared devoid of hikers in which he hoped they could steal a moment alone.*

"Just a minute." Sam knew she was drinking it all in, this scenery before her.

When she eventually removed her hands from her hips and looked up at him beside her, he lifted his pack from the ground and led the way. With the shoulder strap hanging over the crook of his elbow, Sam patted the bottom pocket with the palm of his hand and felt a hard mass within.

It was still there. Not that he had really thought he'd lose the ring when the zipper was secured tightly, but, well . . .

Annie followed behind, holding her backpack by the black handle at the top, the excess material of the shoulder straps gently brushing the weathered rock at her sneakered feet. When Sam halted and Annie moved to his side, he felt himself begin to shake. Why he was nervous, he couldn't say—he had no doubt she'd say yes—but nervous he was as he slowly unzipped the small pocket of his backpack and removed the black velvety box while Annie's gaze was directed past the mountain and into the stunning blue sky.

He held the box to his chest and paused a moment. Annie might have been captivated by the glory of nature, but Sam, at this moment in time, was captivated by Annie's profile: her dark blond hair, her pale skin, her rose-tinted cheeks, small nose, and small pink lips that she was continu-ously smothering with lip balm.

Sam felt his eyes relax, his shoulders droop, and the breath release from his body as he gazed upon the woman he adored.

He would remember this moment forever.

Sam inhaled and removed the box from his chest, bringing it to rest behind him.

"Hey, Annie?" He found he was shaking again, and his voice presented a slight quiver.

Sam had taken a step forward, and Annie turned to look beside her. "Yeah?"

"Beautiful, isn't it?" Sam's gaze didn't waver. He was looking directly at Annie.

"Oh," Annie said as she turned to look once again at the horizon.

"Yeah, it really is. I never tire of this view and don't think I ever will. When I look out there, Sam, I feel like everything makes sense. If I have a day where I question my place in this world, I just need to look outside and see the dirt, the trees, the sky, the lake, and just like that, I belong somehow. I may be insignificant, but just look at this. Everything makes sense. Everything has a purpose. And it's all connected." She paused for a moment.

"Yeah," she confirmed, "it's beautiful."

Goofy or not, Sam grinned. Annie had a way of eliciting this from him. "I love you, you know."

Annie looked into his green eyes. "I know. I love you, too."

That smile! Sam thought as he gazed back into the depths of brown that held such emotion, such appreciation.

"No, Annie," Sam said. "I mean I really, really love you."

"I love you, too, silly!" Annie chuckled.

"Annie?" Sam brought his hand out from behind him and presented Annie with the black box.

Annie's smile faltered.

When she looked up at him, her eyes were pooling with tears.

Sam opened the box to reveal the ring he had chosen for her, a large diamond in the center, two slightly smaller diamonds on either side, with a white gold band.

"Oh, my God, Sam!"

"Annie," Sam said, "I'm not kidding. I do love you." Although his voice wasn't quivering any longer, the box was a bit unsteady in his shaking hands. He held it tightly with his fingers. "Will you marry me?"

Annie didn't say anything for a brief moment, and although Sam could see that she was clearly positively affected, this moment was enough to invoke an immense amount of anxiety within him. Luckily, just as he felt his stomach plummet, Annie spoke.

"Yes!" Her answer was enthusiastic. "Of course I'll marry you!

Sam couldn't hide his relief or his pleasure. He smiled so broadly his cheeks began to ache as Annie threw her arms around him in a tight and fervent embrace.

He held the box more tightly.

When she removed her arms from his shoulders and backed up to look into his face, he saw that tears had made their way upon her cheeks and were now dripping off her jaw. She swiped at them with her fingers and laughed.

Sam reached for the ring and began to remove it from the box but halted. "Maybe you should grab this? I'm shaking." He chuckled.

Annie did as suggested and reached for her new ring, lifting it between her thumb and pointer finger and placing it on the third finger of her left hand. She held her hand extended before her and gazed adoringly at the immense amount of sparkle the sun reflected and that she now donned proudly.

"I hope you like it," Sam said.

"I love it," Annie announced. "Sam, it fits perfectly. How did you know what size to get?"

"Well," Sam said, "I kinda told your mom and dad I was going to propose."

"Seriously?"

"Yeah," Sam said abashedly. "Your mom helped me out. I picked out the ring, but she knew your size."

"I love it," Annie reiterated. "And Sam?"

"Yeah?"

"I would have married you a long time ago if you asked. I've known since we first dated that you were it for me." Though she spoke sentimentally, Annie laughed again as she wiped the ever-flowing tears from her cheeks.

Now it was Sam's turn to cry.

Caroline held the side door of her home open on Annie's wedding day and peeked outside. She thought she had heard the sound of a vehicle in the driveway and her senses were correct as there it was, the white limo she had rented for her daughter and of which Annie was ignorant. It was ten o'clock in the morning, and Caroline had been more than pleased and relieved when she had woken at dawn to see the sun rising in the sky and no evident sign of rain. It was to be an outdoor ceremony for Annie and Sam, and Caroline had been stressing about the weather.

She breathed the summer air in thoroughly and exhaled, then quickly exited the house before Annie had the chance to approach the kitchen and inquire as to her whereabouts. Luckily, her daughter was busy in the bedroom that had been hers throughout her childhood with her three brides-maids, all friends from college.

Caroline rushed to meet the limo's driver, who had opened his door and was climbing out of his seat. Her heels impeded her haste, but she made it to his side rather quickly nonetheless.

"Hi," she said. "I'm so glad you're here. I'm Caroline Bailey, mother of the bride."

"Daniel," the middle-aged man said as he extended his hand for Caroline to shake. She accepted it.

"I'm so sorry," Caroline rushed, "I don't mean to be rude, but my daughter has no idea that you're here or that I've even rented a limo in the first place. I'm going to head back indoors, but I wanted you to know that this is a surprise." She beamed as she expressed her enthusiasm.

"Got it," Daniel confirmed.

"Thank you so much. We'll be out soon! Please excuse me for not inviting you in."

Daniel took the black chauffeur hat off his head and rested it against his stomach, then nodded at Caroline. She turned and ran back to the side door of her home as quickly as her high-heeled shoes would permit.

Caroline was thankful to find Annie wasn't in the kitchen when she returned; she could hear the girls' laughter floating through the hallway from Annie's old room at the back of the house. She slowly walked forward, smiling as she savored the twinkling melody of joyfulness on this day she was sure would proceed in utter bliss.

She poked her head through the open doorway. "Oh, Mom!" Annie squealed. "You look so good!"

Caroline looked down at her mulberry-colored dress and lifted the light, flowy material. When she released the fabric, it slowly drifted to rest back upon her thighs, the hem smoothly halting below the knee. She brushed the palms of her hands down her stomach and then over her shoulders and the tight lacy sleeves that ended just before reaching her elbows. "Thanks, Annie. I've got to say that I kind of feel good."

"Yeah, well, I can see why," Annie announced. "You look hot!"

"Annie!" Caroline blushed; then, despite her embarrassment, or perhaps because of it, she chuckled. After a moment she said, "Thanks, honey."

She looked at her daughter then. Really looked at her. She had grown her dark blond hair out long enough for the hairdresser to have parted it on the left-hand side and swept back to place in a large bun at the nape of her neck early that morning. The black mascara on her large eyes accentuated the deep brown of her irises. A small amount of pink blusher tinted her cheeks, and the color of her lips matched the hue. Her nose was small; her chin, too. Her face was slightly rounded. She stood at a height with her mother, both about five feet, five inches. Her young body was lithe and fit, and her summer-sun-kissed legs were visible under the shorts she wore.

Caroline was looking at herself at twenty-three.

Her mind wandered momentarily, and she recalled the day she, too, had walked down the aisle. John and she had married young. Gosh, was she in love! She was convinced she would never forget the look upon his face as she turned the corner in the church on her father's arm and he caught sight of her. She had blubbered the entire way down that aisle. She supposed she really was quite an emotional woman, so the fact that she could barely see her soon-to-be husband through her lowered veil as she took one step and then another was of no surprise to her in the least.

Twenty-five years they had been married. Twenty-five.

She hoped for at least twenty-five more.

"Well," Caroline said after a few minutes of jubilant conversation, "do you girls think you're ready to go?"

Annie took a deep breath and nodded. "Absolutely!" She reached for her wedding dress, snug on a large, thick hanger inside a heavy dress bag to save it from ruin before the ceremony was to take place and hanging on a hook on the back of her bedroom door. Her veil was strategically placed within. Her friends' plum bridesmaid dresses had been hung in the hallway closet for safekeeping.

Caroline led the way out of the bedroom and to the side kitchen door, *where the five women exited out into the warmth of the summer morning, Caroline with a small camera in hand that she'd been using that morning. She'd let the photographer take over once they arrived at the venue, but for now, she desperately wished to document her time with her daughter on what would be one of the most memorable days of their lives, surely.*

With Annie looking to the side at the ground in her white heels, dress slung over her arms awkwardly, and her mother in front of her, Annie didn't notice the limo straightaway. After a moment, she lifted her head and halted her movements instantly, inhaling a deep breath of surprise. "Mom!" she cried as she reached for Caroline's shoulder and grasped on.

Caroline chuckled with glee. "Surprise!"

"Mom!" Annie's breath left her slowly. "You did this?"

"Your father and I wanted to surprise you on your wedding day," Caroline said by means of explanation.

"You and Dad have already done plenty for me. Seriously!" She looked into her mother's eyes.

"I know, Annie, but here's just one more thing. What do you think?"

"What do I think? I think I'm super excited right now!" She looked at her friends, who were all beaming beside her. They hadn't known about this surprise, either. Annie bent her knees and bobbed slightly as Daniel left his perch at the limo's driver's side door.

"Allow me," he said to Annie as he relieved her of the burden of her heavy dress, lifting it rather easily into his own arms and walking to the limo as Caroline began snapping photos with her camera. He opened the back door and gently brought her dress to hang upon a sturdy hook. When through, he stood erect and motioned with the palms of his hands toward the open door of his white limousine. "She's all yours," Daniel announced with a broad smile.

Annie clapped her hands in front of her, then raised them in the air. "Yes!" she exclaimed. She looked at the beaming faces of her friends and at the pleasure her mother's countenance revealed and led the way happily to Daniel and the open limo door.

Annie bent at the waist in her shorts, button-down shirt, and wedding heels to peek inside the vehicle before climbing inside. Gosh, was it large! The seats were made of light gray leather and wrapped almost fully around the interior save for a shiny black space partitioned off for the bottle of champagne chilling at its center and the several sparkling glasses extended from holders. Lights illuminated the space, shining upon the champagne almost as if it were announcing its presence to the women, beckoning them to relax and celebrate the event that would transpire in just a few short hours. Lights, too, were sparkling around the circumference of the ceiling and Annie could even see a slightly dimmer glow at foot-level, appearing as if it were seeping out of the walls themselves.

She looked behind her, smile wide. "It's huge!"

One last glance and she stepped her right foot inside and made her way to the very front of the limousine to sit. Her back would now be against the partition where Daniel would be driving. Sitting spaces lined the entire side to her left, and the champagne was on her right between two large seats. Her friends followed and hung their dresses next to Annie's. Two girls sat to her left and one to her right. When her mother entered the limo, she sat upon the soft leather just to the right of the door and facing Annie.

Daniel bent to peer at the women inside his limo, black hat neatly placed upon his brown-haired head. "I hope you're all comfortable in there," he said.

"I sure am!" Annie said with enthusiasm. Caroline noticed that her daughter had taken off her heels and tucked her bare feet with red-painted toenails under her bare thighs as she sat cross-legged in her shorts on the large seat she had to herself.

Caroline grinned and looked at Daniel in the doorway, the morning sun now shining a bit higher in the sky, smiling upon them all, offering its beauty and warmth for Annie's day. "I think this is all perfect, Daniel," Caroline said. "Thank you very much."

"Wonderful." Daniel looked at Annie. "Well, Miss Bailey, I hope you have a pleasant ride. If you need me at all, just push that button there"—he motioned to a slight knob next to Annie on the wall—"and you'll reach me up front. Help yourselves to the champagne, and just below that in the refrigerator you'll find some grapes and cheese. They're all yours."

Annie clapped her hands in front of her and bounced in her seat,

tanned legs still crossed. Caroline looked at the French manicure adminis-
tered meticulously to Annie's nails just the night prior. What fun that had
been with Annie and her girlfriends. Even Caroline had her nails shaped
and painted light pink. Never before in her lifetime had she been to a nail
salon.

"Thank you, Daniel," Caroline said.

"You are welcome, Mrs. Bailey."

"Call me Caroline, please."

Daniel touched the brim of his hat and nodded slightly, then stood
and closed the door behind him. A moment later Caroline heard the limou-
sine start and felt it move as it slowly backed out of her driveway.

"Shall we?" Caroline reached for the champagne.

"Oh, yes!" Annie agreed eagerly. Her girlfriends readily concurred,
and excited chattering filled the interior of the limo.

"Here we go," Caroline said as she prepared to pop the cork. She
paused a moment. "I suppose I should do this over the bucket," she said.
"You're all in shorts, but I'm in my dress. How terrible would that be—
having champagne on my dress as I'm walked down that aisle in front of
all our friends and family!" She chuckled.

"Oh!" She hesitated. "Annie, would you like to do the honors? This is
your day."

"Nah," Annie said. "I'll probably pop the darn cork into my fore-
head and have a bright red spot for all our wedding pictures. If that was
going to happen to anyone, it would happen to me!"

Caroline chuckled again. "I suppose that would make for some very
interesting photos."

The girls laughed as Annie unconsciously touched her forehead with
her fingertips. "Go for it, Ma," she said as she lowered her hands into her
lap. "I'll definitely have a glass. And you can fill mine right up," she
announced as she lifted her eyebrows and grinned mischievously.

"I'll fill it up," Caroline agreed with a ready smile, "but be careful,
Annie. We don't want you stumbling down that aisle to Sam."

Annie laughed. "That'd get the guests talking, though, wouldn't it?"
she said. "A wedding to remember for sure."

Caroline, still grinning, looked from her daughter and back to the champagne bottle in her hands. She readied the cork. "Okay," she announced, "here we go. One . . . two . . . and THREE!" she yelled as the cork sounded its airy pop and champagne tumbled out the top and cascaded down the bottle and into the bucket on the side of the limousine. Caroline grasped a white linen napkin in her free hand and wiped at the aromatic champagne, removing it from the bottle and from her hand. Placing the napkin on the shiny black countertop, she removed a sparkling clean glass from its holder and poured the bubbly beige liquid inside. She filled it almost to the brim and handed it off to Annie.

"Girls, some champagne?"

A chorus of "Yes, Mrs. Bailey" and "Yes, please, Mrs. Bailey," and Caroline filled three more glasses and handed them over. The final glass would be for herself. She filled it only halfway and watched as the bubbles floated to the surface. She placed the cork back on the champagne bottle and rested it back in its bucket to keep it chilled. She then lifted her glass in the air.

"A toast," she announced. "To my wonderful daughter, Annie. May you enjoy every moment of today. I love you so much!"

"Cheers!" she heard to her right and saw the brunette Marilyn beaming at her friend.

"Cheers!" Their voices filled the space, and Annie smiled brightly before saying "Thank you" and taking her first sip.

"Mmm . . ." Annie said. "Now, that's good!" She held her champagne flute aloft and gazed at the bubbling contents before lowering it. "I'm so excited," she admitted. "Really, really excited. I bet Sam's gonna look so good. And it's a beautiful day. And we're gonna have so much fun. Oh, I just can't wait to be his wife!"

Sam stood at the altar under the afternoon sun. The slight breeze from the lake to his right blew the front of his hair to the side and helped to cool him down. He wasn't used to wearing a full tux; in fact, he hadn't worn a full tuxedo since his high school prom. Brooks, his college roommate, stood beside him as best man. Brooks now lived in LA, and big-city life

suited him well. The miles between them prevented frequent visits, but Sam was appreciative of his long-distance friendship nonetheless. Add to that the fact that Brooks had convinced Sam to attend the party at which he met his future wife, and his presence here was well deserved. Two other men stood beside Brooks as Sam's ushers, both men who also had attended college with him.

Guests shuffled in the white lawn chairs on the lush green grass. The mountains loomed off in the distance beyond the lake, tall and majestic. The venue's gray stone facade faced him, a pebbled path winding its way along the lake and to the large wooden front door. This was where Annie would emerge when she was ready, he knew.

He waited, eager for his first glance of his soon-to-be wife.

He listened to the merry voices of the guests before him, heard the beautiful, soft melody of the cello playing at the corner of the stone building, turned around to gaze out upon the glistening water of the lake and watch the few boats that grazed her surface. When he heard the cello halt and then abruptly change its tune, louder now but still slow and melodic, he turned his gaze in the direction of the front door. It was opened by a uniformed wedding coordinator provided by the venue, tall and lean and handsome. His father emerged, his mother's hand resting at his elbow. He led her slowly down the pebbled walkway. He wasn't entirely close to his parents, either in proximity or emotion. They had moved from New Hampshire to Rhode Island a year prior, and Sam found he hadn't been affected in the slightest when they had announced their retirement to the even smaller state. His mother had birthed Sam at the age of forty-two, quite old for the '70s, he was told.

A surprise.

This he had been aware of his entire life.

They weren't cruel people, his parents. Just a bit selfish and aloof.

His parents had made it halfway down the walkway when Caroline emerged on her husband John's arm. Now John he liked. In John, he had found an easy camaraderie. Sam had never been made to feel uncomfortable in his soon-to-be father-in-law's presence. John always had a ready smile and a booming laugh that materialized often. With John, he could simply be himself.

Caroline reminded Sam of Annie, in appearance and personality both. She was a kind woman, and Sam knew that Annie adored her. She'd often refer to her mother as one of her best friends.

He saw how much at ease Annie was with her parents, and this pleased him greatly. He felt honored to be inheriting a family such as hers. Sam smiled now at the looks of pure elation on John and Caroline's faces as they made their way to their seats in the front row and sat down.

Gretchen, a friend of Annie's from high school, stood in the doorway and took a heeled step forward in her plum dress. The top was tight around her small bosom, and spaghetti straps rested upon her shoulders. The dress was empire-waisted and flowed freely down to her toes. A slit above the navel allowed some of the soft material to billow on either side of her as she made her way down the walkway a bit awkwardly, with the size of her heels and the pebbles of the path disturbing what could have been a smoother stepping ground. She smiled at Sam as she approached the altar with her bouquet of flowers. The bouquet was small and tasteful. Beautiful, really, Sam could admit, and he wasn't one to truly appreciate the beauty of flowers very often. Roses, he knew. At least those were easy to recognize. White and plum, held together at the green stems with a thick, plum ribbon.

Once Gretchen was in place, Amanda, a college friend, emerged into the sunlight and walked in rhythm to the cello's melody. She, too, approached the altar and stood in place.

It was Marilyn's turn now. Marilyn, one of the friends Annie had been with the night she and Sam met.

The music ceased once Marilyn was in place. The guests stood from their chairs, all eyes directed to the venue's front door. The cello hit its first note, high, piercing Sam's body with its beauty. He knew now why the cello was Annie's favorite instrument. He heard Yo-Yo Ma playing often enough in their home—an appreciation Annie had inherited from her mother—but nothing could compare to the bow hitting the strings this close to your ear, in front of you, the music live and feeling.

The cello's chord was lower now, and he caught a glimpse of her. First the tip of a white shoe, then the hem of a white dress. Her hips now, the dress puffing out as if she were in a Victorian ballroom. She walked *slowly forward, and he saw the dress was tight upon her waist and stayed as such to the top of her breasts. The material was unadorned and looked like it would be soft to the touch. It was sleeveless, this dress, and stunning.*

Then he saw her face.

She was beaming, this woman he cherished. Her hair was parted at the side and swept back. She wore a simple tiara at the top of her head. Her veil must have been held in back, as it wasn't covering her face, but he could clearly see it brushing her bare shoulders. It peeked out from below her elbows as she held her rose bouquet in her hands resting upon her stomach. It matched those of her bridesmaids, though hers was larger. The thick plum ribbon was tied in a bow, and the tendrils touched her hands and fell to rest upon the front of her white dress.

A tear glistened upon her cheek in the sunlight as her brown eyes found Sam's.

John left Caroline at her chair in the front row of seats and met Annie in the doorway. He took her right hand. He kissed it, then lowered it into the crook of his left arm. Sam saw Annie's shoulders shake slightly as she laughed and wiped tears from beneath her father's black-rimmed glasses with her free hand. After a moment of familial togetherness, they both looked toward Sam and began to walk.

Annie smiled brightly and walked closer and closer, until there she was. Right before him.

She and John stopped.

Annie's eyes never left Sam's.

"Who gives this woman to be married to this man?" the justice of the peace asked once the cello's last note left the air.

"Her mother and I do," John announced. Then, when Annie still would not take her eyes off Sam, John cleared his throat audibly and the guests laughed.

"Sorry, Daddy," Annie said. She turned her gaze to him and kissed him on a bearded cheek.

When she embraced her father, Sam heard John whisper, "I love you, Annie Bear."

A fresh pool of tears fell from Annie's eyes. "I love you, too."

John turned and walked to sit beside his wife. The ceremony began. Annie had insisted she wanted it short and sweet, and Sam had no objections. Annie, too, requested they write their own vows. Sam thought he'd have a heck of a time writing his, for a writer he was not, but once his pen hit that sheet of paper, the words flowed freely. He hadn't had any trouble at all. When you loved someone with your entire being, the articulation of these feelings came a bit more freely.

"The happy couple has written their own vows for today," the justice of the peace announced loud enough for the guests to hear. "Sam, the floor is yours."

Sam took the folded sheet of white paper from the inside of his suit pocket. Unfolding it, he cleared his throat. He looked down into Annie's eyes, smiled, then began to read. "Annie," he said, "I stand here today a happy man. You have made me a happy man." He paused momentarily. "I knew it, Annie, I really did. That night I saw you on that dance floor from across the room, I knew it. I had to come meet you, goofy grin and all." He heard Annie chuckle, and the laugh was contagious; he couldn't help chuckling himself. "You were hesitant, and I don't blame you. You didn't know me then. But I was determined to convince you that I was a good guy, a guy deserving of your attention. I didn't know you from any other girl in that room, but I was drawn to you, Annie. God was speaking. I listened.

"That night ended too soon. I went back to my apartment and thought of nothing but you. Your voice, your smile. It's a wonder I graduated." Light laughter from the guests. "Annie, every day I spend with you is a day well spent. We even fight well together." Annie threw her head back as she smiled widely, her white teeth prominent. "I love you. Very much. And I promise to love you always." He folded his sheet of paper and repocketed it.

"Don't throw that away," Annie whispered. "I want to look at that when we're both eighty years old."

Sam reached for her hand and squeezed.

"Annie," the justice of the peace said, "you now have the floor."

"I didn't write my vows down," Annie began. "I know exactly what I need to say to you, Sam, and I've known it for quite some time now."

She looked directly into his green eyes. "You're right about one thing: the day I met you I was initially unsure. I mean, here you are, this guy with a very goofy grin on his face, trying to meet me. We were at a party, for goodness' sakes! I didn't think you were for real. But you just looked at me and I felt like you were really looking at me, you know? At me. We talked and talked, and I just felt so comfortable. Mom and Dad have always told me to go with my gut, and my gut was telling me that night that you were a guy I could trust. We said goodbye and my friends and I left and I only thought about you, too. I couldn't stop smiling. Maybe I looked just like you: a goof!" She laughed. "But seriously, Sam, when you called me the next day, I think I felt my heart thump inside of me. I know that sounds super corny, but that's how I was feeling. And I think from that moment on, the rest was smooth sailing.

"Making the decision to be with you was the easiest thing I've ever done. I want to be with you every day and every night. I want to grow old with you, start a family with you. You make me happy, Sam. I vow today in front of our friends and family to do my very best to make you as happy as I feel at this moment. I can't wait to make more memories with you, Sam. I even see us as hunched-over old people, holding hands as we slowly walk along the beach or go to visit our kids and grandkids.

"I love you."

Sam reached over and wiped the free-flowing tears from under Annie's eyes, then swiped at his own.

Caroline shook her hips on the dance floor, raised her hands in the air. She was typically a much more reserved individual, but today she couldn't contain the pure joy she felt inside.

"Who Let The Dogs Out" blared from the speakers at the DJ table, and Caroline found herself immersed in the middle of the crowd of dancers, Annie by her side jumping into the air with raised arms. Annie's feet were bare on the wood, her heels having been discarded along with her veil as soon as the ceremony ended, pictures were taken, and they moved indoors for an early dinner.

When the song came to an end and a slower song began, Caroline was startled by a pair of hands encircling her waist from behind. When a nose nuzzled her cheek, and coarse facial hair tickled her skin, she knew it was John and smiled. She turned and found herself in his arms.

"You are quite the dancer, you know," John said. His voice was deep and husky, a trait she had always relished. He wasn't much taller than she was, but now that her feet—like her daughter's—were bare, she found her head rested well on his chest, just below his collarbone.

She placed her arms under his shoulders and rested the palms of her hands on his upper back. She closed her eyes and listened to his heart beating slowly but strongly.

She didn't believe she could ever be more content.

When the couple's song began to play, she watched from the side of the dance floor as Sam took her daughter into his arms and slowly moved her around. It was Ben Folds's "The Luckiest." Caroline had been so pleased when Annie had come to her home and played the song for her, told her that it would be the wedding song she shared with Sam. Such a beautiful song it was, and now, as she watched the sparkle in her daughter's eyes, the look of adoration as her head lifted to gaze at her new husband, Caroline knew it was simply perfect.

They truly were lucky to have found one another.

Dancing and conversation continued through the night, and when the last guest left, Caroline helped Annie out of her dress in the bridal suite and into more comfortable clothes. Her daughter and her new husband would be staying at a hotel just down the street on this first night as a newly married couple. In the morning they would catch an early flight to Banff National Park in Alberta, Canada, where they would spend ten days on honeymoon.

But for now, for this moment in time, she'd soak her daughter in.

Several tendrils of Annie's blond hair had come out of her bun. Some were tucked behind her ears; others rested on her flushed cheeks. She appeared to be exhausted, but the smile on her lips hadn't dissipated all night. She peered at the black mascara on Annie's long eyelashes as her daughter looked down at the sandals she was slipping onto her feet, then gazed into the brown eyes that appeared when Annie looked back up.

Caroline held that gaze as she reached for her daughter's hand. "I know I've said this before, Annie, but I am so very proud of you. You are a wonderful person, and you have just married a very wonderful man." She paused emotionally to catch her breath. "The world is a better place because you are in it."

"Mom," Annie began, "I have to tell you something." Annie's smile had faded, and Caroline began to worry.

"Honey, what is it? Are you okay?"

"Yeah," Annie assured her, "yeah, I'm perfectly okay. I just need to tell you, seriously, that I am who I am because of you. You are just the best mom ever, and one day, when I have kids, I hope to be just as great to them as you are to me."

Caroline was truly touched. "Honey, when that day comes, you are going to be a wonderful mother. And it makes me giddy just to think that I might one day be a grandmother." She smiled at her daughter. "But don't you rush things, you hear?" she teased. "You have plenty of time to have children and make those memories."

Annie kissed her mother and father goodbye and left with Sam. Caroline watched as the staff cleared the remaining plates from the white linen tabletops and stripped the chairs of their white wraps. Caroline thought the bows at the back of the chairs had been a simple yet beautiful touch. She thought, too, that the glow of the golden lights around the perimeter of the high ceiling added extra ambiance that fit well with the mood of the wedding.

This had been a perfect day, and she just knew that she would never forget it. She was pleased with the knowledge that her daughter would also have the memories of this splendid day to look back upon.

CHAPTER ELEVEN

Sam

"You're here because I have the results of Annie's MRI and PET scan." It was Dr. Barnard speaking. Sam was in a small room with Annie beside him and Caroline to her left. After Annie's first appointment with Dr. Barnard, they had scheduled an MRI for three weeks later and were extremely fortunate to have had the ability to head back the next day for a PET scan. Sam and Annie stayed in a small room at a hotel a short walk away from the hospital while Caroline remained at home with the kids. Approximately two weeks after that, they had received a phone call from Dr. Barnard's office informing them that the results were in and would they please make a further appointment to drive into Boston to see Dr. Barnard. Thus, at the end of July almost two months after their initial visit to the neurologist, they were once again in his office.

"Yes, that's right," Sam said. He felt as if he were about to jump from his chair, he was so anxious. This had been such a long journey, and he still felt like definitive answers for Annie hadn't been given.

"We'll discuss the MRI first," Dr. Barnard said. He swiveled in his chair and faced the computer propped on the counter. Sam leaned forward. His anxiety and inquisitiveness urged him to stand, to hover over Dr. Barnard's shoulder so he could best see the image of his wife's brain and better understand what it was the neurologist was about to convey, but he held steady, hard as it was to do so.

"Here, we've got Annie," Dr. Barnard began. Sam was looking at a darkened egg-shaped image on the screen before him. The outer portion was surrounded fully by a thick, white line. When he looked at the image inside of this shell, he equated it immediately with that of a sea sponge as some portions were full and dark gray, while others lacked the gray and dark black snaked its way through.

"If you look closely," Dr. Barnard continued, "right here" —he pointed to the uppermost gray-and-black portion of the image on the screen—"you'll find a bit of atrophy in the frontal lobe."

"Atrophy?" Sam was confused. He didn't fully understand what it was he was looking at.

"Yes. Let me further explain," Dr. Barnard said. "This is an image of a healthy brain," he said. He pulled up a separate MRI photo next to Annie's on the computer for comparison.

A healthy brain?

That implied Annie's was unhealthy, didn't it?

"Look just here," Dr. Barnard continued. "With this image, we can clearly see that the front of the brain is quite full, if you will. These gray portions are abundant, and the black, not so much. The gray you see is this person's brain. With Annie's image, these black areas are empty spaces. Annie's brain has begun to atrophy, it's begun to shrink. If you look here"—Dr. Barnard pointed to the bottom of the image now—"we're fairly full, but here both at the frontal lobe and here"—he indicated both the right- and left-hand sides of Annie's brain; Sam thought it looked as if these portions were positioned at Annie's temples—"you see more black, you see more shrinkage."

"Shrinkage? You mean to tell me that Annie's brain is shrinking?" Sam's stomach churned, and a bead of sweat trickled from his hairline down his forehead.

"Yes, that is what I am saying," the doctor confirmed. "We see this even further when we look at an MRI image from the side." Dr. Barnard clicked the computer mouse several times, and two new images filled the screen. Sam could now clearly differentiate between Annie's unhealthy brain and the MRI of a normal brain. There was more black on Annie's. In this image, he could also see a ghost of her facial features. He was looking at her nose, her lips, her chin. He moved his gaze from the computer momentarily to look at his breathing wife beside him, the producer of this image. She appeared to be listening to what Dr. Barnard was stating but had a flat affect in response. Sam locked eyes with Caroline and saw her lip trembling slightly before he turned his attention back to the computer.

"This is the area of concern. As before, Annie's brain is atrophying in both the frontal and temporal lobes. Looking at the image of the healthy brain, you see very strong gray lines that almost rest against the edge here. Compare this image to Annie's and you find that Annie is losing a good portion of that gray. It's shrinking."

"I really don't understand this," Sam said. "How can Annie's brain shrink?"

"First off, let me show you Annie's PET scan. I know you must have a lot of questions right now and I assure you I will answer them, but the PET scan will further corroborate the diagnosis I am about to give you."

Sam nodded, though reluctantly. If the neurologist had a definitive diagnosis, he wanted to hear it. Now. But he understood, also, that Dr. Barnard was doing his best to fully explain how he had come to the diagnosis he was about to convey, so he held his tongue, gritted his teeth.

His stomach felt even more uneasy.

A few touches of the keyboard and new images were displayed on the screen. These scans weren't black and white; rather, they presented a burst of color, bold and forthright. Sam studied these images, looked from the purple to the green, red, and yellow. It was Annie's brain, surely, but he had absolutely no notion of what these colors represented.

"This here," Dr. Barnard began, "is a healthy brain. Just as with the MRI image, you can clearly see that the brain fills the entire space within the skull." He touched his pointer finger to the screen, slowly made his way from the left and arched upward and to the right, tracing the slight green line from one side of the brain to the other. Yes, Sam could see that this was all rather solid.

"Now here," Dr. Barnard said, " we have Annie." He turned the screen an inch on the sterile countertop so Sam, Annie, and Caroline could better view the image.

And there it was.

Sam knew what he was looking at now. After learning just moments before to find the discrepancies in Annie's MRI, to see the areas of the brain that just simply . . . well . . . weren't there, he found the PET scan did indeed offer corroboration, as Dr. Barnard had claimed it would. He was amazed that he was looking at a neon-colored image of the workings of his wife's brain, the mechanism that controlled her entire being, really. Flummoxed that he was staring at what Dr. Barnard had described as shrinkage, as portions of Annie's brain were atrophying.

Wasting away.

He could clearly delineate where the skull began, but where, with the PET image of the healthy brain, Sam could discern the actual brain almost touching that skull, in the image of Annie's brain there was a bit of space. Empty space. On both the right- and left-hand sides of her brain, just at the top of the image. He was reminded this time of one of Hannah's squishies, those silly toys of hers that she'd take along on car rides and press with her fingers as she held one in the palm of her hand. Even when she pressed lightly, the substance would mold to the force of her fingers, would press downward. That's what he was looking at right now. A slight press. If Hannah let go of that toy, it would bounce back up to its true form—the healthy brain.

But there was no letting go for Annie. There was no turning back. Her brain was shrinking. The part of his wife's body that allowed her to think, feel, move, breathe—it was wasting away. And in doing so, it was taking his wife down with it.

Could it be halted?

Dr. Barnard explained the PET scan before them, took his time to show them the exact areas that were affected with Annie. Eventually, he paused, and Sam looked him directly in the eye. "What does this all mean?" he asked. His voice was ragged, though barely a whisper. The palms of his hands were held firmly together and snuggled between his thighs. He pressed. He needed to feel that strain. If he didn't occupy his hands, his legs, he was afraid he'd jump out his seat at any moment. "Shrinkage? It can't be Alzheimer's, can it? I mean, Annie's not yet forty-one years old."

"No," Dr. Barnard said. "Not Alzheimer's. But what Annie has is a form of dementia."

"Dementia?" It was Caroline who spoke. Her voice quavered, and when Sam looked to his left past Annie, he could clearly see the dismay she felt portrayed on her countenance. He gazed at his mother-in-law's profile, so much like his wife's: same dark blond bob, same small nose and chin. She was holding Annie's left hand in her right while the tremoring fingertips of her free hand were swiping at newly shed tears upon her cheeks.

"Yes," Dr. Barnard confirmed. He looked at Annie, leaned forward so he was a bit closer, then spoke directly to her while Sam watched his wife and listened to the neurologist as he sealed her fate with a diagnosis. "Annie, you have what we call frontotemporal degeneration, or FTD for short. Specifically behavioral variant FTD. As you have seen through both the MRI and PET scan images on the computer, the frontal and temporal portions of your brain are shrinking. The frontal lobes of our brain—the front—control such things as emotion, cognition, speaking, sequencing, multitasking, and judgment, while the temporal lobes—the right and left sides of our brain that I showed you on the screen—control memory, hearing, learning, and feelings. In people with FTD, these lobes slowly atrophy, and those functional areas are affected as a result. This is why you have been showing less emotion, wandering, displaying signs of poor judgment, eating more and eating things you normally wouldn't. This is why your family has been so concerned for you." Dr. Barnard paused for a second and studied Annie before him. "Do you understand what I'm explaining to you, Annie?"

Annie smiled at Dr. Barnard, then slowly shook her head. "I don't know," she said gaily.

"What I'm essentially saying, Annie, is that your brain is sick."

"Okay," Annie said in response. "I have a sick brain."

"Yes," Dr. Barnard confirmed. "You do." He sat erect and swiveled his chair to rest beside the counter as Sam heard a definitive sob from Caroline.

Sam attempted to process this new information.

Dementia? Degeneration? Frontotemporal? Shrinkage? Behavioral variant?

"What do you mean by behavioral FTD?" he asked.

"The two major variants we see with FTD are behavioral and primary progressive aphasia. I see the complex look on your face." Dr. Barnard smiled sympathetically. "Aphasia is when a person has difficulty with language: speaking, reading, writing, and understanding. In patients with FTD whose brains atrophy mainly in this area, we don't see the behavioral changes as much as we see these difficulties with language, especially at first. Now, with Annie, you've indicated you are witnessing many behavioral changes, both physically and emotionally. You have also indicated language difficulties, but with the time we have spent speaking about Annie, along with the MRI and PET scan images, she most definitely has FTDbv—the behavioral variant of frontotemporal degeneration."

"But it's not Alzheimer's?" Caroline asked. "I've heard of early-onset Alzheimer's."

"It is not," Dr. Barnard confirmed. "Even with early-onset Alzheimer's, as with Alzheimer's in individuals past their seventies, memory loss is the most prevalent symptom. Behavioral changes come later as the disease progresses. With Annie, with FTD, we see that memory isn't affected greatly in the beginning stages of the disease. Now, Annie's memory will be affected in the later stage of the disease as her brain continues to atrophy, but what we are seeing now are telltale signs of the beginning stage of FTD moving into the middle stage, really. I have seen other patients with this diagnosis, though I admit not as many as with a diagnosis such as Alzheimer's. FTD affects approximately fifty thousand to sixty thousand people, whereas Alzheimer's might affect upwards of five and a half million. With Alzheimer's so prevalent, FTD is often misdiagnosed as early-onset Alzheimer's as our patients are predominantly in their forties and fifties, but FTD can take hold even in your thirties. The MRI and PET scans, oral evaluations, along with my time with Annie and interviews with you, convince me that we are looking at FTD."

Sam inhaled sharply, closed his eyes. When he exhaled, it was audible. He opened his eyes and looked at Dr. Barnard. "You're saying her brain will continue to shrink?"

"I am, yes."

"So, what does that mean for Annie?"

Dr. Barnard looked at Annie before him. "Annie," he said, "I wonder if perhaps you'd like to walk with my nurse down to the cafeteria? Would you like something to eat?"

"Oh, yes!" Annie said. "I want Swedish fish."

"I don't know if we have Swedish fish, but I'm sure you can find something to your liking." Dr. Barnard stood and opened the door. He turned his head to the left and motioned with his hand. When his nurse approached, he asked her to accompany Annie to the cafeteria long enough for her to eat a snack and chat before reuniting with her family. Annie left without hesitation, and Dr. Barnard sat back down.

"Annie will continue to decline," he said. "She will continue to exhibit behaviors that you have been privy to thus far, but her behaviors will also change as her brain continues to functionally struggle. You'll notice more difficulties in language as time progresses. She'll be uninhibited. I know this has all been extremely difficult for you so far, but I fear I must tell you that it only gets harder from here. Annie is not purposefully making your lives harder. In fact, Annie isn't fully aware of what is going on. Know that when she appears apathetic—when she smiles when you feel that's an inappropriate response to any given moment or when she has a flat affect when you feel she should be smiling and loving, reciprocating emotion—these are all things her brain is having difficulty with. She is not doing it purposefully. This, unfortunately, goes with the diagnosis, the disease. It's trademark." Dr. Barnard paused for a moment. Sam's gaze didn't waver. Beside him, Caroline's shoulders shook and a sob leaped from her throat.

"In some cases, it will take years for an individual to

approach the stage of the disease I believe Annie is in, but I feel Annie's case is progressing very rapidly based on the onset of symptoms." Dr. Barnard spoke freely, though his voice was soft, kind.

"So Annie is going to struggle with these symptoms for the rest of her life? Her brain will continue to shrink?" Sam asked

"It will," Dr. Barnard confirmed.

"What does that mean? It just shrinks and shrinks?" Sam was beginning to lose his composure. What was this doctor saying? His wife's brain was going to shrink . . . until when? Until there was nothing left of it?

"Yes," Dr. Barnard said. "Annie's brain will continue to atrophy, and sadly, I do believe it will atrophy rather quickly."

"How can she just live like this?" It was Caroline who spoke. "What will happen to her when this disease progresses even further?"

Dr. Barnard paused. He looked from Caroline to Sam. His gaze was sympathetic. The corners of his brown eyes crinkled, and his bushy eyebrows dipped as his face softened. When he looked back at Caroline, he said, "Annie's brain will continue to atrophy and her symptoms will increase in severity." He paused for a moment and began again, softly and slowly. "She will exhibit a gradual decline in language and will eventually become mute." Caroline gasped, and Sam felt his hands begin to shake. He placed them between his thighs again, hoping to squelch the sensation just to find that his stomach roiled, his jaw clenched, and his arms and shoulders were now shaking.

Dr. Barnard continued. "As Annie's brain continues to atrophy, she will have trouble remembering how to dress, how to brush her teeth, and how to bathe. Annie's brain will eventually fail to tell her how to move. It will fail to remember how to eat."

"Oh, my God!" Caroline placed her right palm over her mouth.

"What are you saying?" Sam's voice quavered.

"Patients with FTD increasingly struggle until their brains don't know how to struggle any longer. Annie will pass away."

Caroline was now sobbing. Sam's head throbbed and his vision blurred as he looked at the neurologist before him. "So this is a death sentence? There's nothing that we can do?"

"Unfortunately, there is not. FTD is often misdiagnosed for years before the patient and family learn what it is that's truly going on. I understand this past year has been rather difficult for you all, but I do hope I have at least aided in your movement forward and that your questions about what is happening with Annie won't go unanswered from here on in." Dr. Barnard leaned forward. "My suggestion would be to find yourselves a support group with other families and caregivers who are also living with loved ones who have FTD. This is no minor hardship. While Annie is functioning fairly well at the moment, she will continue to decline, and it will become necessary to find her around-the-clock care. Many families find it obligatory to place their loved one in a home."

"A home?" Caroline was near hysterical. "My daughter in a nursing home? My *daughter*?"

Sam reached over and took hold of his mother-in-law's hand. Caroline looked his way, though he wasn't sure she was looking at him at all. The sclera of her eyes were red; tears were streaming down her cheeks, down her chin, and landing upon her bosom.

"What caused this to happen?" Sam asked.

"We really don't know," Dr. Barnard stated. "With a smaller number of individuals with this particular diagnosis and the fact that for so many years—and even still—it's continuously misdiagnosed . . ." He shook his head. "Research is continuous and we hope to find answers soon, but for now we know that in many cases, there is a genetic component, though in about half, there is not. I wish I had answers for you."

After a minute Sam said, "So what now?"

"Now I suggest, as I said before, you find a support group. I also highly recommend you review your finances, petition for aid. A support group can better help you with this. Help Annie with a will if she doesn't already have one. There are medications that can help with certain symptoms Annie is exhibiting now or will exhibit in the future. Honestly, I suggest you take it day by day and continue to enjoy the time you have with your wife"—he looked from Sam to Caroline—"and your daughter."

"How long?" Sam asked.

"Excuse me?"

"How long do we have with Annie? When do you think she'll . . . die?" He choked on the finality of this last word.

"It's hard to say. The average lifespan is approximately seven or eight years from the onset of symptoms. Though some individuals live for about fifteen, sixteen years with the disease, some decline rapidly and pass within just a few years. I do believe Annie is in this latter group."

Another sob from Caroline.

Sam's entire body was shaking by now and his insides were plummeting. "So, you're telling me that my forty-year-old wife has only a few years to live and that she'll never get better? That the woman who is not my Annie right now never will be again?"

"I do apologize," Dr. Barnard said, "but yes. I am very sorry. There is a chance that Annie may pass in a couple of years."

"How?"

"How?" Dr. Barnard asked.

"How will she die?"

"I cannot tell you this as there's no definitive way of knowing. Many patients with FTD have trouble swallowing, so many aspirate and develop pneumonia. She might fall and injure herself. She may develop an infection."

"Jesus Christ," Sam breathed.

"Again," Dr. Barnard soothed, "I am very sorry. I've compiled some information for you. Support groups, lawyers, caregiver services and such.

Sam placed his face into the palms of his hands as he listened to Caroline cry beside him. He looked up when there was a knock on the door and the knob turned. Annie bounded into the room, speckles of some sort of frosting lingering on her lips. "Hi!" she announced. She stepped forward and occupied the empty seat between Sam and Caroline. Caroline attempted to compose herself and took her daughter's hand in her own. Sam looked from Dr. Barnard to Caroline, then to his wife.

A few years?

The kids.

What the hell was he going to tell his kids?

He wanted to reach for her, console her. He wanted Annie to embrace him back. He wanted her beautiful brown eyes to gaze into his. He wanted to see that look of adoration in them. He wanted that sly smile of hers to return when she was nuzzling up against him, teasing him.

He wanted to hear her say "I love you."

But that wife was gone. In her place was this woman he didn't really know, this woman who was changing week by week. He wanted to grasp onto that woman, wanted to shake her and tell her to let his wife out, force her to bring his wife back to him.

But he knew he couldn't do that.

His wife was dying.

Sam leaped from his chair and in two long strides hovered over the sink at the counter and vomited. When he was finished, he turned the faucet on and attempted to splash water on the chunks that had been expunged from his stomach. He cupped his hands under the faucet to catch some of the streaming water and rinsed the acidic bile from his mouth. He then slowly turned around, leaned his backside against the counter for support. He looked at Annie before him.

"Well, that was fuckin' disgusting!" she exclaimed.

CHAPTER TWELVE

Caroline

*H*er daughter was dying.

Caroline slid the palm of her hand over Annie's, fingers squeezing, eyes imploring.

They sat upon the Adirondack chairs in Annie's backyard overlooking the small New Hampshire lake. Just this morning, Annie had been given her diagnosis. Just this morning, Caroline had learned that her daughter was wasting away, that her brain was failing her.

She's had a couple of hours now to let this diagnosis sink in, to truly think upon what Dr. Barnard had said to her and Sam. She struggled now to remember it all; she was so emotionally affected by the reason behind her daughter's decline, but she knew she could simply make a phone call to Dr. Barnard's office if she or Sam needed clarification. And there was the internet, right? She had that.

A support group. The neurologist was probably right: she should join a support group. She didn't even know where to begin. Though she was heartbroken, she had to admit that she also felt a slight relief at finally understanding why Annie had been behaving so out of character. Why Annie hadn't initiated an embrace or looked her mother in the eye to speak words of love. That. That's what she was going to miss the most.

When Annie was a baby, she'd look at Caroline with those big, beautiful brown eyes and smile. She had the chubbiest cheeks back then. Gosh, were they amazing! Caroline would run the tip of her finger down those cheeks gently, feel the soft skin. She'd kiss her daughter's forehead and drink in the smell of her Johnson's baby shampoo. Often on a warm summer day, she'd choose not to dress Annie when they were at home; rather, she preferred cuddling Annie with only the cloth diaper pinned to her bottom. She enjoyed nothing more fully than sitting upon their wood-framed wingback sofa, her back against the hard brown floral synthetic velour cushion with Annie's back resting on the thighs of her mother's bent legs. Caroline would prop her bare feet on the egg-shaped coffee table and kiss her daughter's chubby toes and feet, tickle the rolls on her neck and blow raspberries onto the skin of her tubby stomach until Annie would close her eyes tightly and belly-laugh, showing her mother the most amazing gummy smile while doing so.

And oh, the sounds she made when she laughed, the coos she babbled when she was learning to coo.

Caroline was hoping that perhaps Annie's first word would be "Mama," as so many first words tend to be. No such luck. Annie's first word was "no." Caroline had been attempting to convince her daughter to eat some broccoli off the metal tray of her sunflower-splattered high chair when Annie had shaken her head with conviction and crinkled her nose in disgust. When Caroline picked up the broccoli and brought it to Annie's mouth, her daughter had shouted a very assertive

"No!" before flinging her arms in the air and accidentally knocking the broccoli out of Caroline's hand.

"Uh-oh," Caroline said. She leaned forward at the waist and picked the broccoli up off the floor.

The next day found Annie in her high chair again. She looked at her mother and purposefully dropped a blueberry onto the floor. "Uh-uh," she approximated, her eyes never leaving Caroline's.

"Oh, you little stinker," Caroline had teased. She picked the blueberry up, and with it grasped between her thumb and forefinger, she lifted it into the air and pantomimed an airplane, swerving it to the left and to the right above her head. She began to blow raspberries with her mouth in semblance of the airplane's engine. Annie chuckled, the apples of her cheeks lifting with pleasure.

"Open wide," Caroline sang as she brought the blueberry to her daughter's lips. Annie giggled once again and then willingly cooperated. She had always loved her blueberries.

"Mama" had been Annie's third word, spoken just after her first birthday and just days after she had given a vehement "no" to the broccoli her mother was trying to coax her into eating.

It was one of the most beautiful sounds Caroline had ever heard.

"Annie, sweetie." Caroline lifted her finger and began to stroke the cheek of her now adult daughter by her side. Annie was watching a mother duck emerge from the shallow water to stand upon the sand at the edge of the lake. Seven ducklings followed her lead and waddled onto the warm sand, a few shaking their tails to send small water droplets flying.

Annie burst from her chair, a loaf of white bread in her hand. She opened the plastic at the top and lifted a slice as she hurried over to where the ducks gathered. In her haste, she frightened the birds, and they protested with loud quacks and hurriedly waddled back into the water.

"Oh, no, no," Annie pouted. "Come back. Bread. See? I have bread."

Caroline lifted herself from the chair, feeling as if her torso were entirely too weighted down for her legs to carry. But she willed them forward and slowly joined her daughter at the water's edge. "They're just scared, sweetie, that's all," she soothed. "Here, let me." She extended her hand and gently took the bread slice from Annie's palm. Annie looked at her mother with a frown but was soon giggling with delight as the ducks emerged from the water to eat the small portions of bread that Caroline had torn and thrown down.

"See? They're happy now," Caroline stated wistfully. "Why don't you try?"

Annie reached into the plastic bag and threw an entire slice of bread onto the ground. The mother duck scurried over and attempted to break the piece apart.

"That's a little much," Caroline stated. "Let's break it up a bit, shall we?"

Annie removed another slice from the bag, and instead of holding the plastic under her arm or entwined within her fingers, she let it drop the ground so she could break the bread apart. Caroline watched her do so—large chunks that the ducks had difficulty swallowing.

Caroline retrieved the bag from the ground, opened it, and pulled out another slice, breaking it apart into smaller portions and throwing them to the sand. Annie watched the ducks eat with jubilation. When she attempted to walk to them with outstretched arms, they were spooked again and ran into the water, swimming farther away.

"Oh, bye!" Annie called.

Caroline looked at her daughter beside her, looked at her slightly messy bob, at the wrinkled shirt she had noticed in Dr. Barnard's office and that embarrassed her slightly. She looked at her bare feet, the red polish chipped and old, and sighed. She gazed now upon Annie with an entirely new lens.

Messy hair? Had she showered that morning, run a comb through her hair? Did she use her blow-dryer any longer?

A wrinkled shirt? Had she forgotten to iron? Could she iron? Would she burn herself? Was she even aware that her shirt was in need of care?

Bare feet? Annie often wore shoes, Caroline knew. She was always saying how much she abhorred the feeling of grass on her toes. Sand she didn't mind at all, but the grass had always bothered her; she claimed she didn't know if she'd step on a pebble or even an insect. She hated not knowing what lay there. Currently, bare feet didn't seem to bother her in the least.

And the chipped nail polish? More often than not when Caroline saw her daughter's bare feet, they were groomed and summer-ready. Right now she was in desperate need of some lotion for her dry skin and removal of the polish that was staining her nails. Was she aware? Did she care?

So many thoughts ran through her mind as she watched Annie wave at the ducks, watched her sit and begin sifting the warm, dry sand through her fingers, allowing it to trickle onto her thighs.

Annie would continue to deteriorate. The daughter she had always loved, the daughter who had become a best friend, was in desperate need of aid. And Sam—Sam needed help. Caroline saw how the change in Annie had also changed the entire family dynamic. She and Sam were close; had been since the day Annie brought him home to meet her and John. Luckily this fond relationship lent ease when heavy conversations were warranted. Caroline knew he was incredibly stressed, knew his boss had spoken to him. She had been helping out, yes, but as she lowered herself to the sand to join her daughter, she realized her help was needed even more, was needed critically. Sam couldn't run this family on his own, not with Annie's brain hindering her from being the mother she had always been, being the wife and partner he was used to.

Caroline needed to step up.

~

"Absolutely not."

"Sam, I really think this needs to be done. I really do."

"Caroline, I cannot ask you to move in. I can't ask you to uproot your life so completely."

They were seated at the kitchen table once the kids had gone to bed. Annie was watching television. Ben and Hannah knew that their mother had had an appointment at the neurologist, and they had seen the grave faces of both their father and grandmother when they had returned home from school. Caroline had asked Sam if he'd like for her to take Annie back outside so he could converse with the children, and he had gratefully accepted her offer. She walked with Annie around the neighborhood, stopping when her daughter had seen Pumpkin, her neighbor's Yorkshire terrier whom Annie still adored.

She had actually knocked on the front door of her daughter's home when they returned approximately an hour later just to be sure Sam was ready for her to enter. She wanted to ensure her son-in-law had sufficient time to speak with the children. When he called for her to come in, she did so, Annie following behind. Hannah had taken one look at her mother and run upstairs sobbing. Ben stared at Annie. His eyes were red-rimmed, but if he had cried, those tears had since dissipated. His face was expressionless, his lips pursed. Eventually, he turned, shoulders dropping slightly, and walked out the back door onto the deck and into the yard. Caroline watched him from the bay window in the kitchen as he made his way to the distant water's edge and sat down.

For the better part of the day, her heart had been breaking for Annie and for Sam. It had been breaking for herself.

Now it was shattering for her grandchildren, who would never again have the mother they'd had the privilege of knowing until this point, the mother who loved them unconditionally and who had shown it every day prior to the onset of FTD symptoms.

And if Dr. Barnard was correct, Annie would be physically gone from their lives in just a couple of short years. How would this family be affected then? How could they stand by and watch her deteriorate even further?

Caroline inhaled deeply, held the air inside her lungs, and slowly blew it out as she walked toward Sam. Annie had found her way to the couch and had the television set on, flipping through the channels.

"Are you okay?" she asked as she approached his side. She saw the affliction on his face, saw the puffiness of skin below his watery eyes. The green of his irises was strikingly illuminated through the moisture. She held them intensely with her own.

Sam ran his hands through his disheveled dark brown graying hair, rubbed his temples with his fingertips. "I don't even know how to answer that, Caroline. Am I okay? I just found out my wife's brain is mush. I just found out it's not depression that's making her this way. At least with depression, we could have continued to see Dr. Patel. We could have switched up meds until we found one that worked. She could have gotten better. But now? Now I find out my wife won't ever come back to me. Here I've been thinking she's got this issue that will go away. Here I am, pissed beyond belief that she could be so heartless, that she could lose her job, sit on her ass, make us pick up all her slack. And now I find out my wife can't help any of this, I find out my wife is dying? Fuck! I'm such an asshole!"

"Don't you ever say that again, Samuel Carson," Caroline

admonished. "You are far from being an asshole." Caroline never swore. Never. So the fact that she had done so now and Sam didn't flinch, didn't tease her, merely proved that he was past consolation, that he was so utterly tormented he lacked the ability to calm himself, to think straight.

"Sam, look at me." He didn't, couldn't obey. Tears were now streaming down his cheeks, clear mucus dripping from his nose to rest upon his upper lip. His shoulders quaked as he sobbed. He wiped the wetness from his cheeks with the bottom of his shirt, wiped below his nose, but still, the tears came.

"I . . . I—"

"Don't say anything right now," Caroline said, her own tears now emerging. "Sit down, Sam." She led him the few steps to the kitchen table, pulled a chair out, and guided him down. He rested his forehead in his hands and continued to sob. Caroline sat beside him, and the two of them cried together, both thinking of Annie, a woman they loved so dearly. Both thinking of Ben and Hannah, children who were being asked to endure the unendurable. Both thinking of themselves, what they had lost thus far and what they were going to lose day by day until Annie's body ceased to inhabit the earth.

Caroline didn't know how long they sat there together crying. She knew only that the sun had begun to set out the bay window, emitting an iridescent glow onto the kitchen table. She saw Ben remained on the sand at the water's edge, gazing into the horizon. Hannah hadn't come downstairs.

Annie remained on the couch watching television. Caroline surmised she wasn't even aware that she and Sam had been sitting so near, that she and Sam had been pouring forth their anguish for an indeterminate amount of time.

Eventually, the tears evaporated. The waning sun's rays shone through the upper strands of Sam's hair as his attention diverted to his mother-in-law. "I just don't know how I'm going to do this," he admitted. "I'm so sorry, Caroline. I've been sitting here and I've thought of nothing but Annie and myself, but I know you're suffering, too. I know how close you and Annie always were."

"I think we're all struggling, Sam."

Sam nodded his head forlornly. "I feel so much guilt. Guilt for all the negative thoughts I've had about my wife. Guilt that she's afflicted instead of me."

Caroline shook her head. "Don't go there. You had no way of knowing what was really going on with Annie. Neither of us did."

"No," Sam said. "I know. But the guilt is still there nonetheless." He paused, looked at his son through the kitchen's large bay window. "How am I going to help them, Caroline? They've already seen so much, been through so much with their mom being the way she's been. Now they're forced to sit by and watch as she gets worse. Worse and worse until we can't take care of her and she's gone. How am I going to help them when I'm in trouble at work, Annie doesn't have a job. Shit, I guess she never will again, will she?" He rubbed his eyes with his knuckles. Caroline looked at him, gave him time.

"How am I going to help them, Caroline, when the money's running out?"

"Dr. Barnard spoke about some kind of aid, yes?"

"Yeah, I guess so. There's a lot I need to research now. There's a lot that needs to be done.

"Yes, there is. But Sam?" He looked at her. "I'll be here to help."

"Thanks, Caroline. But you've helped so much already. So much. I can't ask you to help even more."

"Of course you can! Sam, this is my daughter we're talking about." She pointed toward the living room. Her voice rose. "That's my daughter over there.

"Sam," she continued after a few heartbeats, "I want to move in."

Sam looked at his mother-in-law incredulously. "Absolutely not."

"Sam, I really think this needs to be done. I really do."

"Caroline, I cannot ask you to move in. I can't ask you to uproot your life so completely."

"My intention is not to make things harder for you but to help. You need to work, right?" Sam nodded his head slowly. "Well, I'm retired. I have savings that can help Annie. My husband has been gone for a few years now. Annie is my only child. I love you and the children, Sam. You are my family."

"Caroline—"

"No, Sam. I want to do this. I *need* to do this. You have that room next to the stairs. All you use it for is books and a computer, if I'm not mistaken. We can move the computer to the living room and I'll sleep there. I can be here each and every day to care for Annie. I can ensure the kids are off to school safely, and I'll be here when they get home. I can take Annie along to after-school activities so the children don't have to lose out on any more opportunities. They're already losing out on enough. I can help, Sam. I want to help."

"Caroline, I really don't know how I can ask you to do this."

"And I really don't know how you can afford not to."

She knew she had him there.

"How can I ever repay you for this, Caroline?" Sam looked at her sorrowfully.

"You won't ever have to. We'll repay each other by simply being together. We'll all need help from here on in."

They paused then, each in their own heads with their own thoughts. Eventually, it was Sam who spoke first. "I don't know how to do this. I just don't know how to do this. How can we be asked to live without Annie?"

～

"Push! You can do it, Annie! Push!"

When Annie had asked Caroline to be in the delivery room with her as she gave birth to her first child, Caroline had begun to weep. She was becoming more emotional these days, it seemed. Annie was her only child, after all. She had watched her grow from a hungry infant into a chubby, adorable baby girl; had watched her grow from a forlorn, though happy (a contradiction, was it not?) teenager into a thoughtful, beautiful young woman. She had witnessed her first crush, her first heartbreak, then the beauty of her falling in love with Sam and their glorious wedding celebration.

She remembered the day well when Annie and Sam had surprised her with the knowledge of Annie's pregnancy. Caroline's birthday was the following day, a Monday. Annie and Sam had arrived at her home that Sunday afternoon in late May after a morning of local hiking with a small wrapped gift.

Annie was beaming.

"Ah, I'm so happy to see you!" Caroline said. Though she had seen her daughter just the weekend prior, she was always pleased to be in her company.

John crept up behind Caroline. *"Come in, come in,"* he said amiably. *"Happy you're here."* His smile was wide on his round face. He wore a neatly trimmed medium-brown beard and mustache, something Annie had never seen him without, though when Caroline had met her husband he was clean-shaven. A pair of thick black-rimmed glasses rested upon the bridge of his nose.

"Hi, Daddy," Annie said as she stepped through the doorway and took off her shoes. Sam followed. *"Hi, Mom."*

"That's gotta be for your mom," John said as he looked at the small package held in his daughter's hand. Caroline turned to look at him, and he winked at her with a sly expression on his face; then he chortled that deep-throated chortle that was his trademark and always made Caroline smile and Annie chuckle herself.

"Yep, it sure is," Annie confirmed. *"Although,"* she said, *"it's actually for the both of you."*

When Caroline looked at her daughter inquisitively, Annie just *grinned widely and walked toward the kitchen table. Caroline turned to Sam and lifted her eyebrows expressively. Sam merely shrugged as if he had no idea what lay inside that box.*

"Come on over, Mom," Annie called. "I'm really wanting you to open this. I'm super excited! Dad, you, too."

When the foursome were all seated at the off-white table, Annie handed the package off to her mother. "I hope you like this, Mom. Sam and I think it's pretty amazing. Happy birthday."

Caroline accepted the gift and slowly unwrapped the balloon-adorned birthday paper from its sides. Before she could see what lay beneath, Annie spoke up again. "Just don't read the side of the box, okay? You need to just open the top and then take it out."

"Okay," Caroline said. She was eager to see what Annie and Sam had gotten for her. They had never, in her recollection, been so excited to bestow a gift upon her as they were right then.

She did what Annie had asked of her and opened the top of the cardboard box that had appeared under the wrapping paper. It was approximately one and a half hand lengths in height, and she was able to fully place her palm on one side, grasping it between her thumb and four fingers.

With the top of the box now open, she peered inside. "Oh, a Willow Tree Angel. I can at least see that's what it is." Caroline had been collecting Willow Tree Angels for a few years now. On a shelf in her living room and on the end table beside the couch stood an angel holding a red heart, an angel kneeling in prayer, and an angel with birds upon her outstretched arms, among others. She was curious to see what angel Annie had chosen for her to add to her collection. Each angel did have a meaning behind her. What meaning had Annie deemed important and exciting on this day?

She reached in and gently lifted the angel into the palm of her hand. It was approximately eight and a half inches. She saw first the angel's sculpted face. No eyes. No nose or mouth. Simply a hard light tan circle looking down, darker brown sculpted hair flowing between her shoulder blades. It took Caroline only a moment to look from the angel's face to the hands placed upon her stomach.

Her swollen, pregnant stomach.

Caroline's hands began to shake. *"Annie?"* She looked up at her daughter. Annie was smiling gleefully.

"Surprise!" she shouted.

"Annie!" Caroline squealed. She had to place the angel down on the table so as not to break it, she was so excited. *"Oh, my gosh, Annie!"*

"What's going on?" It was John who spoke. He looked at his wife, who had leaped from her chair, to his daughter, who had strode and closed the distance between them to embrace her mother. Both were crying joyously; both were jumping up and down in each other's arms.

"What in God's name?" John looked inquiringly at his son-in-law. He couldn't see the gently discarded angel resting on the table as the box was hiding it from sight.

"Annie's pregnant," Sam announced with a huge grin.

"Well, I'll be damned," John said wonderingly. He nodded his head a few times, and slowly, his smile grew. *"Well, I'll be damned,"* he said again, more loudly this time.

"What do you think, Daddy?" Annie had one arm around her mother's shoulders as she looked at her father seated at the kitchen table.

"A baby, huh?" John said.

"Mmm-hmm," Annie confirmed with a smile and a few tears trickling down her cheeks.

"Well, I'll be damned," he said again, which just made Annie laugh. *"A grandpa, yeah?"*

"A grandpa," Annie said.

"Cool." This made Annie laugh even more.

"And you're going to be a grandma," Annie said to Caroline.

"Oh, my goodness, yes!" Caroline enthused. *"Oh, Annie, I'm so happy for you."*

"Me, too," Annie said. *"Sam and I couldn't believe it! We've been trying for a while but were having trouble. And then . . . and then, well, one day I wasn't pregnant, and the next thing I know, I am!"*

"When did you find out?" Caroline asked.

"Just four days ago!"

"Oh, Annie!" Caroline began bouncing in place as she took her

daughter's hands in her own and squeezed with enthusiasm. "Oh, how wonderful!"

Caroline found herself quite fortunate to have been with her daughter throughout her pregnancy and found that she was so greatly appreciative of the fact that they lived close by. She watched as Annie would visit in the following weeks and almost fall asleep on the couch as they spoke. She was visiting Annie at her home when her daughter had run into the bathroom to vomit up her breakfast, something she stated she had been doing quite a lot of in her first trimester. She was present when Annie's belly began to extend and marveled when she'd place the palm of her hand on Annie's stomach and feel a kick or a hiccup.

She was also privy to Annie's waddling attempts when her stomach had extended so far that her back was aching as she moved. A helping hand was required in order for Annie to lift herself from the couch cushions, and when she sat, her legs weren't able to fit directly under that large belly of hers as it rested so low. Rather, she had to rest her legs on either side of her drooping extension as the baby inside demanded the space her legs would otherwise have taken in a seated position.

It was on Caroline's couch that Annie had asked if Caroline would please be in the room with her and Sam when the time came. She was touched and felt truly blessed. She would bear witness to the birth of her first grandchild!

Caroline so desperately wanted to know if Annie was carrying a boy or a girl. When Caroline herself had given birth to Annie, she hadn't known the sex of her child. Having an ultrasound to determine the sex of a child simply wasn't common procedure in the late '70s. When Annie and Sam had announced that they wanted to be surprised after delivering this baby, Caroline was slightly disappointed. She would have loved to start shopping for little pink or blue clothes and decorations. Gender-neutral clothes just simply weren't as adorable in her opinion. But the decision wasn't hers to make, and she quickly got over her disappointment. Boy or girl, this child was to be her grandbaby.

Her grandbaby!

Annie had gone into labor just after midnight on Sunday, the twenty-

sixth of February, several days past her due date. She had called Caroline from her home.

"My water broke."

"Oh, my goodness, Annie!" Though she had answered the phone groggily, she was now fully alert.

"Nothing's happening, though. The doctor said to stay home until contractions started."

"They haven't begun yet?"

"No."

"Okay, then," Caroline said. "Would you like me to come over?"

"No," Annie answered. "Sam's here. I'm a bit nervous, I have to admit, but other than the fluid still trickling out of me, I have no other symptoms, so I'm going to try to sleep. The doctor said I should sleep."

"That's a very good idea," Caroline said. "This could take a while, especially with no contractions yet."

"I know," Annie said. "Okay, I should go. I'll try to relax. I'll call you when we're headed to the hospital, okay?"

"That sounds good. Annie?"

"Yeah?"

"I love you so much."

"I love you, too, Ma. I'll call you."

Now, hours later, Caroline placed her hands over her cheeks and watched as her daughter grasped her legs, Sam by her side on the bed, and bore down, her face reddening from the efforts.

"That's it," the petite and kind Dr. McConnell said. "Just a bit more, Annie. Let's see this contraction through."

Annie pushed for forty-five grueling minutes. Caroline felt powerless as she stood by the doctor's side and watched as her daughter worked strenuously to deliver her baby. When Annie sat back after a heavy push and looked at her husband and said she didn't have the energy to do this much longer, Caroline let a tear trickle from her eye. She watched as Sam smoothed the hair from Annie's forehead, watched as he offered words of comfort into her ear. She watched the look of exhaustion on Annie's face, but the look of utter love and adoration as well.

"I see hair," Dr. McConnell said.

"You do?" Annie leaned forward a bit, slightly renewed.

"I do," the obstetrician confirmed. *"Would you like to feel?"*

Annie merely nodded and slowly guided her hand to rest between her legs.

The tears were now plentifully running down Caroline's cheeks.

"Oh, my gosh!" Annie exclaimed. She turned to Sam and smiled brightly. Sam stood and leaned over to take a look himself, and the expression he wore after having done so tickled Caroline. She was pretty confident Sam would be sitting by Annie's head for the remainder of his son or daughter's delivery.

"We've got another contraction coming," Chloe, the nurse, announced as she looked at the monitor.

"All right, Annie, let's get this little one delivered," the doctor said.

Annie pushed a few times more through her contractions until Caroline saw a forehead, then a nose, then an entire head! She placed her fingers on her lips, let the tears stream freely.

"Hold up just a minute, Annie," the doctor said. *"Okay, give it all you've got!"*

Annie grunted with the exertion of her last push, and then the baby was crying in the doctor's hands.

"It's a boy!" Dr. McConnell announced.

Caroline was sobbing now as she watched her grandson transferred from the hands of the obstetrician to his mother's chest. Annie looked at her son through bleary eyes, looked at her husband, who was beaming brightly and wiping the tears that had found their way out of his eyes. He kissed his wife's forehead and stroked his son's hair with the tip of his finger.

"You did such a good job," Sam said to Annie. *"I'm so proud of you."*

The baby rested in Annie's arms for a bit longer and was then whisked to a bassinet that had been placed in the corner of the room to be weighed and measured by Chloe while Dr. McConnell delivered the afterbirth and cleaned Annie.

"Nine pounds, two ounces, and twenty-one inches long," Chloe announced. *"He's a big boy."*

Annie's eyes didn't waver. She was watching her newborn son the entire time from her perch on the bed.

Caroline watched Annie and was flooded with an immense amount of unconditional love for her daughter. She had birthed this amazing woman; she and John had raised her. She had been there for her wedding to an absolutely incredible man. And now this couple had gifted her with a grandson.

Life couldn't get much better than it was today.

When the baby was wrapped in a blanket, he was handed back to Annie, who accepted him with eager, open arms. She showered him with kisses from the cotton-capped crown of his head to his small nose, and then handed him off to his father. Held by Sam, the baby looked tiny.

Caroline's heart soared.

She didn't think she could be more full.

Then Sam walked the few steps to Caroline and transferred her grandson into her empty arms. She marveled at the fact that something weighing less than ten pounds could fill her so completely, could cause the sensation that her heart might just explode with pure joy, with such exhilarating fulfillment.

"So now you have to tell me," Caroline said as she looked at Annie propped up in bed. "I can't believe you wouldn't tell me his name, but now I just have to know what you've called my grandson."

"Do you think maybe you can go get Dad?" Annie asked.

"Of course. Oh, my goodness. I forgot about your father!" Caroline laughed out loud as she handed her grandson back to Sam and left Annie's room for the waiting area down the hall. "He's here!" she announced enthusiastically the moment she spotted her husband.

"He?" John's eyebrows lifted. He closed the book he had been reading and rested it on his lap.

Caroline nodded. "We have a grandson."

Together they walked back to Annie's room. Dr. McConnell and Chloe were still present, though Annie had been cleaned and a blanket now covered her legs.

"Hi, Daddy," Annie said.

"*Hi, Annie Bear,*" *her father replied softly.* "*I hear I have a grandson to meet.*"

Sam walked forward and offered the baby to his father-in-law. John lifted the small bundle into his arms. A tear shimmered in his eye. "*Well, hello there, little guy,*" *he said. His nose twitched in an effort to hold back the tears that were threatening to let loose and spill beneath his black-rimmed glasses. A morsel of cracker had found comfort in his brown beard, which only endeared him more to Caroline.*

"*Okay, can you tell us now?*" *Caroline asked.*

"*Tell us what?*" *John displayed his confusion, though his gaze hadn't wavered from his grandson.*

"*The baby's name,*" *Caroline said.* "*I want to know his name!*"

Annie paused, looked at Sam beside her.

"*His name is Benjamin. After Grandpa.*"

Caroline felt it in the pit of her stomach. The love, the honor. Benjamin had been her father.

"*Benjamin John.*" *Annie finished.*

John looked up, his grandson in his large arms, his beloved daughter before him. He didn't utter a word. But the tears that had threatened to flow were now released beneath his glasses to land on the blanket warming his first grandchild. His namesake.

Caroline placed her hand over her heart and inhaled, looked around. At Sam, whom she knew loved her daughter immensely. At her husband, who was such a kindhearted soul. Had she been given the choice to do life over, she would have searched for this man beside her. She desired no one else.

She looked at tiny Benjamin, whom she already knew she'd bend over backward to protect.

And Annie. She looked at her daughter. At the radiant expression upon her face. At the glow of motherhood. She'd do anything for Annie, she knew.

Her heart swelled.

Life was beautiful.

CHAPTER THIRTEEN

Ben

*B*en didn't know what to think. He just didn't get it. How could his world be so fucked up?

He knew now why his mom was acting so strange, and according to his dad and grandmother, this wouldn't stop. It was going to get worse. And then—

Death.

He was lying in bed, staring at the white ceiling. His window shades were drawn and his light was off. School had been out since the beginning of June, and where his mom had taken him and Hannah outside of the house almost daily during summer vacation in years past, this wasn't the case anymore. No museums, no strawberry picking, no blueberry picking. No soccer fields or hikes. No urging Ben and Hannah to play outdoors.

He had often complained about all these activities before. He just wanted to be in his room or with his friends playing soccer or *Fortnite*. He didn't want to berry pick. He didn't want to go into Boston to the Museum of Science or any children's museum.

But now that his mother hadn't even attempted to get him out in the sun, hadn't once urged them to do things that they normally would have done, he found he was pissed.

Yeah, okay, his dad said it wasn't his mom's fault at all; said it was her brain and she couldn't help it.

He couldn't figure out if he was pissed at his mom or pissed at the world.

Or both.

His earphones were in and his phone was in hand. Imagine Dragons poured from the buds. He figured he could listen to something else, couldn't he? Something that raged, something that his mom would have caught and disapproved of when she did one of her periodic phone checks. She wouldn't be doing those any longer. She didn't care what he listened to. Especially if he listened in his room, with his earphones. And his dad wouldn't be checking. That was his mom's thing. His dad was too stressed out right now to think about checking Ben's phone. Yet he didn't want to listen to other music. He wanted his typical music, his Imagine Dragons, his Nico & Vinz, his Marshmello. He wanted what was normal.

His phone chimed. He had a text.

He lifted the screen to rest above his face. It was Tyler.

Man, you ok? Heard about ur mom.

Of course he had. Bitsy Bower would have told her son. She was, after all, his mom's best friend, and her son was Ben's.

He didn't answer. What was he going to say, anyway? *Yeah, I'm good?* That was bullshit. *Na, not okay?* That was more truthful, but he didn't want to go there. Not now. Not even with Tyler.

He lowered his phone, turned his music up. Returned his gaze to the ceiling, where the sticky remnants remained of glow-in-the-dark stars that his mother had placed to shine in the darkness of the night to help alleviate the fear a small child had of the monsters under his bed.

∾

He was in the second grade.

Seven years old.

He and Tyler were playing on the monkey bars during school recess, their favorite outdoor activity on the playground.

"Hey, watch this!" Tyler exclaimed. He climbed to the top step of the play equipment and tightly grasped the horizontal bar in front of him.

"Count to three," he instructed.

"One . . ." Ben began, "two . . . three!"

Tyler, still grasping the bar in his right hand, pushed off the step with his sneakers and lunged, skipping the next bar entirely and just managing to take hold of the metal bar that came next. He hung there, arms widely extended, then let go and dropped to the ground.

"Cool!" Ben said, a bit in awe of his friend's ability. "Let me try."

Tyler stood aside, and Ben climbed the steps of the play gym. He held tight to the front bar. "You count for me," he instructed with enthusiasm.

"Ready, set . . . go!"

It wasn't a numerical countdown, but Ben was barely aware of that fact. As soon as he heard the word "go," he pushed off with his feet and leaped into the air, turning his hips to the right and swinging his left arm forward.

He reached and reached, extended his small arms as wide as he possibly could and lightly brushed the third bar. Without his having fully grasped the solid metal in his palm, his momentum swung him backward and he hit his calves on the step and lost his grip entirely, plummeting to the ground and falling on his bottom.

He pouted but lifted himself to his feet and wiped the gravel from his jeans.

"Bummer," Tyler sympathized.

"Your arms are longer," Ben said.

"I guess," Tyler agreed. "Hey, let's go kick a ball."

"Okay."

The boys ran to the large blacktop area and chose a soccer ball that was currently not in use. They were surrounded by other second grade boys and girls playing catch or kicking balls. Others were playing hopscotch or four square.

"Go over there," Tyler instructed, not unkindly.

Ben ran several steps away, and when he turned, he saw the soccer ball careening his way. He charged and stopped it before it could go any farther.

"Here it comes!" he yelled before he kicked it back to his best friend.

Tyler stopped it with his foot and kicked it back, though this time the ball was unsteady and had been sent completely off course. It passed Ben's left side and continued to roll and bump along the black pavement. Ben ran after it but halted as the ball came to an abrupt stop under the black-sneakered foot of Mike Da Silva. Mike was a bit larger than Ben himself and quite the opposite where physical appearance was concerned. Although Ben wasn't short of stature, he was slight of build. Mike was stalky, though not overweight. Ben mirrored his mother and sister with his blond hair, though his eyes were blue instead of brown. Where Ben wore his hair short, Mike's dark hair concealed his ears and almost covered his brown eyes. Ben knew a couple of the girls had crushes on Mike, and even at the tender age of seven, he could understand why. Mike stood with an air of confidence and was extremely outgoing. Ben was not.

Mike also made him uneasy.

Mike bent at the waist and picked the ball up from the ground. "This yours?" he asked.

"Yeah." Ben's voice was small, hesitant.

"You gotta watch it," Mike chastised. "We're playing here. You messed me up."

Ben paused for a moment and then offered a meager "Sorry."

"Just watch it," Mike warned. He threw it over Ben's head, and Tyler ran to catch it midair. Ben walked away from Mike and back to his best friend to resume their game.

The boys gaily kicked the ball to each other for a few minutes longer *until Tyler kicked with a bit too much momentum and the ball soared toward Mike and his friends once more. Mike dribbled a soccer ball of his own and was attempting to keep it away from his opposition on the blacktop when Ben's ball bounced its interruption and another boy took possession of the ball Mike had at his foot just a moment before.*

Mike lifted Ben's ball from the ground with outward annoyance and surveyed his surroundings. When he found Ben and Tyler looking at him, he walked a few steps toward them, jaw clenched and a grimace on his face. He lifted his arm in the air, then behind him, and pelted it toward Ben. Ben was so utterly surprised at Mike's reaction that his instincts failed to take hold and the ball hit him directly in the face. The moment it bounced to the ground, Ben cupped his nose with the palms of both hands, one over the other. Blood was pouring out, too fast for him to catch it all. It dripped through the cracks in his thin fingers, dribbled down his wrists. It painted his chin, stained his shirt, and droplets hit the ground.

"Oh, no!" Tyler exclaimed. He ran off to get help from a teacher on recess duty.

Ben just stood there, pained and stunned.

Mike had gone back to playing ball.

Through the tears in his eyes, Ben saw a teacher jog over to him, following his friend's lead.

"Oh, goodness," she said. "Let's get you inside." Ben felt her arm around his shoulder, felt her lead him forward. He stepped blindly. His eyes were too blurry for him to walk of his own accord.

When they reached the door, the teacher led Ben through the threshold. Tyler attempted to follow. "You stay here," the teacher instructed. "Go play."

Tyler didn't leave. He didn't turn to play. He just watched his friend —hands still cupping the blood flowing from his nose, shoulders slumped —walk farther into the building without him.

Ben soon found himself in the nurse's office. He was ushered into the bathroom and instructed to lean over the sink. He lowered his hands from his nose and watched as his blood dropped and splashed to brightly color the white porcelain below him.

Eventually, the nurse was able to stanch the blood flow, though his nose was incredibly sore. His hands were washed, his shirt scrubbed. Dried blood stained the area under his fingernails.

He sat on the nurse's cot, his slight frame shaking, his nose and head throbbing.

The nurse picked up the telephone. After a moment's pause, she began to speak. "Hey, Annie, it's LeAnn." Ben watched the nurse's eyes gaze out the window, then back at Ben. "I have Ben here. He's okay, but there was a bit of a mishap outside at recess. He says he was hit by a ball. He had quite the bloody nose, but it doesn't appear to be broken. His forehead is a bit red and I think he's just a little shocked." She smiled at Ben, sympathetic, encouraging. "No, no . . . I don't think that's necessary." Another pause then, "Yes, of course. Hold on just a moment."

She handed the cordless phone to Ben. "Your mom would like to speak with you."

He took the phone, placed it to his ear.

"Mom?" His voice choked. His mom was on the other end of this phone, and he knew she was just down the hallway in her classroom. His mom always made him feel better.

"Hi, baby. I'm here," she said. Voice soft, comforting. "Mrs. Walker says you were hit by a ball?"

"Yeah."

"I hope it was an accident, baby."

Ben didn't answer.

"Are you okay?"

"I guess."

"Well," she chuckled lightly, "that didn't sound very convincing."

Again, he remained silent, the tears beginning to well in his eyes, his small lips beginning to tremble.

"She says she thinks it was just a nasty nosebleed, that you aren't hurt otherwise."

"Okay," Ben answered.

"Are you hurt somewhere else?"

"No."

"Your recess is over. Do you think you're okay to go back to class?"

"I guess."

"Okay, I'll tell you what," his mom said. "You stay there in the nurse's office for as long as you need to calm your body down and feel better, okay? Then you go back to class. If you feel like you need me to come and get you and take you home, then you let your teacher know and the nurse can call me again. I'll come and get you. How does that sound?"

"Okay." He wanted nothing more than to go home with his mom. He didn't want to see Mike. He was thankful they weren't in the same class together. That would have made matters worse for sure. But the nurse said he was okay. His mom wanted him to try to go back to class.

"Okay?"

"Yeah, I'll go back to class."

"You call me if you need to, Ben."

He nodded.

"Ben?"

"Okay," he vocalized.

"All right, then," his mom said. "I love you so much, baby. So much! We'll talk more after school. I'm going to head back to my kindergarten class, but like I said: you call me if you need to. I'll get someone to cover me and I'll walk on over and get you. Yes?"

"Yeah."

"I love you, Ben."

"Love you, too."

"Bye for now," his mom said.

"Bye."

He finished the day off at school, then met his mom in her classroom as he did every school day once the bell rang dismissal. At this moment, he was extremely grateful that he went to the same school his mom worked at.

"Hey, Ben," she greeted him as he walked through the doorway. Her children had already left the room, though the hallways remained packed with children walking and jogging to their end-of-school dismissal stations, hallway monitors guiding their way and attempting to slow the steps of the overzealous.

His mom walked toward him. He held the straps of his Trans-formers backpack with his fingers and looked up into her brown eyes. She

167

knelt down in her black skirt, bare knees resting against the area rug, and gently lifted his chin. "I can see you were hurt," she acknowledged. "Your nose is really red, baby." She smiled sympathetically.

Instead of smiling back, Ben began to cry.

"Oh, my goodness, sweetie, what's wrong?" His mother remained on her knees and held his face in the palms of her hands, wiping his tears with her thumbs as they fell. "What is it?"

Ben shook his head, averted his eyes.

"Ben," she said gently, "look at me."

A large tear fell as he looked at his mother once again. "Why are you crying, sweetie?"

"I don't know."

"You don't know?" His mother grinned, unconvinced. She raised her eyebrows.

Ben wasn't sure he should tell his mom that Mike had done this, that Mike had thrown the ball purposefully. That Mike didn't care he had been hurt.

He was embarrassed. If other kids knew, maybe they'd think he was a crybaby.

But, on the other hand, his mom was right here, right now. His mom was looking intently into his eyes with a look he knew well: love.

"I got hit."

"What do you mean you got hit?" his mom asked, an expression of worry now crossing her face.

"I got hit with the ball."

"Yeah, baby, I know. That's how you got hurt, right?"

"Yeah," he confirmed. "But it was by purpose."

His mother stiffened. Just a small amount, but he felt it nonetheless. "On purpose?"

Ben nodded his head, looked to the ground.

"Baby, look at me." His mom was stern, though Ben knew she wasn't angry at him. She just got like this. "Someone hurt you? What happened, Ben? What did they do? Mrs. Walker said a ball hit you in the face."

"It did," Ben confirmed, "but it was by purpose."

"*How?*" *His mom's eyes were searching his own.*

"*A boy got mad at me and Tyler. We were playing at recess. We were playing soccer. And Tyler kicked it too hard and it went and it ruined his game and he got really mad. We ruined his game before, but it was by accident and he got really mad then, too. But when we ruined his game again, he looked at me and he threw the ball really, really hard, and I didn't duck and it hit me in the face. It hurt so much, and my nose was bleeding.*" *Ben's tears began again.* "*And it still hurts.*"

"*Baby,*" *his mom said softly,* "*why didn't you tell anyone that this was done on purpose?*"

Ben shook his head. "*I don't know.*"

His mom paused and gave him time to dry his tears. "*Take a deep breath,*" *she instructed. He did so.*

"*Now out.*" *He exhaled.*

"*Who was it, baby?*"

Ben looked at his mom, at the concerned expression upon her features, at the pale lashes above her brown eyes. He bit his lower lip and then, "*Mike.*"

"*Mike?*" *She waited for further identifying information.*

"*Mike Da Silva,*" *Ben clarified.* "*He's in my grade.*"

His mom nodded. "*I know him,*" *she said.* "*He wasn't ever in my class, but I know him.*" *She lifted herself from the floor and stood. Ben could tell she was becoming angry.*

"*Did he apologize, Ben? You were obviously hurt. I mean, your nose was bleeding quite a lot.*"

Ben shook his head in negation.

"*No teacher saw what happened?*"

"*No.*" *His voice was soft, meek.*

He watched his mom's face, watched as her lips moved ever so slightly, watched as her eyes creased. He knew she was thinking; he knew her emotions were taking hold.

"*Nope,*" *she said.* "*No freaking way! Come with me, baby. We're going to talk to Mrs. Daily.*"

Mrs. Daily? Mrs. Daily was the principal. Ben didn't want to get in trouble.

He took his mom's outstretched hand and followed her hesitantly, feeling incredibly anxious. They rounded a corner, dodged straggling children in the hallway, and entered the office area. He had only ever been in here to say the Pledge of Allegiance through the intercom system on those special occasions when he was chosen to do so. He had never been here before because something bad had happened, something involving him.

He squeezed his mom's hand tighter when he saw Mrs. Daily talking to another teacher through the open door of her room. The principal of his school looked up at his mother, then looked at Ben by her side. She must have sensed something was wrong because she said goodbye to the lady she was talking to and welcomed him and his mom into the room, closing the door behind her.

Ben was afraid he was going to cry again.

"Lucinda," his mom began, "we need to talk."

"Never a good way to start a conversation, is it?" Mrs. Daily, the principal, said. Luckily, Ben could see her thin lips were lifted in a small grin. "What is it, Annie?" And that was a kind voice, wasn't it?

"Ben was hurt today," his mom said. "He was on the playground. I know he was taken to see LeAnn, and she called down to my room to let me know that he had been hit by a ball and had been bleeding quite a bit from the nose. She said she was able to stop the bleeding and he seemed to be doing all right. I talked to Ben and convinced him to go to class and end his day here at school, but what I didn't know until just now is that Ben was hit in the face with a ball on purpose."

Mrs. Daily looked from his mom to Ben. Her eyebrows creased and she pursed her lips. "Ben, is this true?"

Ben's lower lip quivered.

"Here." Mrs. Daily sat down at a small round table. Three other chairs were tucked underneath. "Come sit with me, Ben. You're not in trouble. But I would like very much to hear what happened to you today."

Ben looked up at his mother, who nodded her consent. "Go ahead, baby."

He slowly walked to the table and climbed into the indicated chair next to Mrs. Daily. His mom pulled a chair out from under the table and sat next to him. She reached over and took his hand in her own, squeezed. Her understanding smile gave him courage.

He began his tale, told Mrs. Daily how he and Tyler were playing and how Tyler had accidentally kicked the ball a bit too far and interrupted Mike's game. He told her of their first altercation and then of their second, when Mike had looked directly at him and thrown the ball. Hard. He told her how much it hurt when it hit his face. And he told her how Mike saw him bleeding and merely continued with his soccer game.

"Well, then," Mrs. Daily said, "I wish you would have told the teacher who took you inside, Ben. Or told Mrs. Walker in the nurse's office. No, no," she assured him as she saw his expression of worry, "I'm not chiding you at all, young man. I'm just very pleased you are telling us about this now."

"I'm not happy," his mom said. "Not at all, Lucinda. I completely understand that accidents happen, but this was no accident. And I even understand that sometimes children become upset and have difficulty controlling their emotions and behaviors, but then I would have expected Mike to have at least had some sort of reaction to hurting Ben so badly, you know? I would have expected him to walk over to him, to ask if he was okay, even though he could clearly see he was bleeding. But Ben got none of this. Nothing. That makes me think this boy did this maliciously." His mom sighed. "I'm not happy," she repeated.

"Nor am I," Mrs. Daily agreed. "Annie, please know that I'll be making a phone call home tonight. I think right now he has probably left the premises. But I will call shortly, and I assure you I will be speaking to a parent or caregiver."

"I know you will, Lucinda. Thank you so much." She looked at Ben. "That's my boy right there," she said, her features softening, "I think my mommy claws just came out." She laughed then, and when Ben looked at Mrs. Daily, he could see she was smiling.

"All right, Ben," his mom said as she leaned forward and caressed his cheek with a finger, "are you ready to go get your sister and then head home?"

Ben nodded.

"Mmm," she mumbled. "And . . . how about some hot chocolate?"

"With whipped cream?" His eyes widened. Hot chocolate was usually a weekend treat.

"Absolutely!" his mom said with enthusiasm. "We can't have hot chocolate without whipped cream!"

Ben smiled brightly.

His nose didn't even hurt all that much anymore.

He took his mom's hand as they left the office. They returned back to the classroom so his mom could clean up a bit and gather her belongings, and then they walked out the front door of the building and to their waiting van.

When she opened the side door for him and he bounced in, he looked at his mom and felt nothing but her love.

He knew he was safe as long as she was there to protect him.

CHAPTER FOURTEEN

Sam

The end of August marked the first day of school for Ben and Hannah. Sam couldn't believe that his son was now in high school. High school! Had Annie been herself, she would have been a wreck on his first day of school, seeing him off as he stepped out the garage door and into the driveway on his way to the bus.

But not before pictures. She had always taken pictures on the first day of school. She even had Hannah in Ben's first-day-of-kindergarten photo. Hannah had been only thirteen months at the time. She was clinging to her big brother's leg. She knew he was leaving, though at the time she simply didn't understand what school was. She just knew she didn't want her Benny to go. Annie's favorite picture of that morning was still thumbtacked to their communication board. In it, you saw a toddler Hannah pleading. She was standing, though at the time she couldn't stand without holding onto something to steady herself, and that day, that something was her big brother's leg. Her eyes were closed and her mouth open as she cried her protestations. Tears clung to her cheeks. Ben was looking at the camera, his face contorted. He hadn't any sympathy for Hannah that day. He wanted to go to school! He just didn't know how to shake her off, and her tantrum was annoying him.

On a typical weekday morning, Sam already would have left for work before it was time for Sam to catch the bus. But this morning he wanted to be there for his children.

Caroline was nursing a cup of coffee at the kitchen table, and Annie was still sleeping. Hannah's bus wouldn't arrive for another hour.

"I gotta go." Ben was ready. He had dressed in a pair of black Adidas athletic pants and a white Adidas sweatshirt to stave off the morning chill.

"Ah," Sam started, "wait a minute. Pictures. I've got to get pictures."

Ben was silent, though he waited for Sam to retrieve their good camera—a large black Canon—from the upper shelf in the mudroom closet.

"Got it," Sam announced as he met his son in the kitchen. "Hannah," he called. "Hannah, come down. Your brother's leaving, and I need to get first-day-of-school pictures."

"Coming," Hannah called back.

Sam heard loud, fast footsteps descend the stairs and walked to open the garage door. He exited and kept the door open for Ben, who was directly behind him, then Hannah, whose body emerged from the hallway to follow.

"I gotta go," Ben repeated.

"Yeah, I know," Sam said. "I'll make this quick. Promise."

Ben and Hannah stood next to a particular tree in the front yard, wide and tall. It had been the tree Annie had always had them stand by. Sam was pleased Ben and Hannah routinely made their way over there, had remembered that this was where first-day-of-school pictures were taken, because Sam would have just snapped the photos wherever they stood. This was Annie's thing. She had often remarked how she loved to see the progression through the years, how their children had grown, how their hair colors changed, how styles changed. She loved their choices of clothes. Even when an outfit wouldn't have been something she would have chosen for them, she appreciated the fact that their children were becoming their own advocates, were beginning to discover what they liked, who they were. Sam didn't want to mess that up.

Though the irony wasn't lost on him: Annie wouldn't care about this year's picture. Or any first-day-of-school photos from here on in.

He paused for a moment, looked at the large black camera in his hands.

"Dad," Ben protested, "I gotta go."

"Yeah," Sam whispered, "I know." The day would go on. His children would head to school, and he'd find himself back at work, performing a job he was liking less and less as time progressed, but a job that was crucial to his family's survival.

He lifted the camera to his eye. "Okay," he said. "Smile."

Hannah smiled brightly. She had always loved the first day of school. Ben's expression didn't alter. He stood in front of the massive tree, gray backpack slung over his shoulders, hands in the pockets of his black pants. His blond hair was disheveled, and now that Sam was intently looking at his son, he found it was also in desperate need of a cut and was devoid of gel, which he typically used.

Hopefully, he had at least put some deodorant on.

Sam concluded he would have to pay more attention to his son. He wasn't entirely sure when he had lost interest in his physical appearance. With summer being what it was, a time to relax and recuperate, Sam hadn't been aware that anything was amiss.

"Okay," Sam said to his children. "I think that should do it."

Ben turned to walk down the driveway.

"Hey," Sam called with a smile. "No hug goodbye?"

Ben didn't slow his steps, didn't turn around. He merely placed his right hand in the air, then back into the pocket of his pants.

"Jesus," Sam breathed. "'Thanks, Dad. You have a nice day, too.'"

He turned to Hannah, plastered a smile on his face. "Okay, Hannah Banana, we should get you ready for school."

Hannah smirked and rolled her eyes. "I can get myself ready for school, Dad."

"Yeah," Sam agreed, "I know you can." He placed his arm around her shoulder, brought her closer to his chest in an embrace, then ran the knuckles of his fist across the top of her head, back and forth vigorously, so the long blond strands of her hair stood in a scruffy mess.

"Daaaad," Hannah protested with a giggle.

"Hannaaah," Sam mocked affectionately.

Together they walked back indoors.

Not only did the end of August mark the first day of school for the kids, it also marked Sam's first meeting with a support group he had found online. He'd be driving forty-five minutes to get there, but deemed it necessary. He needed someone to talk to who had been through this process before or who was going through it right now.

He felt lost.

Caroline had attended just last week, but with their schedule, Sam couldn't swing it then. He had work, dinner, his kids. He thanked God for Caroline. Without her, he wouldn't be able to juggle daily life.

It was a Friday. Sam would leave work and head directly to the meeting. He had packed an extra sandwich he could eat in the car for dinner. Soccer had started up again. Bitsy Bower would bring Ben to and from practice with Tyler so Caroline could stay home with Hannah and Annie. Thankfully Hannah had no after-school activities to attend tonight. Sam knew how exhausted Caroline had been lately.

Sam shut his laptop down at the end of the day and placed it in its bag. He grabbed his coat from the back of his chair and put it on.

"Good work today, Sam." Sam turned around and looked into the weathered face of his boss, Steve.

"Thanks," he said with a close-lipped smile and slung his laptop bag over his shoulder.

"I want to see more of that," Steve said. He turned on a heel and left the cubicle area.

Sam watched Steve's backside walk away, his tall, wide frame and long legs in their black suit pants. He closed his eyes momentarily and took a deep breath before gathering his lunch box and making his way to the parking lot.

Yeah, he had done a good job today, at the meeting especially. Steve was his boss, but his boss also had a boss, and he was present in the conference room. Steve wanted to look good, and depending on Sam's performance, Steve either looked like he had his shit together and could manage his ever-growing team, or looked like he couldn't do his job. On those days, the days when Sam had tripped up, Steve steamed.

Sam had done well today—but at the expense of his family life since he had put in countless extra work hours both in the office and at home.

He needed to be there for his wife, for Caroline, and right now most especially for his children.

But he also needed this job.

Once he reached his maroon Subaru Outback, he lifted the door handle to unlock the vehicle and climbed inside, thinking for the umpteenth time that he should sell Annie's minivan. She wasn't driving it any longer, and Caroline had her own car. Plus, they didn't really need it, did they? The kids could fit in his Outback well enough, and they could certainly use the money from the sale.

He started the car and plugged the support group's meeting address into the GPS before pulling out of the parking spot. His stomach began to rumble, so he reached into his lunch box and took out his turkey sandwich, throwing the square-shaped reusable plastic container onto the passenger seat of the car before driving out of the lot and merging into traffic on the main road.

The radio was playing for the forty-five minutes he was driving, though he rarely listened. He was stuck in his mind, thinking about what this meeting would entail. He did hope he'd get the answers to some pressing questions about Annie's diagnosis that only other families struggling with FTD could answer. He hoped this meeting was worthwhile.

His GPS indicated the destination was on his right. He turned the wheel and pulled into the small parking lot of a brick building. He parked his car, turned the ignition off, and took a deep breath before opening the door and stepping outside onto the pavement. He surveyed his surroundings. He was in a small city now, denser and more populous than the town he lived in. Cars lined the sides of the road and sped past faster than they should have in this particular area. The building he was about to enter was just one of many, and the air he breathed felt stagnant.

He hoped he was in the right place. The building itself didn't seem to have any identifying markers.

Sam pocketed his keys and walked to the door closest to where he stood on the side of the building. He turned the metal knob and found it unlocked. He peeked his head through the doorway to look left, then right before slowly entering. He stood in a silent narrow hallway with empty white walls and several closed doors.

He shut the door behind him but initially made no further move, as he wasn't sure where to go until he heard muffled voices in the distance. He followed and found a door at the end of the hallway had been left ajar. He smelled coffee even before he hesitantly stepped a foot inside.

Eight metal chairs were oriented into a circle. A white rectangular-shaped folding table was erected next to the wall on which snacks rested: doughnuts and muffins, some navel oranges as well. A coffee maker stood in the center of the table, some sugar packets and small plastic cream containers beside it. A middle-aged woman was sitting in a metal chair facing Sam's direction. He could clearly see she was silently crying, her eyes downcast, a tissue in hand. A similar-aged man sat to her right, consoling her with soft-spoken words, and a young woman, perhaps in her twenties, had an arm around the woman's shoulder.

"She lost her husband last week." Sam turned. A burly man with curly black hair and a bushy black beard and mustache had approached. He held a paper cup of black coffee in his left hand and extended his right.

"George," he said.

Sam took the proffered hand and shook. The man had a strong, firm grasp and held Sam's gaze steadily. "Sam."

George took a small sip of his hot coffee. "You here for the FTD support group?"

Sam nodded slightly. "I am. I'm guessing I'm in the right place?"

"Sure are," George confirmed. "I run this group. We'll get started in just a couple of minutes. Glad you're here, Sam, though I'm never glad for what brings us all together. Help yourself to a cup of coffee if you'd like."

"Thank you," Sam said. He started for the table as George made his way to an elderly woman standing behind a chair.

Sam lifted a paper cup from the table and filled it three-quarters of the way with hot coffee. He added two packets of sugar and three containers of cream, stirred, and placed it upon the white table. He picked up a small napkin that read

"Happy Birthday"—probably a leftover that George had brought, Sam surmised—and chose a large chocolate-glazed doughnut from the small platter. His turkey sandwich just hadn't done much to satiate his hunger.

Grasping his coffee in one hand, his napkin and doughnut in the other, Sam turned around and walked toward the metal chairs, choosing the one closest to him and sitting down. He noticed the middle-aged woman was no longer weeping. The young woman in her twenties was whispering in her ear and holding her hand.

Sam took a bite of his doughnut as George made himself comfortable in a chair to his right. "Let's get started," George said. "Dotty"—he looked across the way to the middle-aged woman who had just lost her husband—"I'd like for us to talk about Bill today if we could." The middle-aged woman, Dotty, nodded her head and clung to the white tissue in her hand. "Before we do so, we have a new face to welcome. This is Sam." George momentarily motioned to Sam with his hand, then lowered his arm and placed both palms on his upper thighs.

Sam acknowledged this with a slightly uncomfortable smile.

"Can you all introduce yourselves to Sam," George suggested. "Tell him why you're here?" He looked to the elderly woman on his right.

"Oh, yes," she said. Her voice was hoarse, though soft. Her white hair was short on her small head and looked to be curled or at least styled to lend a puffy, thicker appearance to strands that must have once been lusher and more filling. She looked directly at Sam, who had swallowed his bit of doughnut and now held his coffee and napkin on his lap.

"I'm Grace," she said with a smile. "I've been coming here for, oh, goodness gracious me, what is it—eight years now?" The pronounced wrinkles of her face contorted as she frowned in concentration. "Yes, about eight years." She nodded her head, the strands of her white hair bouncing ever so slightly with the momentum of her movements. "My daughter is the one with FTD. She was diagnosed about eight and a half years ago, I think it's been. My husband and I had each other to help us through this time, but he passed on just a year ago. It's just me now. And my friends here." She grinned at the individuals around her, all smiling in return, even the middle-aged woman clinging to her tissue: a circle of camaraderie.

"My daughter is in a home now closer to her family in Virginia. I don't make it down to visit all that often. I'll be eighty-seven on my next birthday, you know! But I do what I can. And even after eight and a half years, I still can't believe it." She shook her head. "My Ginny—that's my girl—she's my baby, you know? Even at sixty-three, she's still my baby girl." Grace's face dropped, dejected and forlorn.

Sam nodded. He didn't know what words he could use to console this woman whom he had just met, this woman who was so obviously suffering as he was.

"Thank you, Grace," George said. He turned his gaze from Grace to the young woman Sam thought might be in her twenties.

"Nanette?" George prompted.

The young woman, Nanette, looked at Sam. "I'm Nanette," she began. "I go by Nanette but also Nan. I like them both." As Sam looked at her, he realized that she was lovely. Long black hair that fell to the middle of her back, unblemished skin the color of the coffee he held in his hand. She wore a pair of high-rise milk-colored ripped jeans and a lightweight black woven short-sleeved sweater that just barely brushed the button at the top of her pants. Her legs were crossed, and she wore a pair of black Converse sneakers on her feet. Sam marveled at her youth, that someone so young was struggling with a loved one diagnosed with FTD.

He immediately thought of Ben and Hannah.

"I'm here because of my dad," she said. "He was diagnosed four years ago when I was starting my senior year of college. When I graduated, I moved back in with my parents to help my mom out. I had plans to head straight on to grad school, but I just couldn't do it. My brother is five years older than me and he doesn't live close by. He's got a family to take care of, anyway. So it's me and Mom. She usually works until seven. She comes when she can but couldn't make it tonight. There's another group she attends more often. My dad's still living with us at home. We have a full-time nurse that helps care for him during the day, and friends have been great. Mom's best friend is with him now. We're not where Grace is just yet since Dad is still at home, but he can't be left alone anymore. I think we realized that when he walked to the convenience store down the street from us and stole some candy and a soda. Just walked right in, took what he wanted, and walked right on out." She shook her head and her eyes widened with disbelief—tinged with a slight smirk—as she recalled her tale.

"Luckily, we're friendly with the owners since we've lived in that house all my life. I used to walk to that store all the time as a kid to get snacks with my friends. And they had this penny candy . . . Anyway . . ." She trailed off for a moment. "Yeah, I'm Nan." She lifted her hand in the air and waved shyly.

"Hi, Nan," Sam said. "Thanks."

"Thanks"? Such a stupid thing to say, but what else could he have imparted?

"Dotty?" George looked now to the middle-aged woman who still clung to her tissue.

"Yeah," she said. "I'm Dotty, as George said." Her bottom lip began to tremble. "Oh, Jesus Christ," she said, "here I go again." She held the tissue to her eye. "First thing you need to know about me? I swear a lot. And I mean no disrespect, but I make no apologies for it, either. If there's any place you should be able to get it all out, it's here." She dabbed below her eyes and lowered her hand.

"FTD sucks, let me tell you, Sam. It's shitty that you're here, but I'm glad you're here, too. This place is a saving grace. I don't have a lot of friends or family, and I sure as hell have no friends or family around that know what I've gone through or what I'm going through now. But these folks. Yep, these folks have saved me." She paused, looked around the room, then rested her eyes back on Sam, tucking a strand of her fine shoulder-length light-brown hair behind her ear.

"I lost my husband just last week," she said. "His funeral was just a couple of days ago, and every single person in this room was there. Can't tell you what that meant to me." A few tears trickled down her cheeks.

"Fuck it! I tell ya, I'm done with all this crying. For Christ's sake, you'd think a person would run out of tears, but I just find I've got more and more in me. Jesuuus!" She laughed then.

Soft giggles were sent forth around the room.

"My husband's dead and gone, but I lost him a long time ago. He was diagnosed with FTD ten years ago, but I know now that he had symptoms for several years before that and it took a good couple of years to even get the damn diagnosis right. Can you believe they said he was depressed?"

Sam unconsciously inhaled sharply and grasped his coffee a bit tighter. "Me, too," he admitted. "I mean, my wife."

"Yep," Dotty confirmed. "Pretty typical. Good thing you're here, Sam," she said. "Not a lot of people can truly say they know what you're going through right now. But us? We know." Another tear found its way down her cheek.

"Thank you, Dotty," George said after a lull in the conversation. He looked to the man seated at Dotty's right.

"Hector here," he said as he lifted his arm in the air then placed it back on his thigh. "My wife got the diagnosis less than a year ago. Thinkin' it's the hardest thing I ever done, and I done lived a hard life. We live up north. No meetin' up there, so I drive an hour and a half to get here. But Dotty right: these people good people and you all help me out a bunch. I knew somethin' ain't right with my wife, but we don't got a lot of doctors up there that know about brain troubles, you get me? We had to travel a bunch and my Doris, she get carsick real easy. Pukes a whole lot when we have to be in the car for more than twenty minutes. I learn real quick to bring a good puke bag or two." Hector chuckled then, deep-throated and hearty, then touched the palm of his hand to his dark brown hair peppered throughout with gray. "She still okay to be alone for a bit, but I gettin' nervous these days, you get me? I gettin' nervous. And we ain't got money, so beats me what I gonna do when she get sicker." He shook his head. "Just me and Doris, don't got us no kids, Lord don't bless us there. But I got my Doris still. And I holdin' on as long as I can." He lowered his gaze.

"Thank you, Hector," George said. Sam remained silent, this man's pain soaking itself into his soul. It sounded to him like Hector had only his wife in his life, and she was slipping away. Sam desperately hoped he had a few friends who helped him out up where he lived. He knew some of those deep northern New Hampshire towns were minuscule and remote. Sam felt extremely thankful, even though they were all suffering, that he had Caroline and his kids and Bitsy Bower.

"And," George said as he looked at Sam, "we've met. I'm George and I run these meetings. My mother passed away several years ago now. She was just sixty-eight years old and had been living with FTD for approximately nine years after diagnosis. I was thirty-five when we learned she had FTD. My kids were just two and four at the time, so they've grown up watching their nana decline. I won't lie to you, Sam. This is real and it's hard. But we're all here. Every person in this room has a loved one with frontotemporal dementia."

"Dementia?" Sam asked. "Our neurologist called it degeneration."

"Yeah, that's the term they seem to use more these days. But it is a form of dementia, and back when my mom was living with FTD, that's what it was called. 'Degeneration' is newer. But it goes by both, really. Call it what you'd like."

Sam nodded. "Makes sense," he admitted.

"Would you like to introduce yourself?" George asked.

"Sure," Sam said. "I'm Sam. My wife's name is Annie. She was diagnosed last month, but she's been different for a while now. I'm glad I know what's going on, but I still haven't come to terms with the fact that she's only going to get worse." He looked at the coffee in his hand, now cool to the touch, at the doughnut with only one bite mark.

"We have two kids. Ben is fourteen, and Hannah turned ten last month. Hannah's hurting, but she's a talker and seems to be taking this diagnosis pretty well. I mean, not well, but she hasn't been acting out or seeming depressed or anything. She has her moments when she breaks down and needs consolation, but she seems to pick herself back up. I don't know how this will all affect her as Annie's disease progresses and she gets worse. I just don't know." Sam pursed his lips before continuing.

"Ben . . . Ben I can't figure out. He's fourteen, so I guess I expect some teenagerish behaviors to begin with, but since this diagnosis, he's shut down even more. And I feel like I'm not there for him. My boss hasn't been happy with all the time I've taken off work, and my mind has been elsewhere. But I can't lose this job. Annie's diagnosis has touched us in so many ways, ways I wouldn't have even thought about. She lost her job a while back. She was a kindergarten teacher and a damn good one. But she was speaking inappropriately to the children and she had even wandered off out of the classroom a few times, leaving the children alone." Sam took a deep breath and lifted his eyebrows.

"Our neurologist says that Annie is progressing unusually fast. My mother-in-law has moved in with us to care for Annie during the day, and I seriously don't know what I'd do without her. Not only does she care for her daughter, but she takes the kids to after-school activities so I can work. But I know Caroline is exhausted. She's sixty-five. I can't imagine she ever thought she'd be taking care of a family again. And I feel guilty. Guilty that I can't take care of my own kids. That I can't take care of my wife."

Sam willed himself not to cry. He didn't know these people, not really. Sure, they all had FTD in common and they certainly wouldn't judge him if he did cry, but he just couldn't go there. If he began, he didn't know if he'd be able to stop.

Perhaps he and Dotty were kindred spirits?

"Can I say something, Sam?" It was Grace, her cloudy hazel eyes searching his.

Sam nodded his assent.

"As a mother, especially if I were Caroline's age, I would drop everything to help my daughter out. At eighty-six years old, I have trouble getting from place to place, so even if my Ginny lived close by, I still would not be of much assistance to her family. But if I were in Caroline's position . . . I just want to say that I imagine she wouldn't want it any other way. Like I said before, Ginny will always be my baby girl. Caroline feels the same way, I assure you."

He couldn't stop the lone tear that trickled down his cheek and hastened to wipe it away. "Thanks, Grace," Sam said. "I'm just . . . it's just really hard."

A murmuring of agreement surrounded him through the circle of chairs.

Dotty spoke up. "A long time ago, I would get so mad at Bill," she admitted. "He'd be such an asswipe. Sometimes I didn't want to be around him at all, and this even though I knew he was sick. He had the behavioral variant of FTD."

"So does Annie," Sam said.

"Most do," Dotty said. "Except Hector here. His wife has that aphasia kind, where it's mostly her language that's messed up."

Hector nodded.

"So, I'd get mad," Dotty continued. "So, so mad. There was yelling, there was swearing, and even when I'd swear my ass off, yell till I thought I'd break the windows in the house, he'd just look at me with this blank expression on his damn face. This face that I loved for so many years. Our kids are older. The youngest is finishing college now. But both boys were there when he was first sick and I know it was hard on them, too. So I made a decision one day. Yelling wasn't gonna get me anywhere but to where you are right now in feeling guilty. There's nothing to feel guilty about. If you're doing what you need to do to survive right now, then you're doing everything right." Another tear found its way out of the corner of Sam's eye.

"Can't say I don't swear anymore, I like it too damned much, but I stopped yelling. What was that accomplishing? Guilt all around, guilt that I was now being an ass to someone who couldn't help it, and guilt that my boys were seeing their mother losing her shit. Instead of yelling when I wanted to yell, I'd walk away. Walk away, close my eyes, and force myself to think of a time where Bill made me smile. I can tell you, I had a lot of those memories. Now that he's gone and I came to terms with the diagnosis a long time ago, I can even laugh at some of the shit he did when he was sick. I've learned that you've got to take life by the balls, that sometimes life just plain sucks ass, but you gotta hold on."

Sam didn't lift a finger now to wipe the tears that were falling freely. Dotty continued to hold his gaze intently.

She leaned with her back resting against the metal chair and crossed her arms upon her ample bosom and chuckled. "There was this one time I was gonna head out to an event for work, a dinner in the ballroom of a hotel down the street from the office. We did this once a year as a fundraiser for our organization. Bill always came with me. This was the first year he stayed back. I just couldn't deal with the embarrassment and felt guilty that I was even thinking my husband was embarrassing—there's that guilt for you again. I took my black dress out of our closet and laid it on the bed while I took my shower that night. I toweled off and walked to the bedroom to dress and found a white stain right in the middle of my damn dress. Didn't take me long to realize Bill had masturbated and left me a little gift. Man, was I pissed off." Dotty laughed. "Pissed. Off. I took that dress to the bathroom and scrubbed and scrubbed, ended up wearing a pair of work pants and a blouse to this fancy fundraiser of ours." She continued to laugh, her bosom shaking, her arms rising in the process.

"Hope that's not too much information for you, there, Sam, and I hope it didn't make you uncomfortable, but I think you'll find out soon, if you haven't already, that FTD has many demons and we can air them here. Bill was always a sexual being, but as his FTD progressed, he didn't know what it was to be inappropriate and he'd do things any normal person just wouldn't do in places you just shouldn't do them in. Luckily, I can laugh a bit about some of these now. Hell, he even woke me up one night because he was having a bit too much fun with himself, making all these noises. Yeah . . . right next to me in bed." Dotty shook her head with a reminiscent smile.

"So yeah," she concluded, "try your best to get rid of your guilt and realize that you need to do whatever you need to do to survive this."

George stood from his chair and walked to the white folding table to the left of the room, returning with a small box of tissues that he handed off to Sam. Sam thanked him with a slightly embarrassed smile.

"But," added Nan, thin legs still crossed in her milky

ripped jeans, "while trying not to feel guilty, also allow yourself to mourn. There's a difference."

"Oh, yeah," Hector concurred. "Your Annie probably ain't who she was when you married. That tough. I miss Doris and she ain't even gone and she still herself a lot. She still have all her memories, and she don't act out none, you get me? But she don't talk like she used to. Sometimes she forgets words all out or sometimes we be talkin' about one thing and she change the subject just all a sudden, like that." Hector snapped his fingers. "Sometime she talk and she don't make no sense. Sometime she open her mouth and close it again. I think she give up a lot. I miss talkin' with my wife. Took three years to know she got FTD. Three years, I think, from when she first have trouble."

"Three years from when she first showed symptoms!?" Sam was incredulous. "It took us a year or so, I believe. I know Dr. Barnard—Annie's neurologist—said it often took much longer because of misdiagnosis, but I guess I'm just surprised."

"Yep, took a long time," Hector confirmed.

Sam shook his head. "I was going out of my mind in just that year not knowing what was wrong with my wife. Less than a year actually, because when she first started displaying symptoms I didn't think anything of it. I can't imagine if it had taken three years instead of one. I wonder if the fact that Annie is declining rapidly has something to do with it."

"Could be," Hector said. "Could be." He nodded his head, ran his fingers through his day-old stubble.

"I guess Dr. Barnard was right when he said we were lucky to get the diagnosis so early. In a way, I suppose, anyway."

"Give you more time to accept," Hector said. "More time to live with your wife, even if she ain't who she was. She still your wife."

Sam walked through the garage door and into his home later that evening. Pizza boxes littered the kitchen countertop and the smell of fresh-popped popcorn permeated the air.

"Hi, Dad!" Hannah called from the living room. "Grammie's letting us stay up late to finish watching *Pirates of the Caribbean*. And she's even letting us have popcorn this late at night." Sam could hear the giggle in Hannah's voice.

He put his bag and lunch box down on the kitchen floor and walked to the living room. "How'd it go?" Caroline asked.

"I'm glad I went," Sam said. "We can talk more later."

Caroline nodded.

"Where's Annie?" Sam asked.

"In the bedroom. I checked on her not too long ago and she's doing well. She was just playing with her phone."

Sam wasn't surprised in the least. "Hey, Ben," he said.

"Hey."

"How was school today?"

"Boring." Ben didn't look at his father. Instead, he continued to pop kernels into his mouth and watch the movie.

"That's all I get?" Sam chuckled.

Ben shrugged his shoulders.

"Look at me," Sam said. Ben turned his head, popped another kernel into his mouth.

"Tell me one good thing about your day at school today," he said.

Ben turned back to the television set. "It's over," he said.

Sam gave up. It had been a long day.

Survival, right? He had to pick and choose his battles with his son right now.

CHAPTER FIFTEEN

Ben

Fall waned and winter announced its presence in southern New Hampshire. The first snow fell in late November, and by Christmastime, the earth was blanketed in heavy whiteness.

This was the first Christmas his grandmother was living in the house and the first Christmas since his mother's diagnosis. If this had been two years ago, he and Hannah would have woken early, waiting eagerly in their bedrooms or even together in Ben's room for their parents' room to creak open. Ben knew Hannah still believed in Santa Claus, but he had guessed the truth when he was ten, the age his sister was now. He wondered how long his father would be able to keep up the charade, especially now that he had witnessed how difficult it had been to get out of the house to shop for gifts. He wondered how the gifts were even wrapped with his mother getting into everything these days. Where did his father and grandmother hide them?

Two years ago, they would have waited it out in their rooms on Christmas morning because his mother insisted they do so. She wanted to make sure all was good downstairs in the living room and to grab their camera before her children bounded down the steps in eager anticipation. She always had that camera up to her chest as they emerged from their rooms, looking at the small video screen as she recorded their every movement as they bounced into the living room, their awe at the gifts under the Christmas tree and in the stockings hanging from the stone fireplace and filled to the brim.

Last year Ben and Hannah had headed downstairs with their father when their mom wouldn't get out of bed. Though he remained in his room this morning, Ben knew he was doing it out of habit and to help Hannah. He didn't want to be the one who would eventually break it to her that Santa wasn't real.

How could a jolly old man in a red suit deliver gifts to all the children in the world, bringing peace and happiness to each household, when his mother's brain was mush?

That was enough real-life shit to trump the Santa card.

But Hannah didn't know. If remaining in his room before his father went downstairs helped his family adhere to tradition, then he'd do it.

Even if it was bullshit.

"Can I come in?" Hannah was in his doorway. Ben had woken an hour ago. He didn't sleep as well these days.

He pulled the earbuds out of his ears. "Yeah."

"Whatcha doin'?"

"Nothing, really. Just listening to music."

"Can I listen, too?"

"Hannah, you don't like my music," he said.

"Then do you have the iPad?"

"It's charging downstairs."

"Then can I play on your computer?"

"Dad wouldn't be happy with that."

"Then let me listen to music with you, silly," Hannah settled.

Ben handed over one of his buds and placed the other back in his ear. Hannah climbed under the blankets with him and rested the back of her head on the edge of his pillow. This was closer than he liked his sister to be, but whatever.

They listened to music for twenty minutes and then Ben turned his head when he saw his father's figure in the doorway. He wasn't sure how long he'd been standing there peeking in.

"Sorry I slept in," his dad said. "It was a long night last night." He winked at Hannah, and she giggled.

"I'm pretty sure your grandmother is already up," his dad said. "I smell coffee." He smiled. "Your mom's still sleeping. We'll just let her sleep for as long as she needs to. We can head on down."

"Yay!" Hannah exclaimed. She yanked the bud out of her ear and handed it back to Ben before leaping from the bed and running downstairs to join her grandmother. Ben slowly placed the earbuds on his nightstand and pocketed his phone. He pulled the blankets from his body and let his legs hang loosely off the side of the bed momentarily before coming to stand. He walked toward his door with his eyes averted from his father, but his dad stood firm in the doorway and wouldn't let him pass.

Ben looked up and held his father's green-eyed gaze.

"I love you, Ben."

Ben had been expecting some kind of reprimand, not an "I love you." He nodded and averted his eyes again, slightly abashed. His father lifted his chin with the tip of his finger. Ben allowed his face to rise, but his eyes remained downward.

"Look at me," his father said, kindly but firmly.

Ben obliged.

"I love you, Ben. Very much." Ben nodded to acknowledge he'd heard his father's words. "I know this has been tough on you; it's been tough on us all. Please know you're not alone." He paused, searched his son's eyes.

"Are you still active on that online support group for teens?"

Ben nodded again.

"Good," his father said. "I fully understand that I'm not a kid anymore, and I know that although we're both struggling with your mother's . . . decline . . . it may be affecting you differently than it's affecting me and I'm not able to fully help you as much as I wish I could. Do you find the group is still helpful?"

Ben nodded.

"I'm glad." His dad paused. "Are you going to say anything this morning or just keep nodding your head?" He smiled.

Ben smiled back.

"Well, at least I got you to grin," his dad said. "Ben?"

"Yeah?"

"I love you."

Ben willed himself not to cry. He'd been doing that enough in private lately. "Love you, too," he choked, then looked down toward the ground once again.

His father moved to let him pass, but as Ben walked a step forward, his dad grabbed him by the shoulder and crushed him in a large, warm, and feeling embrace.

And that's when Ben lost it.

That's when he found himself on Christmas morning grasping onto the back of his dad's nightshirt and sobbing into his chest while his mother slept on, her camera catching dust on the mudroom shelf.

The new year began and Ben found himself back at school. At least in school, he was surrounded by his friends, even if he didn't enjoy school itself. Such bullshit, really. So frickin' boring! His grades had slipped a bit, and his father had been less than happy when he received Ben's last progress report.

He lived life day by day now and found himself spending ever more time at the Bowers' house. Tyler didn't ask Ben too many questions about his mom, and he appreciated that immensely. Appreciated the fact, too, that Tyler treated him just as he always had instead of with the pitying eye he found some of his teachers gave him from time to time. Even Bitsy Bower was cool. She was always taking him to and from soccer practice and games his father couldn't make it to, and she often let him spend the night on the weekends so he could get out of his house.

The snow of winter melted, and his mother continued to decline. She was bumping into things now, mimicking the gait of a person slightly intoxicated: a bump of the hip on the counter, a trip of the foot as she ascended the stairs. She had even fallen out of bed the other day.

He knew his gram cared for her during the day when he and Hannah were in school and his father was at work, but this still tripped him up sometimes, the fact that his mother— his *mother*—required care as a toddler would.

It was now a Saturday afternoon in April, and he had a soccer game. He played for his high school junior varsity team in the fall and for a local soccer club in the winter and spring seasons.

It was the one thing he was able to hold on to, one of the things he still found pleasure in doing.

They piled into his dad's Outback, his grandmother in the passenger seat of the car and he, Hannah, and his mother in the back—they had sold his mom's old minivan just the month prior—and drove to the soccer fields.

"Dad, can I go play on the playground?" Hannah asked as they pulled into the large dirt parking lot.

"Yeah, go ahead," his father said. "Just check in with us in about twenty minutes, okay? You've got your watch on?"

"Yep," Hannah confirmed. She was stuck in the middle seat of the car, so she looked at Ben beside her to move.

"Hold your horses," Ben said. "I gotta get my stuff together."

"I didn't say anything!" Hannah protested.

"Well, you're looking at me," Ben countered with agitation.

"Oh, my God," Hannah mocked. "I'm loooking at you!" She rolled her eyes.

"Cut it out," his father said sternly from the front seat.

Ben gathered his bag from between his legs and pulled on the door's handle. Once he exited, his sister hastily scooted her bottom to the side and made her way to the seat he had just vacated before plopping a foot to the hard dirt ground and hoisting herself outside.

"Bye," she said cheerily as she ran toward the metal fence that partitioned the parking lot from the fields. Ben knew she often found friends on the playground during soccer games so intuited this was the cause for her swift exit.

His mother was having an off day, even more so than was typical. She just seemed out of it. He watched as his grandmother exited the front of the car and opened his mother's door, watched as she helped his mom out of the car. His father had already stood and pocketed the car keys.

Ben began to walk away, slinging his black soccer bag over his shoulder.

"What?" his dad joked. "No goodbye?"

Ben turned. "Bye," he said stoically.

His dad smiled. "Good luck," he said. "And have a great time today."

"Thanks," Ben said.

"I love you," his father finished. He had been saying this more and more lately.

Ben gave a slight smirk. "Love you, too," he said before turning back to the metal fence and walking forward to meet the few members of his team that he could see were already off in the distance on the middle soccer field—there were three—kicking a ball to each other. As he walked, he closed his eyes and lifted his chin to the sky. The sun was bright today and lent a warmth that had been desperately needed of late and was much appreciated by so many, Ben included. He felt that warmth on his face now, heard the crunching of dirt and a few pebbles as his cleats slightly bore into the ground with each step he took.

As he neared his team, he saw Tyler was already there. That meant Mrs. Bower was probably somewhere close by, no doubt accompanied by Tyler's father, and would soon find her way over to Ben's mom. Though he could tell she was uncomfortable and pained at times to be near his mom, her best friend, he knew she was making a conscious effort.

He wasn't sure why, since his mom was clueless. But he supposed he thought that was pretty cool of her all the same.

"Hey," Tyler said as Ben approached.

"Hi," Ben said.

"We're playing the Blue Devils today," Tyler said. "They're tough."

"Yeah," Ben said. "But we're gonna win." That made Tyler smile.

"Damn right," Tyler said. Ben ditched his bag and joined Tyler and the two other boys already warming up. Together, the foursome kicked a ball from boy to boy until a few more team members arrived and they broke off into twos and threes awaiting the arrival of the coach. They didn't have to wait long, as the coach announced his presence by demanding the boys sprint around the fields, a total of a quarter mile. If Ben wasn't warmed up prior to the run, he certainly was now.

Forty minutes later, the game was about to begin. Ben and his teammates huddled and placed their hands in the center of the standing circle they had made. Coach started them off with a "One, two . . . three——" and the boys all finished with "Eagles!"

Ben ran to his starting position on the left side of the field. He cleated the ground as the head referee brought the game ball forward. Ben looked down, ensured his black athletic tape adhered strongly to his black soccer socks; it helped keep his socks in place so he wasn't forced to bend down and lift them up throughout the game. He tucked in his red jersey. Coach liked them tucked in, said the refs could see when the opposition was too handsy because they'd take the shirt right out of your black game shorts.

He loved this jersey. Red was one of his favorite colors to begin with, but he had also gotten lucky and snagged the number nine: his lucky number. So far it had done its job as his team was undefeated. Sure, it was still the beginning of the season, but they were on a roll nonetheless. Add to this the fact that his last name, Carson, was written in large black letters on the upper back of the jersey, lending a sense of pride and ownership, and he was set. Blue Devils, watch out!

The whistle blew. Tyler, as striker, passed back to Mike Da Silva (the only team member Ben thought was an asshole), who played defense for the team. Mike took possession and dribbled forward before passing off to the right. The game progressed and Ben worked it. He zoned in. He often found his mind was nowhere else but where it had to be: on the ball and on his team. Today was no exception.

Seventeen minutes down and his friend and teammate Cole passed the ball to Ben. Ben dribbled off to the left side of the field, sprinted forward. The Blue Devils defender was on him, but Ben was faster, made it closer to the net. When another defenseman came to take the ball, Ben knew he wouldn't get off a shot, so he found Tyler in the center of the field and passed. The moment that ball left his foot, he sprinted up the field again, losing the defensemen, whose attention was now honed on the ball in Tyler's possession and not on Ben.

Tyler saw him. He kicked the ball through the defensive line where Ben was waiting. Ben shot and scored a beautiful goal in the upper right-hand corner of the net. He clenched his fists and shouted "Yes!" as he bounded toward Tyler. The two high-fived and jogged to center field, where the game would soon resume.

At the whistle, one Blue Devil passed to another. Ben jogged forward, getting into position. He saw his chance! He sprinted, approached the player currently in possession of the ball and—

The whistle blew, loud and piercing, then blew again.

And again.

"Hey, lady," the ref called. "Get off the field."

Ben turned to look behind him.

Shit! You had to be kidding.

It was his mom.

On the damn soccer field.

Wandering around aimlessly.

Ben watched as his father and grandmother were suddenly cognizant of the situation and ran to his mother, coaxing her gently back to the sideline. Bitsy Bower stood next to the area they'd vacated with her hands over her mouth.

Ben clenched his eyes shut, breathed.

With his mother back on the sideline, the ball was brought forth to begin again. Mike Da Silva stepped forward so he was closer to Ben now and said, just loud enough for Ben to hear, "What's wrong your ma, hey? She stupid?"

Normally, Ben would have let that slip by him; he had been dealing with Mike Da Silva's shit since the second grade, when he had hit Ben in the nose with a soccer ball. He had become proficient at ignoring the kid.

But not today.

Today Mike had hit him where it hurt too damn much.

Ben spun around and lunged at Mike, pushed him hard against his chest.

"Hey," Mike spluttered, "what the fuck!?"

"Don't you ever"—Ben punched his right fist into Mike's cheek—"ever"—his left fist landed on Mike's jaw—"talk shit about my mom again!" he yelled.

He pulled his right elbow back, hand fisted, and was going in for another blow when he was held firmly from behind. Ben was heaving, breathing heavily. He was fighting off whoever it was that held him firmly.

Another pair of hands held him back, then pushed him to the ground. A knee to the chest that Ben couldn't shake off.

"Easy, man!" Tyler's voice, Tyler's face above him.

Coach's knee, coach's strong hands holding him down.

"Chill, Carson!" Tyler again. He knelt next to an outraged Ben.

Ben was breathing heavily, his chest heaving up and down with each large inhalation, with each exhalation. The warmth left his open mouth, his dry lips.

"Calm down, man," Tyler said, a bit more softly now. "Look at me."

Ben was still worked up but lucid enough to look at his best friend hovering over him.

Tyler nodded. Coach loosened his hold.

Tyler helped Ben to stand. Coach walked to check on Mike Da Silva and speak with an extremely irate referee and an explosive father, who had charged the field at Ben's first blow to his son.

Tyler placed the palm of his hand on Ben's shoulder. "I heard," was all he said.

Ben hadn't known until that moment that his cheeks were warm and wet from shed tears.

CHAPTER SIXTEEN

Caroline

*T*he door alarm chimed, loud and clear.

Caroline startled, awake now, and turned over in bed. She had inhabited the room next to the front hallway for a year now. She pulled the light comforter off her pajama-clad body and frantically leaped out of bed and hastened to the front door in a discombobulated manner.

No. No, it wasn't the door alarm they had installed when Annie had snuck out of the house undetected one too many times for their comfort. It was her bedside alarm clock announcing it was six o'clock and time to wake for the day.

Sam got up by five each day to shower and get ready for work. Hannah often woke around six thirty during this summer vacation, but Ben slept later. Sometimes he'd wake around the same time as Hannah, other times not until closer to nine o'clock in the morning. Caroline never really knew when Annie would wake as her times altered from day to day, but Caroline always woke around six o'clock, setting her alarm clock to ensure this was the case, so she'd be up and ready both physically and emotionally when her daughter rose for the day.

Caroline's heart began to relax its heavy beating as she retraced her steps back into the bedroom to shut the alarm off.

She sighed.

She did *not* want to wake up this morning.

She was so darn tired!

But wake she must.

When she exited the room, she smelled the morning coffee and heard Sam rummaging around in the kitchen.

She and Sam had developed a routine this past year, a routine they had to alter often based on Annie's decline and specific needs at any given time. But they worked it, and they worked it well. Each morning, Sam would rise, shower, then start the coffee for both him and Caroline. While that coffee started brewing, its aroma lifting to fill the air—a most welcome scent when Caroline was loath to rise from slumber —he'd make his lunch for the day. Sam used to head to the gym before work. That had ceased quite a while ago. There just wasn't time any longer to do so.

"Good morning, Sam," Caroline said groggily, though kindly, as she entered the kitchen.

"Morning, Caroline," Sam replied. "I've got to rush today. There's a bunch of work I need to get done before my nine o'clock meeting this morning. Annie's still sleeping."

Caroline nodded her head. "All right, then," she said. "I'll go take my shower, but I won't be long." Caroline had learned rather quickly that if she didn't shower while Sam was still present in the house each morning, then she wouldn't get a shower until he returned home that evening. She didn't like this much if she were being honest. She didn't enjoy the greasy feeling of an unbathed body and a head of hair that stuck up on end from a night's fitful tossing upon her pillow.

She reentered her bedroom and gathered the day's clothes

in her arms. She then climbed the stairs and opened the baby gate secured in place at the top for Annie's safety now that she was more unsteady on her feet. Closing the gate behind her, Caroline continued down the hallway and placed her clothes on the countertop in the master bedroom, then poked her head farther into Sam and Annie's room. Annie's face was hidden under the blanket, so Caroline approached the side of the bed. Her daughter's eyes were closed, and she was breathing slowly, deeply.

Caroline ran the tip of her finger gently along Annie's hairline, felt her smooth, warm skin. She cupped her daughter's cheek in the palm of her hand, careful not to disrupt her slumber.

She studied her daughter now, watched the blanket rise with each inhalation of breath. She looked upon the pale white skin of her daughter's face, the small freckles the sun of the summer had birthed, the small pores that dwelled comfortably on her slight nose. She gazed upon the few wrinkles that lined the corners of her eyes. She watched as those eyes darted from side to side beneath the thin skin of the eyelids that protected them. She thought of Annie's beating heart, thought of the blood coursing through her veins.

Thought of the brain that would one day forget to do the most menial of tasks to keep her daughter alive.

But she wasn't going to go there. She pondered this macabre situation all too often these days as she bore witness to her daughter's rapid decline. In sleep, she looked like Annie. In sleep, she resembled the daughter who, in her younger years, would wake and smile as soon as she saw her mother and breathe a "Morning, Mama." The innocence of childhood, carefree features, no lines of worry for the future.

While Annie slept, Caroline could believe, even if just for a moment, that everything was as it should be.

One last lingering look upon her beautiful daughter and Caroline composed herself and walked back toward the master bathroom. She turned the knob on the tub's faucet, pulled the plug on the spout, and let the water cascade down from the showerhead. She closed the curtain and began to remove her nightdress.

The tepid water felt remarkable on her warm skin. She closed her eyes as it pelted her head and ran down her neck, her back. Bliss would ensue if she were granted the ability to bask in this glorious feeling, if she were able to simply stand there under the flow with no worries, no time constraint.

She slowly opened her eyes. This reprieve wasn't permitted today. Sam needed to get to work, and she was responsible for her daughter and her grandchildren.

Caroline rubbed the white soap on a cloth, amassing thick bubbles. She scrubbed her body, then washed her hair with a coconut-scented shampoo. Finally, she placed a small amount of conditioner into the palm of her hand, then into her wet, short dark blond hair, rinsing it out soon thereafter.

She allowed herself a moment, just a moment more under the running water, before she shut the spout off and pulled back the curtain with a sigh.

She was tired already and the day had only just begun.

She toweled herself dry and dressed. She very quickly blew her hair dry, then checked on Annie once more (she was still sleeping) before heading back downstairs to relieve Sam for the day.

"Hannah's not up just yet?" she asked Sam as she entered the kitchen. Sam was already placing his shoes on his feet in the adjacent mudroom.

"She's not," he confirmed. "Hopefully it'll be a nice morning for you, Caroline."

"I'm sure it will be," Caroline said.

"Okay," Sam said as he reentered the kitchen to retrieve his laptop bag. "Have a wonderful day."

"Thanks, Sam. I hope you do as well."

Sam shut the mudroom door behind him, and Caroline

heard the garage stall door announce loudly that it was lifting. Sam started his car, and Caroline heard him pull out. She took a mug out of a cherrywood upper cabinet and poured herself a cup of coffee, adding a teaspoon of sugar and a dash of half-and-half. Warm mug in hand, she walked to sit at the kitchen table and gaze admiringly out the bay window into the backyard and the awakening lake, the tethered family boat they hadn't yet used this season motionless beside the dock. She would have loved to head outside, to sit on the wicker chair on the deck and feel the cool morning breeze upon her skin, the sun upon her face as she turned it skyward, but Annie would be up soon, she was sure. If Caroline were outside, Annie might wake unnoticed.

Bounding footsteps on the stairs. "Mornin', Grammie," Hannah said cheerily. My, but this girl could wake easily. Caroline wasn't, and never had been, a morning person herself.

"Good morning, honey," Caroline said, then took a sip of her coffee.

"Can Grace come over today?"

"Perhaps," Caroline said, "or maybe we can head to the pool or the playground? Maybe she could meet us there if her schedule permits."

Caroline knew that Hannah and Grace had been friends for quite some time. Hannah spoke of Grace often, and Caroline had seen them play at Halloween parties she had attended in her daughter's home since Annie, Sam, and the kids had moved to this small town when Ben was just a toddler. If she wasn't mistaken, Annie and Grace's mother, Audrey, had met when the girls were just babies and had become fast friends. The girls followed suit.

Yet Caroline knew, too, that Audrey didn't take Annie's sickness well, to say the least. She had confessed to Caroline last year that she preferred the girls to meet out of the house, where situations could be better monitored by her, Audrey.

She wanted to be present when her daughter was around Annie.

And what was Caroline to say to Hannah? *"Oh, baby girl, I'm sorry, but Grace's mom doesn't want her to come to our house"?* Or perhaps, *"I'm so sorry, Hannah, but Grace's mom doesn't trust your mom"?*

She understood it all; she really did. Annie had fits. Annie swore. Annie bumped into furniture. Annie spoke her mind on days her words didn't fail her.

But at the same time, it devastated Caroline. She was just pleased that she was often able to redirect playdates to public venues. Harder on her, yes, but it made Hannah incredibly happy to be with her best friend. And Ben was able to get together with friends easily in this manner as well. Often Tyler and sometimes Cole. Caroline found Bitsy Bower to be a godsend, a blessing.

"Okay," Hannah conceded easily. "Let's do the pool!"

A membership at a local tennis and pool facility was the one luxury Caroline had allowed herself for these summer months. She had the ever more stressful job of caring for Annie during the day, and in the summer, she cared for Hannah and Ben as well. Ben was extremely self-sufficient, but she still wanted to see him happy. He wasn't yet old enough to apply for a summer job, and she simply wouldn't permit him to lie in bed or play on his computer all day long. Though Hannah could care for herself, she complained often of being bored. She was one who needed constant stimulation. This was where friends helped immensely, but getting together with a friend—even if it was Grace, who was soft-spoken and polite—only added to Caroline's stress and responsibility, so it was far from a daily occurrence.

"Well, then," Caroline said, "the pool it is!" Sam had tried to insist on paying for the summer membership, but Caroline had refused. She knew Sam continued to struggle financially, and this was something she was still able to provide. She wanted to help as much as she possibly could while also attempting not to deflate her son-in-law's pride.

"Yay!" Hannah exclaimed joyously.

Caroline grinned and took another sip of her coffee. When she swallowed, she said, "I'll text her mom in just a minute."

"Okay," Hannah said. "I'm gonna get myself some waffles for breakfast."

"Of course, honey," Caroline said. "But you pick up after yourself," she teased with a wagging pointed finger. "Yesterday I had to scrub hardened syrup off the kitchen table."

Hannah laughed. "Sorry," she said before walking to the freezer below the black stainless steel refrigerator and pulling it open.

Caroline smiled and took another sip of her now cooling coffee. She was given a few more minutes of reprieve as Hannah munched her waffles. Caroline was always amazed at how much syrup she poured over the small mound. It was no wonder how that syrup landed on the tabletop and solidified —there was entirely too much!

A few minutes was all she was given before she heard small, shuffling footsteps at the top of the stairs.

This was not the sound Ben made, so she knew Annie had woken up.

"That's your mother," Caroline said to Hannah beside her.

"Okay," Hannah replied through a mouthful of waffle.

Caroline gently placed her mug of unfinished coffee on the kitchen table and lifted herself from her chair. She met her daughter at the baby gate at the top of the stairs and held her hand as she guided her slowly down to the first floor. Annie watched her bare feet the entire time.

When they were safely on the first floor, Caroline lifted Annie's chin so Annie would look her way. "Good morning, sunshine," she said with a smile.

"Morning," Annie replied, smiling back. From that one smile, Caroline predicted a good day for Annie, which pleased her tremendously.

"Hungry," Annie said.

Caroline grinned knowingly. Annie was often hungry.

Annie turned and walked into the kitchen. Caroline followed. Annie opened the refrigerator and peered inside. Not finding anything to her liking, she walked to the pantry. Caroline closed the refrigerator door that her daughter had left open. Annie took out some peanut butter and bread as well as a Hershey's chocolate bar and brought them to the counter, leaving the pantry door ajar. Caroline closed it and walked to stand beside Annie.

Annie opened the jar of peanut butter first (Caroline always ensured the top was just barely twisted closed), lifting a chunk out with her finger and placing it into her mouth. She opened the bread and took a slice out. She attempted to dip it into the peanut butter, breaking the bread apart in the process. This didn't deter her; she simply placed the broken portion into her mouth and began to chew.

Caroline moved to the silverware drawer and lifted a knife out, bringing it to her daughter. "Here you go," she said.

Annie took it from her mother and dipped it into the peanut butter. Instead of tilting the knife to scoop, she dabbed it up and down, leaving only a smear of peanut butter on the smooth, silvery surface of the utensil. She brought the knife down, pointing the blunted surface to the bread and brushed it softly back and forth. When she lifted the knife, only a minute portion of peanut butter had been spread.

"Would you like some help?" Caroline asked.

"Okay," Annie replied.

Caroline took the knife from Annie's hand and spread a small amount of peanut butter onto the broken bread. She then took another slice out of the plastic bag and placed peanut butter on that one as well. Just enough to coat the bread but not stick to the roof of Annie's mouth.

"A chocolate bar for breakfast, Annie?" Caroline looked at her daughter skeptically.

"Yes," Annie said. "Pizza . . . okay . . . pizza." She turned from the counter, quickly discarding the bread from her mind, and opened the refrigerator. Caroline followed.

"There's no pizza in the refrigerator, honey," she told her daughter as she placed the palm of her hand on Annie's shoulder. "And we don't have any in the freezer, either."

Annie turned down the hallway and into the mudroom toward the garage door. Caroline closed the refrigerator once again and followed at a quickened pace.

"Where are you going, Annie?"

"Pizza. Going . . . going . . . pizza."

"You can't head to the store right now, Annie," Caroline said as gently as she was able amidst the frustration that was beginning to well. Annie had attempted on several occasions to walk to the general store down the street when she got it in her mind that there was something specific she'd like to eat that they didn't have in the house.

"Plus," Caroline continued, "you don't have any shoes on and you're still in your pajamas."

"But—" Annie began.

Caroline quickly interceded, attempting to coax her daughter back into the kitchen. "How about we eat that peanut butter bread, yes? And maybe you can even have a little bit of that chocolate bar, too." She gently took her daughter's hand in her own and pulled slightly. It was enough to convince Annie to walk back toward the kitchen counter and her awaiting breakfast.

"Pizza?" Annie asked as she stood over her bread, a quizzical, confused look on her face.

"Not right now, honey. But later, okay? Here, let's take this to the table." Caroline led Annie to sit, passing Hannah, who had gathered up her empty plate to take to the kitchen sink.

Hannah rinsed her syrupy plate in the sink and left it there for her grandmother to take care of later that day. Then she made her way down the hallway and toward the stairs.

"Forgetting something, Hannah?"

"What?"

"It would be very helpful to me if you could please wipe down your space."

"Oh," Hannah called. "Yeah. Forgot. Sorry, Grammie."

"That's all right," Caroline replied as Hannah reemerged into the kitchen area.

Annie began eating her chocolate. Caroline regretted that she hadn't broken the bar in half before leading Annie to the kitchen table. She attempted to do so now, but Annie grabbed the broken half Caroline held in her hand and bit a large chunk off while cradling the other half of the milk chocolate bar in her palm.

A battle Caroline wouldn't win, nor did she want to attempt it.

Caroline lifted her coffee mug and brought it to her lips, taking a small sip.

Cold now. Caroline grimaced and walked to the sink, dumping the remaining liquid down the drain and pouring herself a fresh cup. When the sugar and half-and-half were added, she stirred with a silver spoon and sat back down next to her daughter at the kitchen table. Annie was biting into her bread now, leaving thin smears of peanut butter on her lips and cheeks.

Caroline watched her daughter eat and smiled forlornly before taking her first sip of hot, fresh coffee. She then gazed back into the yard, at the morning sun glistening off the water's surface, at the awakening birds soaring in the sky and skittering from tree to tree.

"Grammie, can I watch TV?" Hannah asked.

"It looks like you've still got some syrup there, Hannah. Wipe a bit more and you should be all set."

Hannah did so begrudgingly but didn't verbalize her dissent.

"Now?" she asked when she had finished.

"You may. Thanks for cleaning up."

Hannah threw her cloth into the kitchen sink and leaped into the living room, her long legs bare and sun-kissed beneath her pink polka-dotted pajama shorts, pink polish on her toenails.

Hannah plonked herself onto the brown leather couch and clicked the button on the remote control to turn the TV on. She surfed through Netflix until she settled on Nickelodeon's *Nicky, Ricky, Dicky & Dawn*. Her granddaughter had watched this silly show often enough, but it was harmless and therefore a choice Caroline had no issue with.

The moment the speakers sounded and the vibrant colors were emitted from the screen, Annie stood from the kitchen table and began to walk toward the living room.

"Annie, aren't you going to finish your breakfast?" Caroline asked her daughter's back.

Annie didn't answer. She continued to move forward, bumping into a kitchen chair with her hip.

Caroline sighed and let her go, picked up the one unfinished slice of bread from the kitchen table as well as the discarded candy bar wrapper and threw them away in the rubbish bin. She sat back down at the table, coffee in hand, feeling the warmth of the mug on her skin. She was secretly pleased that Annie had made herself comfortable in front of the television; there was no way she could pass by without Caroline seeing her, so she knew her daughter was safe and Caroline could finish her morning coffee in peace and relaxation.

A door sounded its closing upstairs and she knew Ben had woken from his slumber. His door was never left ajar; he always closed it whether he was in his bedroom or not. Caroline recalled Annie's teenage years. She, too, had often closed her door. For privacy, Caroline supposed. She assumed it was the same for Ben, though until now she'd had no experience raising boys; they remained quite an enigma to her.

"Hi, Gram," Ben said as he drowsily entered the kitchen.

"Good morning, Ben," Caroline replied. "Did you sleep well?"

"Eh." Ben shrugged his shoulders.

Caroline smirked behind her coffee mug. "I suppose that's a no?"

"It was okay," Ben said. He moved to the refrigerator and took out the carton of eggs followed by salsa and shredded cheese. He found the skillet in a lower cabinet and placed it on the black stovetop, turning the burner on high. An omelet, Caroline knew. He often made himself omelets for breakfast. Though she was highly pleased that Ben made his own breakfast and that it was healthy, too, she would have also liked very much if he'd offer to help her with lunches or with dinner before his father got home. She could use the aid, especially as cooking was often interrupted and done with her eyes averted to her daughter. Caroline often reverted to asking for help from Ben when he didn't take the initiative and offer. Hannah was often pleased to help, and though Caroline wanted very much to acquiesce, she also found it an added stress when Hannah helped in the kitchen. She tried not to let this show.

"We're thinking of heading to the pool today," Caroline said. "Oh, goodness. That reminds me that I promised Hannah I'd get in touch with Grace's mom to see if she'd like to meet us there."

Ben turned from the stove to look at his grandmother. "Can Tyler come, too?"

"Perhaps you could text Mrs. Bower to see if Tyler would like to join us," Caroline suggested. "I can pick him up if need be. I know the two of you like being together very much."

"'Kay," Ben said, then went back to cooking his omelet, the aroma of sizzling, spicy salsa filling the air and tickling her nostrils.

Caroline leaned over and picked her phone up off the kitchen countertop, where it had been charging during the night. She scrolled through her contacts and texted Grace's mom, Audrey, to see if they would like to join her family at the pool later that day. She could see out of the corner of her eye that Ben was doing the same, one hand on the spatula and one hand texting Tyler. He was never without his phone, it seemed.

When it was cooked, Ben brought his omelet to the table and sat next to his grandmother.

"Ben," Caroline said, "I need to start a load of laundry. Would you mind terribly looking after your mother while I head downstairs to do that? I'll just be a moment."

"Sure," Ben said through a large mouthful of egg.

"Thank you." Caroline left her coffee on the table and headed down the basement steps and toward the washing machine. When she returned, Annie was in the kitchen and Ben was struggling to remove a steak knife from his mother's grasp.

"Whoa!" Caroline said as she hastened her steps to her daughter. "Annie, that's not safe, honey. Let me have the knife." She extended her arm, the palm of her hand facing up. Annie looked at Caroline's hand, then at the knife, and slowly positioned it in her mother's waiting hand. Caroline quickly grabbed it and placed it back in the knife holder on the countertop. This hadn't been an issue prior to today. Looked like it was time to hide the knives or at least place them somewhere Annie wouldn't easily be able to reach.

"She always listens to you," Ben said, his lips pursed in a scowl.

"She doesn't always listen to me," Caroline protested

gently. "I've just really been working on how to speak and approach her."

"Well," Ben said, "it's frustrating."

"I really can understand that, Ben," Caroline soothed. "Really, I can." She placed her hand on her grandson's shoulder, higher now than hers. She had to lift her head a bit to look into his eyes, sapphire blue and gorgeous. She often marveled at the fact that this young man before her was her grandson, that she was *old enough* to have a fifteen-year-old grandson.

She marveled, too, though in a different way, that she was caring not so much for this fifteen-year-old grandson of hers, but for her almost forty-two-year-old daughter instead.

Caroline helped Annie to a snack; apparently she wasn't through eating breakfast after all. She received a text back from Grace's mom indicating that they'd be at the pool after lunch that day and would be happy to meet Caroline and the kids there. She didn't mention Annie. When Ben announced that he had heard back from Tyler and that yes, he was able to accompany them if they could provide a ride, Caroline decided that she'd do the grocery shopping that morning. It really did need to be done, and she wasn't sure she could wait until the weekend when Sam was home. They'd leave for the pool after lunch and pick Tyler up on the way.

Once Annie was done eating, she called over to Hannah in the living room. "Hannah, I'm taking your mom upstairs to get dressed. I need you to dress for the day as well and don't forget to pack a bag for the pool. We'll head there after lunch. Grace will meet us there with her mom."

"Yay!" Hannah cheered. She shut the television off and bounded up the stairs to her room. Caroline helped Annie climb the stairs, slowly, one by one, then guided her down the hallway then into the master bathroom. She left her there momentarily as she turned for the walk-in closet and brought back a pair of jean shorts and a blue T-shirt as well as a fresh pair of panties.

"Let's get dressed, shall we?" Caroline said upon her return.

Annie pushed the elastic waist of her pajama shorts down her legs and clumsily stepped out of them. She then tugged on the arm of her short-sleeved shirt, which did nothing in the way of helping her to undress.

"Arms up," Carline said, feigning a smile.

Tired. She was just too tired this morning.

Annie raised her arms in the air, elbows bent, and Caroline shimmied the shirt over her bare bosom and over her head, careful not to nick her nose in the process. She remembered the first time she had seen Annie's naked chest as an adult. It had been shortly after moving in with Annie and her family. Annie's lack of bathing ability had presented itself, requiring Caroline to help her scrub in the shower while Sam was at work one day. She had seen a very naked Annie born into the world, scrunch-faced, skin slick with vernix. She had wiped the bottom of a baby Annie, rolls of chunk creasing the skin of her fat legs, kissable, tickleable. She had helped a toddler Annie dress, often in knee-length dresses for kindergarten and first grade as Annie refused to wear anything else then. She had helped a preteen Annie shop for her first bra, but even then she hadn't gazed upon her naked chest; Annie was too modest, too embarrassed by her budding breasts. So, really, she hadn't looked at her daughter's naked body since she was just a child, and hadn't thought she ever would again. She thought perhaps it was her body, Caroline's, that her daughter would gaze upon in old age, when the brain that controlled the mechanisms of Caroline's own body no longer worked well, when her body, pride lost, demanded help to live before her heart beat its last and expired.

Never had she thought the roles would be reversed.

Seeing Annie's naked breasts, her naked body, did not

unsettle Caroline in the least. In fact, she had always believed that a body was simply a body. What unsettled her was the fact that this body of her daughter's couldn't function without Caroline's loving hands.

When the shirt had been lifted from Annie's torso and discarded upon the floor, Caroline helped Annie remove the adult diaper she wore in the nighttime. They had been purchased for Annie when Sam and Caroline came to the realization that Annie just simply lacked the ability to hold in her urine for longer periods of time and needed a gentle reminder to use the restroom multiple times during the day. She breathed a sigh of relief that Annie wasn't menstruating. Caroline had been there before. It was not a pleasant endeavor to help her clean.

"We'll get your bathing suit on when we get to the pool. I think that'll be easier today, yes?" She didn't expect Annie to answer so went on, "Lift a foot for me, honey. That's it." Annie ever so slightly lifted a leg and Caroline snuck the underwear underneath. The same went for the other leg; then Caroline lifted them up her daughter's thighs and onto her bottom and ever-expanding waist.

"Okay," she said. "Can you sit for me?" Caroline guided Annie gently to the toilet. Annie lacked the ability now to lift her legs high enough for Caroline to get shorts or pants on over her feet without stumbling and threatening to fall. When Annie stood again and Caroline pulled the shorts up to her waist, she couldn't push the metal button through the buttonhole.

"Oh, damn," she said. "And I just bought these a couple of months ago." She sighed. "That's okay," she said as she patted Annie's cheeks. "We'll leave it unbuttoned. Your shirt should cover the top of your shorts, anyway." She grabbed Annie's shirt. "Arms up," she said again.

When Annie was dressed, Caroline threw Annie's pajamas into the closet hamper before guiding Annie back downstairs.

On the last stair, Annie tripped and stumbled. Caroline fought to hold onto her daughter. She was able to steady Annie and then brought her to sit in front of the television set once again so she could dress herself for the day. She was fairly certain the TV would hold Annie's attention long enough for her to do so, but she'd warn her grandchildren that they should be on the lookout for a few minutes until she returned.

Caroline dressed and then checked on both Ben and Hannah, informing them that she'd be leaving in just a minute for the grocery store with their mother. In times such as these, she was very thankful that she trusted both Ben and Hannah alone at home.

Caroline allowed Annie to watch a few more minutes of TV before turning the set off and guiding her to the mudroom, where she helped place socks and sneakers on Annie's feet as she sat on the hard wooden seat of a cubby. She had developed the habit of placing a pair of clean socks in one of Annie's sneakers before she went to bed at night so they'd be there in the morning, ready to go. Annie wasn't entirely steady on her feet when wearing flip-flops, and although it was more difficult to place Annie in sneakers every time they left the house, she'd much rather make the extra effort than have her daughter trip and take a fall.

"All set," Caroline said once Annie's sneakers were secure. "Shall we?" She smiled at her daughter, who smiled back. Annie probably thought they were going for a neighborhood walk. She did still love to see Pumpkin, the Yorkshire terrier, out and about.

Caroline opened the mudroom door and leaned over to push the button on the garage door opener. As the large door moved upward noisily, Caroline began to lead Annie by the hand to her car parked in the driveway. Although there was ample room in the garage for Caroline to store her car when not in use, she found it much easier to park in the driveway. This way, she could guide Annie to her seat and easily reach over her hips to fasten her belt securely. Luckily, with it being summer, the weather often lent heightened ease and accessibility to a car parked outdoors.

Caroline backed out of the driveway and into the street. "The kids and I were thinking of heading to the pool today, Annie. Would you like to go?"

Annie looked at her mother beside her. "Yeah," she said. "Pool." She turned to stare out the front window. "Like pool. Like when . . . when . . . Like pool."

"Yes," Caroline said, eyes on the road, "I know you do. You like to splash, don't you? And you like the hot tub they have."

Annie nodded. "Yeah," she said. "Thing . . . thing up . . . thing . . . we going . . . with feet."

Caroline had become accustomed to Annie's speech patterns and thought processes. She was with her almost every moment of her waking days. Each week, each month, the decline was more pronounced, but she was still able to follow what her daughter was attempting to convey.

"Yes," she said. "I know you like the bubbles in the hot tub. And no, Annie," she continued, "we're not going for a walk right now. We're in the car. We need to get some groceries. We need food."

"Pizza," Annie said, though the word wasn't in the form of a question as much as it was a statement.

"Yes," Caroline said. "We can get you some pizza."

They pulled into the parking lot at the grocery store and Caroline found an open spot. Luckily at this time in the morning on a weekday, there weren't often many people present, which was beneficial as shopping took a while with Annie and she didn't do well with crowds.

Caroline turned the key in the ignition and lifted her purse from the center console of the car. Annie was toying with her buckle release and having a difficult time. Caroline leaned over and pushed the button. Annie pulled the knob on the door. Not wanting her daughter to step into the path of an oncoming car, no matter how slow it was going in the parking lot, Caroline rushed to open her door and hastened to Annie's side. When she arrived, she saw that Annie's door was only partially open as she had failed to pull her elbow out of the seat belt and was struggling, flailing her arm up and down. Caroline opened the car door fully and helped Annie out.

After opening the trunk of the car and retrieving her reusable grocery bags, Caroline held Annie's hand, and together they walked into the air-conditioned grocery store.

"All right, Annie," Caroline said as she released her daughter's hand from her own, "here we are." She pulled a metal cart free of the others in line and wiped it down with a disinfecting wipe from a canister provided by the store.

"Ready, Annie?"

"Yeah."

Aisle one was where they picked up some tuna and nonstick spray. When they approached the pickle and olive jars, Caroline cut in front of Annie so she'd be closer to the items and Annie would be a bit farther into the aisle. Annie's curiosity never wavered, and she was very handsy when at a store. Well, she was handsy anywhere, really, but her fingers weren't as dexterous as they once were and she often dropped items she was holding. Two weeks ago, she had dropped a glass pickle jar, the smash loud and sharp, the smell pungent, and the mess extensive. Caroline had been mortified, but Annie merely stepped in the puddle of pickle juice and walked along as if nothing were amiss. Caroline had been too stupefied to immediately follow; instead, she watched as her daughter trailed wet sneaker prints down the aisle's tan floor.

She wasn't bound to let that happen again if she could help it.

They moved on, turned a corner. Caroline grabbed Annie's hand and pulled her closer to her body so she was able to careen into aisle two without Annie wandering. She picked up some oatmeal for the kids—blueberry-flavored was their favorite—then some Cheerios. Caroline reached for a brown box of pancake mix when Annie grasped onto a syrup bottle and placed the cap in her mouth.

"No, Annie," Caroline gently admonished. "That's really gross. Here," she said as she extracted a soft fig bar from her purse and opened the wrapper, "have this instead." Caroline removed the wrapper fully and discarded it into a pocket in her skirt. Annie might try to eat it, otherwise.

The bar kept Annie occupied, but it also slowed her down as she had a difficult time chewing and walking simultaneously. Caroline left her cart abandoned and retrieved items down the aisle hurriedly while checking on Annie every few moments to ensure she was still standing and too engrossed in her snack to divert her hands and attention elsewhere.

With aisle two done, Caroline lifted the remainder of the bar from Annie's loose grasp. "I'm not taking it away," she promised her daughter. "I just want to get us to the next aisle."

And so it went.

Moving was slow, and Caroline was continuously forced to divert Annie's attention, but she was able to get most of the groceries that were needed for the remainder of the week. She'd come back during the weekend without Annie to get anything she had missed and to make a larger run.

While in the checkout line, Annie reached for a Hershey's chocolate bar. Caroline opened her purse and discovered that she had run out of snacks for her daughter. "You know," she said to the attendant, "we'll just get this, too." She knew if she placed that Hershey's bar back on the rack, Annie would just reach for it again, or reach for another candy bar instead. She unwrapped the bar for her daughter and handed the wrapping over to the counter to be scanned.

Annie took a large bite, then looked up, first at the attendant, then at the woman bagging their groceries. She walked forward until she was by the bagger's side and grinned at her, chocolate noticeable on her teeth and on her lips. The bagger placed the items in Caroline's reusable bags a bit more slowly as she eyed Annie beside her. Annie giggled, then leaped forward and flung her arms around the woman's shoulders in a clumsy embrace, giggling still, her chocolate bar rubbing against the woman's white shirt.

The bagger's eyes widened, and she lifted her hands in the air, her torso stiffening with discomfort.

"Oh, my gosh!" Caroline exclaimed as she removed her daughter from the stranger. "I am so sorry," she said, highly embarrassed and apologetic. "My daughter's not well."

"Sick brain," Annie said, then snickered, a bit of chocolaty saliva spurting from her mouth. She smiled as Caroline wiped her lips with a napkin. "Sick brain." She smiled at her mother.

"Yes, love," her mother said, tears welling in her eyes. "You have a sick brain."

Annie finished her Hershey's bar while Caroline paid for their groceries, eyes downcast. She then led her daughter outside, attempting to hold her hand and steer the cart concurrently, and finding this rather a difficult task to tackle.

When they made it back to her Honda Accord, Caroline left the cart of groceries by the trunk and helped Annie into the car, locking her into the seat belt before placing the bags into the trunk and wheeling the cart away. She entered the car, purse in hand, and started the ignition.

"Are you ready to head home?" she asked her daughter.

"Yeah," Annie said.

They drove home and pulled into the driveway. Caroline helped Annie into the house and asked Ben and Hannah to watch their mother so she could gather the groceries and put them away.

By the time Caroline had put the groceries away and allowed herself a few much-needed minutes to breathe, it was lunchtime.

"All right, everyone," she called. "What shall we do for lunch today?"

"Mac and cheese!" Hannah called back. She did love her macaroni and cheese.

"I'm good with whatever, Gram," Ben said as he followed his mother into the kitchen. "Want some help?"

Caroline paused to look at her grandson. She gave a slight smile, her lips upturned, her eyes softening. "I've got it, Ben, but I have to say that I really appreciate the offer."

Ben said nothing in return as he stopped his mother from opening a package of brown sugar. He distracted her with a small handful of goldfish, instead, and led her to the living room couch, where he turned the TV on.

Macaroni and cheese it was, then. Caroline got to work boiling the water on the stove. Annie and the kids seemed content on the couches for the time being, so she packed a bag with towels and sunscreen and Annie's swimsuit as well as a full change of clothes. She grabbed sunglasses and a sun hat for Annie and goggles for the kids. She placed the bag in the mudroom and headed back to the kitchen to finish cooking lunch.

"Okay, everyone," she called soon thereafter. "Lunch is ready."

Hannah came barreling into the kitchen. Annie was next, Ben following behind.

"Ben," Caroline said, "I want your mom to go to the bathroom before she sits down."

"Okay," Ben said. He guided his mother to the bathroom down the hall and Caroline took over. When Annie had urinated and Caroline helped her wash her hands, they walked back to the kitchen area, where Caroline found Ben had ladled some macaroni and cheese onto four plates on the kitchen counter and added carrot sticks to all but his mother's (a bit difficult for Annie to chew on now). He removed forks from the silverware drawer and placed those, along with the plates, on the table.

"Thanks so much, Ben," Caroline said.

"Welcome."

Annie sat, and Caroline helped to move Annie's chair closer to the table. She secured an adult-sized plastic bib around her neck. Annie picked up her fork and tried to scoop some pasta. She succeeded only in forking a few morsels to her mouth, where she poked her lip with a tine.

Caroline pushed back her chair and walked to the kitchen for a spoon. "Here you go," she said to Annie as she extended the spoon her way. Annie took it, and Caroline brought the fork to the kitchen sink. Though Annie still had a bit of difficulty scooping and maneuvering the spoon to her mouth, Caroline was nothing if not patient these days and gave her daughter the time she needed to succeed. Ben and Hannah finished their meals first.

"We'll head out soon," Caroline told them. "Make sure you've got everything you need."

The children brought their plates to the sink and rinsed them off. Hannah bounded up the stairs. Ben followed behind, his pace lagging, though Caroline could tell he was pleased they were headed to the pool.

Caroline finished eating and placed the dirty dishes in the dishwasher. When Annie decided she was done at the table, she stood and began walking away. Caroline halted her daughter's movements before she reached the living room and removed her dirty bib. By this time, Hannah was back downstairs.

"Hannah," Caroline said, "I don't want your mother to get settled right now. If I put the TV on, I might not be able to get her off the couch easily to get to the pool. Go run and get your brother, please. Then I'd love your help in getting your mother's sneakers on so we can leave the house. I just need to get this food off the floor and run the dishwasher quickly."

"Sure, Grammie," Hannah said merrily and sprang up the stairs once more.

Hannah came back to the first floor with Ben on her heels carrying a black backpack. "Gram, there are no more beach towels," Ben announced.

"Ugh," Caroline grunted on her hands and knees, sweeping the sticky macaroni and cheese into a damp cloth. She stood from the tiled floor, her knees cracking in protest. "For now, you can just use one of the towels we used the other day. I think they might be out on the deck still. They'll be all dry, at least."

Ben grabbed a towel that had fallen from the deck's balustrade onto the wooden floorboards below and brought it inside. Annie was sitting on a stool in the mudroom, and Hannah was helping her place socks and sneakers on her feet. Caroline placed a soap pellet into the appropriate slot in the dishwasher and closed it tightly. She turned the dishwasher on, and it began to run noisily as she walked to the mudroom.

Ready to go, the foursome piled into Caroline's car and headed to the pool.

The afternoon ran smoothly. It was thankfully a gorgeous day outdoors, so Caroline didn't mind wading in the outdoor pool with her daughter. Annie's body didn't seem to process temperatures well, so even on the coolest of summer days she wanted to splash in the water, which left a miserable Caroline drenched and shivering, goose bumps perceptibly raised on her skin.

This was a fantastic facility, really. There was a large, Olympic-sized pool outdoors with a small waterslide and a hut that sold snacks and drinks. Tennis courts lined a long walkway, and there was an outdoor playground. Though her grandchildren were too old for that, she could appreciate it nonetheless. Walk indoors and you'd find another (smaller) pool, this one heated. There was an indoor café that sold such things as smoothies and grilled cheese sandwiches for the kids. There were also more tennis courts as well as a workout room with treadmills and elliptical machines and spinning bikes. There was a basketball court that Ben and Tyler frequented as well as two racquetball courts. Though the water of the lake at home was inviting, this facility got the kids out of the house and together with children they knew, whether the outing was planned or they happened to find a friend who had come to the pool for the day.

Caroline bemoaned the fact that she wasn't able to utilize most of what this facility had to offer, but her grandchildren loved coming here, and it passed the afternoons nicely. It also helped to keep Annie occupied, and today was no exception. Annie splashed in the outdoor pool, and Caroline treated her to some french fries with ketchup. Audrey came with Grace, and though the two girls gleefully ran off to be by themselves, Audrey didn't stay with the women. She had Grace's sister, Sophia, with her and ventured to the indoor pool.

By four o'clock in the afternoon, Caroline was beyond exhausted. She texted Ben asking him and Tyler to meet her in the lobby by four thirty and went looking for Hannah in an effort to rally her up and head home. It would take at least a half an hour to have Annie use the restroom again, dress her, and pack to go.

At home, the kids draped their wet towels over the back deck's balustrade. Caroline guided Annie indoors and took her immediately into the downstairs half bathroom as soon as they entered the house. She simply didn't want to take any chances, and she knew she'd be making dinner soon and thus her attention would be diverted elsewhere.

With Annie's attention happily on the television set and Ben and Hannah occupied, Caroline allowed herself a few minutes of respite at the kitchen table with a cup of warm chamomile tea with honey. During the summer months, the children's extracurricular activities waned considerably, but Hannah still played the violin. Though during the school months she'd had lessons on both Tuesday and Thursday evenings, Caroline was finding it increasingly difficult to transport her to and from with Annie in tow, so Hannah now took violin lessons on Tuesday nights alone. Ben had only a summer soccer program he'd committed himself to, and this would occur tonight, Wednesday. This necessitated an early dinner for the family. Sam would meet his family on the soccer field and take over Caroline's responsibilities so she could head back home for some much-needed relaxation time.

When she lifted her mug and the last drop of tea was tasted on her tongue, Caroline heavily stood from the kitchen table to start on dinner. She'd make a tofu curry tonight—a simple meal that was very easy to make and provided leftovers. The tofu was frying in the skillet when she heard Hannah exclaim, "No, Mom!"

Caroline whipped her head around in the direction of the living room and saw Annie walking out the back door and onto the deck. This lock was one in which Annie was still able to succeed in turning upon occasion, and one of the children must have forgotten to slip the new upper lock (installed by Sam so Annie couldn't meander outside) in place when they reentered the house after hanging their wet towels to dry.

Caroline dropped the stainless steel spatula onto the black granite of the countertop and left the frying tofu on the stovetop, not even bothering to turn the heat down—she needed every second she could muster to reach her daughter before she fell down the narrow, rickety wooden stairs of the deck.

"Sorry, Grammie," Hannah said, her bottom lip beginning to tremble with guilt. "I wasn't paying attention."

"It's okay," Caroline said hastily as she ran past her granddaughter to catch up to Annie outside. "It's okay," she called again.

Annie was at the top of the stairs, one foot listlessly

hanging limp in the air above the first step leading to the grass below. Caroline grabbed her arm and pulled her back. "Not right now, Annie," she said. "I'm making dinner."

"Pizza?" Annie asked.

Caroline shook her head. "No, honey, not pizza."

"Want . . . want . . . woof." Annie mimed a dog panting.

"We can't go see Pumpkin right now, Annie. I'm making dinner."

"Pizza?"

"No," Caroline repeated. "Not pizza."

She led Annie back indoors where the smell of burned tofu filled the air and smoke from the skillet rose thickly to embrace its surroundings.

"UGH!" Caroline clicked the door's upper lock in place and ran to the stove. "Oh . . ." Caroline worried. "Shit!"

"I'm—" Hannah began to quiver. "I'm sorry, Gram!"

"It's not your fault, Hannah," Caroline called with a bit of exasperation as she took the spatula to the tofu and peeled it from the bottom of the skillet. When Hannah began to cry, Caroline turned the burner off and removed the skillet. She walked to her granddaughter, placing her hands on her cheeks and bending down to eye level in consolation.

"It's NOT your fault, Hannah," she repeated with conviction. "Look at me."

Hannah raised her brown eyes, so much like Caroline's. So much like Annie's.

Caroline held them intently with her own. "It's not your fault." Hannah's tears were plentiful, but she bit her bottom lip and nodded her head, indicating to Caroline that, even if she didn't believe Caroline's words, she was at least listening to them.

Annie was moving toward the mudroom. Had Caroline locked the door? It was a habit to do so, but just then, she wasn't entirely convinced, and so she released Hannah's wet cheeks and ran to her daughter again.

The door was locked. And this one, being the lock on a thick garage door, was too strong for Annie to twist all the way.

Once Annie was situated in front of the TV once again, Caroline went back to the stove and her now cooling burned tofu cubes. She turned the burner back on, this time to low, and repositioned the skillet on the stove. She added two glass jars of curry sauce and a full large package of frozen mixed vegetables. She'd apologize for the tofu. She stirred until everything was incorporated and warm, turning her head to look behind her often to be sure her daughter was still in the living room. Luckily, the open concept of the home's floor plan allowed her to do so.

"Dinner," Caroline called from the kitchen. Hannah couldn't be seen from Caroline's position at the stove, so she assumed her granddaughter had gone upstairs to her room. She knew Ben had been in his room since shortly after they returned home from the pool.

"Ben," she called. "Hannah. Dinner's ready."

Footsteps on the stairs and her grandchildren were in sight.

"Smells good, Gram," Ben complimented.

"Thanks," Caroline said. "Can you get your mother for me?" While Ben went to the living room to retrieve his mother, Caroline used the spatula to plonk some tofu curry into four bowls and then dug spoons into each one. Hannah helped her bring them to the table.

"Gram," Ben called. "She's sleeping."

"No, no," Caroline called back. "If she sleeps, your father and I will never get her to sleep when we'd like to tonight. Could you wake her up, please?"

Ben brought his groggy mother to the kitchen and pushed her chair closer to the table once she had seated herself, and Caroline fastened her bib to her neck. Annie lifted her spoon and managed to get most of the concoction into her mouth, spilling only a small amount. The others began to eat.

Annie ate for a while longer and left the table on her own accord when she was through, saying nothing to her family. Caroline dropped her spoon and removed her daughter's bib. She led her to the kitchen sink, where she could more easily wipe her mouth and hands. Hannah had ceased her chewing and watched her grandmother care for her mom. Ben averted his eyes and paid entirely too much attention to the bowl of food before him at the table. He often did this when his mother was finished with a meal.

Caroline knew that the children were young. She knew that Hannah was just barely eleven years old; that, though she had done well enough accepting her mother's illness, she was still confused and simply trying to acclimate to a different life-style, a different family dynamic, as best she could. She couldn't fault her for this no matter how much she wished she'd had more help throughout any given day.

She couldn't fault Ben, either. At fifteen, the boy had enough to worry about with high school, with hormones, with puberty. He had friends he was making, societal expectations he was attempting to explore, to figure out. No young man should have to also figure out how to live with an ill mother, a mother who, as she put it herself, had a "sick brain."

A mother who presented more like a child than her teenage son had for years.

Caroline understood this all and she was sympathetic to it, really.

She was just tired.

So very tired.

Caroline emptied the now clean dishwasher and placed its contents in their appropriate places in the cupboards. Annie was wandering the first floor but so far wasn't doing anything unsafe. Caroline broke for a moment and convinced Annie to sit on the living room couch. Caroline took her cell phone out of the back pocket of her shorts and turned it on to the camera setting. Annie now lacked the ability to turn a phone on by herself—numbers and passwords eluded her, and she wouldn't maintain her thumb's position on the home key long enough for the phone to recognize that it was her, so Sam had gotten rid of Annie's phone a while ago—but she could randomly swipe left and right. Annie busied herself on Caroline's phone now, looking at photos of Pumpkin and of her family.

Caroline asked Ben to wash the skillet and fill the dishwasher with dinner dishes.

With the dishes done, they were set to leave the house for Ben's soccer game. Caroline coaxed Annie to the bathroom before they left. They once again piled into the car, this time with a bag containing a change of clothes for Annie and a sweatshirt in case there was a chill in the summer night's air. The family headed eight minutes down the road to the soccer field at the elementary school.

Caroline didn't mind these nights, and she found them to be an easier, more manageable portion of her Wednesdays. A metal gate circled the entire circumference of the field, and Annie rarely attempted to climb over, and even when she did, she was far from successful.

Ben ran off to play, ball in hand, cleats on his large feet. Hannah spotted a girl she knew from school, and the two youngsters sat down picking blades of grass and chatting cordially. Annie began to wander and Caroline simply followed, attempting to converse with Annie until Sam arrived half an hour later.

"Hey, Caroline," he greeted her, looking rather haggard from his day at the office.

"Hi, Sam," she replied. "Did you have a good day?"

"It was a bit hectic, actually. But I'm sure it was nothing like the day you had." He winked at his mother-in-law.

"I'm tired," Caroline admitted. "If you don't mind, I'm

going to rush off. I'd love nothing more right now than a cup of hot tea and the house to myself."

"Of course," Sam said empathetically.

Caroline said her goodbyes to both Annie and Hannah (Ben was in the midst of his game) and climbed into her car. As soon as her bottom touched the cushiony seat, she grasped the steering wheel tightly with the palms of her hands and let out a sigh of relief.

She wasn't getting any younger, was she? Though she would do anything for her daughter and her family, long, tiring days such as these were not what she'd had in mind when she had thought of her retirement years ago.

At home, she pulled into the driveway. She lifted her purse from the center console and deposited her keys in an inside pocket. She opened the garage door with the remote and walked indoors.

It was quiet in the house.

Blessedly quiet.

Caroline filled the silver kettle with water and placed it on the stove's burner. She turned the knob to high and walked into the living room. Unlocking the back door both on the handle and at the top, she opened it wide and stepped into the inviting, cool evening air. She closed her eyes, breathed deeply.

The wind rustled softly, playfully tickling her neck with the strands of her hair. She lifted her face, felt the sun upon her skin, heard the birds chirping their evening song. Across the lake, the laughter of children.

Opening her eyes, Caroline walked forward and sat on the cushion of a wicker chair on the deck. She rested her heels on the footrest, crossed her arms upon her bosom, and gazed at the twinkling water before her. A yellow kayak passed by. A swimmer, too, arms extending, hands scooping. A neon pink bubble bobbed in the water behind them, announcing their presence to others.

Caroline breathed.

In.

Out.

A tear trickled down her cheek.

A child's squeal across the lake.

The motor of a boat starting, then a child screaming with glee as they were pulled on a tube attached with a hefty rope at the back of the boat.

Caroline had visited often in the summertime when she was living across town. Had witnessed on many occasions her grandchildren in their thick, large tube. Had seen the delight upon their faces as they were pulled, yanked, spun.

They hadn't been tubing yet this season. Caroline didn't think they would. The days passed by and the weekends crept up on them, passing before they knew they had begun.

Another tear worked its way from the corner of her eye to her upper cheek, trickling down, then landing with a warm plop on her bare forearm.

Listening to the laughter of children, watching the waves the boat produced land on the sandy shore, feeling the sun, the wind upon her face, Caroline wept, uninhibited.

She wept even as the teakettle shrilly announced its contents were boiling. She wept as she stood from the wicker chair and poured the water over honey and a teabag in a mug.

She wiped the bottom of her eyes with her fingers as the tea steeped on the counter.

By the time she brought her hot mug back outdoors and sat down to enjoy the warm liquidy taste of chamomile, she had made a definitive decision, heartbreaking though it was.

She couldn't do this any longer.

She loved her daughter immeasurably. She felt nauseated to think of her entering a care facility, was devastated at the thought of her daughter no longer being with her family, but it was because of this love, too, that she knew it must be done.

She would never forgive herself if Annie was harmed on her watch.

She was tormented by conflict, an inner tumult. Guilt for feeling she was no longer able to care for one so loved, a woman such a part of her very being, yet, within the depths of her soul, she knew it was a decision, a step, that was inevitable. Had been inevitable since the day of Anne's diagnosis.

Sam would be heartbroken. The children would be shattered.

But what was she to do?

Caroline lifted her mug, sipped, and felt the warm liquid spread within.

She allowed herself to weep, to feel, to lament the next step in Annie's plummeting decline, a step that would even more greatly affect her family.

She sat there on the deck in thought, cradling her cup between her palms, the tips of her fingers laced together, until she heard a vehicle in the driveway.

Sam.

She'd have to tell Sam. And she'd have to tell him tonight before she lost her nerve, before she changed her mind and convinced herself she could care for her daughter indefinitely.

The mudroom door opened, and she heard the children come barreling through, Ben bouncing his soccer ball in the hallway, Hannah talking animatedly to her father.

Sam laughing at her antics.

He wouldn't be laughing much longer.

Caroline had left the deck door open, and Annie walked outdoors.

"Hi!" she said cheerily.

"Hi, honey," Caroline replied.

"Thing . . . got . . ." Annie trailed off, her eyes glued to the water. She began walking toward the deck's stairs. Caroline placed her mug on a small wicker table with a glass top that nestled next to the chair she was sitting in and stood to grab her daughter.

"Let's head back inside," she suggested.

"I . . . I . . ." Annie attempted to wrestle herself away from her mother. She wasn't rough, but she was driven.

"Hey, Annie." Sam had walked outdoors to join the women. "Maybe a bath is a good idea right now while the kids are busy? You know, since you were in the chlorine today and all." He approached his wife, placed a large hand on her shoulder.

"What do you think, babe?" he asked. "Bath time?"

"Okay," Annie said. She didn't sound convinced and her face betrayed her disapproval, but Sam had a way with Annie, a soft demeanor, a consoling presence.

Even as Annie's brain was failing her, Caroline was convinced the attraction that had always been there between the two of them was still there. Perhaps altered, but still there. Her daughter knew. Knew that this man before her was a wonder, was special.

Perhaps she could still feel his love? Caroline hoped that wasn't just wishful thinking, but even so . . .

"Sam, I'll take her up," Caroline said.

"I've got it," Sam protested.

"I know you're willing, and I appreciate that very much," Caroline continued. "But you've been working all day and I know your job is stressful."

"Not as stressful as a full day at home, I'm sure," Sam said with a smile.

Caroline grinned back, feeling seen, supported.

"Thanks, Sam," Caroline said. "I've got it tonight. Thanks for the rest. You still need to eat dinner, but I'd love for you to take over at bedtime."

"Deal," Sam agreed.

Caroline led Annie back indoors and upstairs to the bathroom. She shut the door behind her and turned the faucet on in the bathtub.

When Annie was situated into a standing position, Caroline gently, lovingly, scrubbed. She watched the water stream down her daughter's back, down her slightly sagging bottom, down the thighs that had become increasingly thick with time and an insatiable appetite.

She brought the cloth to Annie's chest and her sagging breasts. The breasts that had nourished two beautiful children. Down her extended stomach, the stretch marks evident, nestled comfortably in her pale skin. Across the moles that had appeared recently to mark her transition into middle age. The cloth moved farther down, touched her hips, then her thighs. Annie tried to move, giggling at something, though Caroline was ignorant as to what her daughter found so humorous. The cloth continued its descent until it hit the water.

"Okay, Annie, could you sit down for me?" Caroline helped her daughter sit, then lifted her legs out of the water so she could scrub. Forget shaving. She had given up on that a few months ago when she had nicked her daughter one too many times. Annie was pale of complexion, and the hair on her legs was light and scarce, anyway.

Caroline leaned back and sat on her heels, her knees cracking in the process. She rubbed her forearm over her cheek, attempting to remove the strands of hair that had stuck. All she succeeded in accomplishing was making her cheek wet and the strands stick even more fiercely. She moved the cloth to her left hand and brushed at the strands with her wet fingertips.

Now her cheek was itchy.

"Okay, hair time," Caroline announced.

When through, Caroline brought the tip of her finger to Annie's chin and gently pushed so Annie would look at her. "It's time to stand," she said. When Annie made no move-ment, Caroline stood herself, her knees again protesting the transition. She placed her hands under Annie's shoulders and gently guided her to a standing position and out of the tub. She rubbed a thick, clean bath towel over Annie's body and hair and led her to the bedroom, where she opened a dresser drawer and took out an adult diaper. She helped Annie dress into her nightclothes and brought her back downstairs, where Sam, Hannah, and Ben were playing Uno Attack.

As Ben was often in his room these days, Caroline intuited that Sam had probably had to coax his son into playing this game tonight.

She knew this used to be one of Annie's favorite games to play with her family. She so wished her daughter had the ability to join in just now, had the ability to converse, laugh, tease.

Recognize numbers.

Recognize colors.

Fan seven cards in her hand.

"Hi, Mom," Hannah said as she looked up from the cards she was holding.

Annie smiled at the small gathering at the kitchen table, then walked into the living room.

"Would you like some TV?" Caroline asked as she followed in her daughter's wake.

Annie smiled. "TV," she repeated.

Caroline found the remote while Annie sat on the couch. She turned the television set on and settled on an old Mickey Mouse cartoon.

"I'm exhausted, Sam," she said as she reentered the kitchen. "I'm going to head to bed early." She looked at her son-in-law at the table with his children, haggard, in desperate need of a haircut. The past months hadn't been good to him. His hair was considerably grayer now, and his eyes were lined with wrinkles and puffy, dark bags. She determined at this moment that although she had convinced herself earlier that Sam needed to know of her decision straightaway, she wouldn't have the much-needed conversation about Annie with him tonight. She'd save that for the weekend, when they had more time to process and grieve together.

"Yes," Sam said. "Yes, of course! We've got this, Caroline.

Really." He stood, placed his cards facedown on the tabletop. "Thank you so much for today. The kids said they had a great time at the club."

Caroline smiled wearily.

"Good night," Sam said. He reached for his mother-in-law. She knew he was only going to touch her arm, his way of showing appreciation, but she moved forward, wrapped her arms around his neck, and brought him in for an embrace. He stiffened slightly, but soon relaxed and returned the affection.

"Good night, Sam," Caroline said as she lifted her hands and patted his cheeks.

Caroline kissed Hannah and hugged Ben.

"Love you, Grammie," Hannah said.

"I love you, too. Both of you." She paused for a moment, looked at Sam. "All of you."

Caroline turned, walked forward. She rounded the corner and entered her makeshift bedroom, closing the door behind her. She stood for a moment, unmoving, looking out the window onto the front yard.

Caroline took a step, slow and unsteady. Then another. She pushed the button on a small speaker that was connected to her phone. She then took her phone out of her back pocket and clicked on her Spotify playlists. A touch of her finger and her Yo-Yo Ma station began.

She pushed the volume button up. Up some more.

She recognized the music instantly, a tune entitled "*Dinner.*"

The cello played. Entered.

She closed her eyes.

Listened.

With each push of the bow, with each movement upon the strings, the melody filled her.

She opened her eyes to her bedroom, tears streaming.

The music enveloped her, surrounded her, clutched her in

its melodic embrace. She felt it inside, running through her, pulling her.

Calling to her.

She stepped back, sat on her bed, the cushion soft below her.

She closed her eyes once again, tears wet upon her cheeks.

She brought her feet to rest upon the bed, her heels against her bottom, her chin resting on her raised knees.

Her arms hugged her shins. Her eyes were still closed, but the tears continued to flow.

She let them.

The cello played; her heart answered.

Her soul mourned.

Grieved.

Loved.

Memories: Annie, doughy rolls of fat on her baby thighs, looking at her mother with big, beautiful brown eyes. Smiling. Laughing. Reaching.

Annie learning to walk, wobbly, unsteady steps toward the outstretched arms of her father, the giggles as she'd fall on her cloth-diapered bottom, her father's deep-voiced words of encouragement.

Annie's first day of school, her hair in pigtails, her favorite white-and-blue-checkered dress, red buttons down the front, puffed short sleeves. Immense smile.

Annie on her pogo ball at the playground—an awkward child's contraption of the '80s that Caroline had attempted to jump with, failing miserably—singing Madonna's "*Like a Virgin*" at the top of her lungs to Caroline's utter mortification.

Annie's tenth birthday party held in the backyard of their home. Surrounded by friends at the wooden picnic table, blowing out her candles, making a wish, her future holding so much promise.

Annie bringing her first boyfriend home, a gangly boy of fifteen. Kind and awkward.

Annie's face when she told her mother about a boy she'd met at a college party. A boy named Sam.

Annie's wedding. The look of pure love and adoration she gave her new husband with those big brown eyes of hers as Sam held her tightly and danced her slim, lithe body around the floor to Ben Folds's "*The Luckiest.*"

The Willow Tree Angel and Annie's pregnancy.

The birth of her first grandchild. The scene unfolding before her: Annie, Sam, Ben; John, who was gone now. The tears, the love permeating throughout the small room.

Hannah. Three generations of strong, loving, healthy females. The completion of a happy family.

Caroline wasn't aware when the door to her room creaked open. She wasn't aware when Sam entered, shut the music off, and gently laid a blanket over her sleeping body to rest below her chin.

She didn't feel her son-in-law sweep the stiff strands of hair from her cheek.

Didn't feel the soft kiss upon her forehead, like a butterfly taking flight into the dawn of a new day.

CHAPTER SEVENTEEN

Sam

"*M*an, that suck." Hector was sitting next to Sam at support group on a Friday evening in late August, a week before the kids were due to start another year of school.

"Yeah," Sam said. "We've packed her things, and Caroline, the kids, and I will head over Sunday." Sam shook his head. "I'm still having trouble trying to process the fact that as of this weekend, my wife will no longer be living in our home."

"It's really hard, isn't it?" Nan asked, her hands folded in her lap, her black hair held back in a ponytail at the base of her neck. Sam knew her father had been living in an assisted care facility for several months now.

Sam nodded, leaning forward in his metal chair to place his hands between his tightly clenched thighs. "I'm just having trouble with it all, really. I mean, I knew this day would come. I did. And I knew with Annie it would come sooner than anticipated because of the fast progression of the disease, but . . . even with a wife that's been so far from the wife I married and the woman I've known . . . I just . . . she's there. She's home. We may not have held a meaningful conversation together for quite some time now, but she's there. I can still look at her, I can still touch her." He paused for a moment before continuing.

"The facility is half an hour from our home, so I know I can visit her, and I'll be visiting her often, but I'm used to coming home after work and having her there. Caroline and I are both used to caring for Annie, making sure she's safe and loved. Caroline is just entirely too overwhelmed now, and I get it. I really do. This is all just too much. Annie's not safe, and no matter how much we want to provide an environment for her that is conducive to her needs, we just can't anymore. We just can't."

Sam looked up at Nan, then to Dotty, who still attended the FTD support group meetings even though her husband, Bill, had been deceased for a year now.

"But even though I know we can't help Annie anymore, even though I know this is the best thing for us all, I can't help but think that there's no way they can love her like we do." Sam's bottom lip began to tremble and his nostrils flared slightly. "I know they'll take care of her, and I know that she probably can't tell the difference if someone is loving or not, but damn it! This is my wife! She deserves more than just a bath and someone giving her food. And I can't help but wonder, is that all she'll get there?"

The tears were coming now; he could feel them. A lone droplet trickled from his eye and he wiped it away.

"No," Sam said. "No. I know they'll be good to her. We did a lot of research, and this is supposed to be a really good place. Caroline is helping with the cost. She's been a rock, really. I'm not sure I'd pull through this without her. My own parents aren't in the picture much, and I don't talk to them often at all. They know about Annie, but they haven't been up to visit in a couple of years. And we don't bother going down.

It's just more stressful. And attempting to get some sort of financial assistance through this all has been a nightmare."

"Mmm-hmm . . ." Dotty confirmed. "Was for me, too, when Bill was first diagnosed. Bullshit, I tell ya!"

"I got the Medicaid to help. Had to fight to get it, but my Doris got it now. It help us," Hector said.

"See, I've had to fight, too," Sam said. "And for the most part, things didn't go my way. I didn't qualify for Medicaid." He shook his head. "But through it all, I was able to purchase some long-term care insurance, so that's helping. In a last-ditch effort, I tried to take out some of my 401(k) money, but the particular company my place of employment goes with was going to penalize me pretty seriously for doing so. I ended up getting a loan. I borrowed against the amount in my account right now. I have to pay it back—and soon—or I owe taxes and a penalty fee, but I really didn't know what else to do. I'm just taking it day by day and hoping in the long run that I don't have to sell the house. I haven't done that yet because of my kids. My kids need as much normalcy in their lives as I can possibly give them, and this house is what they know. And I need to keep them at their school and in the town I live in. I just have to. So I'll make it work somehow." Sam spoke the words out loud as much to convince himself as to convey his hardships to these men and women who had become, in the last year, incredibly supportive friends.

Sam looked around the room, saw heads nodding and pursed lips.

He wasn't alone.

"I'm really sorry for all of this." Grace's aged hoarse yet soft voice sounded at his right. She reached over and patted Sam's forearm, his hands still clenched between his thighs. He looked at her, into her cloudy hazel eyes, the embedded wrinkles in her worn, mottled skin. Her look was intense and one of extreme empathy. Though her situation was quite different from his own, he knew this empathy was genuine.

"Thanks, Grace," he said, another tear trickling from his eye to leave a wet stroke down his cheek.

"Okay," Sam said. "Okay. That's enough about me for now. Dotty, last time we met, you said your youngest was waiting to hear if he had been accepted into that graduate program, right?"

"Ah, yeah," Dotty confirmed.

"And?"

Dotty's smile was indication enough that the news she was about to convey would veer the conversation in a more positive direction. "He got in," she said.

"Oh, yay!" Nanette exclaimed by her side. A few hands clapped, smiles abounded.

"That's great news," Sam said. "Congratulations to him."

"Thanks," Dotty said, her smile widening. "Now my Jimmy, he's gonna make a damn difference. We had never heard of FTD before his father was diagnosed, I can tell you that, but it fucked up his childhood. Fucked us all up. Shit!" She shook her head with disgust. "Both my boys, they've learned to heal now, they're much older than they were when their father first got sick. But we both had this idea in our head about how our kids were gonna be raised, and FTD blew us a new one. Jimmy says he's gonna go into research. They're learning more these days, we all know that, but the research still needs to come. We need to know more and this needs to end. All of it. All dementia. Fuck dementia!"

Dotty raised her fist in the air. "Fuck dementia!" she said again, louder. Eyes creased, countenance determined.

Nanette raised her fist in solidarity, looked at Dotty beside her. "Fuck dementia," she yelled, her smile wide.

Dotty's eyes softened as she smiled back.

Hector and George, the group's burly moderator, were next. "Fuck dementia."

Frail Grace beside Sam, Grace with her white hair and

gentle demeanor, raised her fist in the air. "Fuck dementia!" she rasped, then giggled abashedly.

Sam laughed, then raised both fists and leaped from his chair and shouted, "Fuck dementia!"

All six chairs scratched the hardwood floor as bodies propelled forward and shot up, erect and fierce. "FUCK DEMENTIA," they all yelled, smiles broad on their faces, tears trickling down Sam's cheeks and upper lip to land in his open mouth, the saltiness stinging his tongue.

"FUCK DEMENTIA!"

CHAPTER EIGHTEEN

Ben

*B*en woke the following morning to laughter in the backyard. At fifteen he was sleeping later and later on the weekends. He liked his sleep. When he was sleeping, he didn't have to think about the fact that his family was breaking, didn't have to think about all the shit that was going down.

Didn't have to think about the fact that his mother was leaving tomorrow.

He closed his eyes, tried to get back to sleep, but it was ten o'clock in the morning, after all, and his body was rested well enough. His urgings to slumber further proved futile.

Ben lifted the light comforter from his waist and sat up in bed. Rubbing his eyes, he placed his feet on the floor and walked to the oversized window that overlooked the backyard. His father was chasing Hannah in the grass. Hannah would periodically look over her shoulder as she ran. A giant smile adorned her face, and Ben could tell his father was chuckling by his wide grin, by the slight bob of his head and the subtle stooping of his shoulders.

His mother was sitting on an Adirondack chair in the sand at the water's edge, his grandmother by her side.

Ben slowly made his way to his bedroom door, opened it, and stepped into the upstairs hallway. He didn't particularly want to leave the comfort of his room, but he was hungry, so made his way down the stairs and into the kitchen. While he was preparing a cheese omelet, his father opened the back door and entered the living room.

"Ben!" he enthused, apparently in an ebullient mood. "Good morning, sleepyhead."

"Morning," Ben answered.

"I was just coming in for a snack. I was going to bring something out for everyone to enjoy, maybe make some lemonade while I was in here. Why don't you bring your breakfast out and enjoy it with us, yeah?"

"I'm okay."

His father approached him, waited for Ben to look up from the stove. "Today's our last day with your mom, Ben. I know you don't want to talk about this, but there we have it. It's our last day with her here. And I want this to be a family day, okay? We were thinking of ice cream cones, the big ones that drip with chocolate sauce we used to make for you kids when you were younger, and"—he paused—"waterskiing and tubing."

Ben flipped his omelet and removed the pan from the burner. He turned the stove off and looked at his dad again. "Can't," he replied nonchalantly. "Have to be thirteen to be a lookout. Hannah's only eleven, and Gram can't leave Mom alone."

"Yeah," his dad said. "Well . . ."

Ben raised his eyebrows, waited for his father to finish.

"I don't care today."

"What do you mean you don't care?"

"I mean just that," his father said. "I don't care about the rules today. Honestly, I don't give a shit if I get in trouble. We need this."

His father rarely swore in front of his children, not even now that Ben was fifteen. This in itself defined the gravity of the situation, how determined his father was to enjoy their last day with his mom, to commit this to memory.

"Mom won't remember," Ben said, forlorn. He pulled a plate from an upper cabinet and scooted the omelet onto it.

"No," his father replied. "She won't remember. But Ben?" Ben looked from his plate to his father. "We will. We'll remember." He paused, looked at his son.

"So," he said. "You in?"

Ben pierced his omelet with a fork, took a large bite into his mouth. "I guess," he mumbled, chewing.

"That's the attitude," his dad said as he tousled his son's hair, the son who, within the last year, had grown an additional three inches.

"Jesus, Dad," Ben protested. "I'm not eight anymore."

"Nah," his father replied. "But you're still my son!" He grabbed Ben's neck with his arm, wrestled his son's head to his chest.

"Cut it out!" Ben laughed. "I'm gonna choke!"

When his father let go and Ben stood erect once again, they were both chuckling.

"I'm going to get that snack and make the lemonade I promised. Meet us outside?"

Ben nodded his head. "Yeah," he said. "Okay."

The sunny August morning waned and lunch arrived. Instead of the typical fare of sandwiches or macaroni and cheese, Ben's father brought a tray to the beach and rested it on a stand that had been erected next to the Adirondack chairs. Cookies-and-cream ice cream (Ben's favorite) along with sugar cones and Hershey's syrup.

His father scooped a generous portion of the ice cream

onto a cone and poured a large amount of the chocolate syrup onto the top. He handed the cone off to Ben's mom.

"She's gonna get so messy!" Hannah squealed, laughing.

"And I don't care one bit," their father answered. "She's got her bathing suit on, doesn't she? We'll just take a little dip in the water afterward."

His mom held her cone clumsily in between both hands and took a large bite out of the top. When she pulled back, Ben saw chocolate on her nose, her cheeks, and her chin, watched as the syrup ran down her hands and dribbled onto her sitting thighs. When she was finished, Ben knew, his mother would be covered. He'd seen it plenty of times with food before, practically every day now, in fact. She'd have syrup and ice cream on her face, her hands, her chest, the red tankini bathing suit she wore now that the sun had risen and warmed up the early-afternoon air. Although Ben had seen pictures of his mother wearing a bikini in her earlier years, back when she and his dad had first met, her body fit, firm, he had always known a woman who was more modest and wore one-piece suits with stylish cover-ups around her waist that fell to mid-thigh when she wasn't submerged in the water. Even a tankini was something unfamiliar, but he knew his grand-mother had purchased this particular suit to make it easier to help his mother in the bathroom.

The bathroom.

She couldn't even piss and shit without a reminder anymore.

Nope. Not going there.

"Earth to Ben." His father was holding out a large cone. Ben took it.

"Syrup?" his dad asked and Ben nodded.

His father squirted an immense amount of chocolate onto the top of his mounded ice cream.

"Stop!" Ben shouted with a chuckle. "It's getting all over the place."

"Better hurry," his father said gleefully. "Like when you were a kid. Hurry! Lick the syrup before it gets all over your hands." He was laughing now and his laugh was infectious. Ben laughed himself as he tipped his head to the side and licked the dribbling chocolate syrup. It had already found its way to his hand and was dripping down his wrists, but he found he didn't care. For just this moment he remembered what it was like to be eight years old again with no worries but whether or not he'd beat the syrup before it reached his skin.

Hannah was licking her cone, and his gram was enjoying one, too. His father scooped the last of the ice cream onto a sugar cone for himself, squirted syrup on top, and began to eat.

The five family members ate their ice cream in companionable silence, then—because they were fitted into swimsuits —waded into the water to wash off and cool down. His father led his mother, and she followed willingly, splashing with the palms of her hands and wetting his dad. It didn't upset his father in the least, as Ben had assumed it would. On the contrary, his father was laughing, splashing himself. Hannah joined in; then even his gram gently splashed the water.

Well, damn! He might as well join in, too.

Ben splashed, jumped like a little kid. Hannah squealed when Ben splattered her face with the warm summer water of the lake.

And so it went for a few minutes longer.

"Well," his dad said, "what do you say? Boat time?"

"Yay!" Hannah exclaimed. "I want to tube, Dad. We haven't been at all this summer, and I can't wait!"

"Then I guess you're first, Hannah Banana. Why don't you and your brother grab the towels, and I'll go get the tube. Ben, do you want to ski?"

"Yeah."

"Okay, then. I'll grab the skis, too." His father made his way toward the garage, where the large, inflatable water tube was stored as well as the skis. He came back shortly thereafter, awkwardly lugging the procured items. Ben and Hannah had grabbed the towels and plopped them down on the metal dock and were now unbuttoning the navy blue protective boat cover. Sam discarded the tube and skis onto the sand and joined his children. When all large snaps were unfastened, Sam threw the heavy blanket onto the dock, and the kids climbed into the front of the boat. Sam grabbed the tube and skis and placed them heavily into the back. He then untethered the boat from the thick rope attached to the dock and stepped into the driver's seat.

Starting the engine, Sam slowly backed the boat away from the dock.

"Bye, Grammie!" Hannah called. "Bye, Mom!"

Caroline waved at her grandchildren from her perch on the shore. Their mother sat at the water's edge, feet kicking, sending droplets into the air. Her dark blond hair—to her shoulders now that she hadn't had it cut in a while—was stringy and wet, and strands stuck to her cheeks and forehead. She paid no heed to her children.

As Sam sped up, Ben closed his eyes, felt the wind in his damp hair, on his face. He lifted his chin, faced the sky. The bright sunlight seeped through his thin eyelids.

He felt unhindered.

Free.

His dad looped the small lake twice before coming to a stop and cutting the engine.

"All right," his father said. "Hannah, you're up." He dropped the large, sturdy tube into the water and attached the end of the thick rope to the back of the boat. He leaned over and held the tube in place with one hand while guiding Hannah with his other. Hannah stepped onto the back of the boat in her swimsuit and life jacket and leaped onto the tube, bending her knees and grabbing the black handles with her hands to catch and maintain her balance. She then pushed her feet from under her and lay down, her stomach hovering over the large hole in the center of the tube, her feet dangling above the water, and her hands continuing to hold tightly to the black handles before her.

Sam slowly uncoiled the thick rope and placed it in the water. When done, he started the boat back up. Hannah gave him a thumbs-up to indicate she was ready, and Ben moved from the front of the boat to the back to sit and keep watch on his sister.

"Here we go!" his dad yelled.

The boat jerked slightly and the rope pulled taut. The front of the tube was propelled out of the water. Hannah held tightly as the boat sped up and the momentum forced the tube to glide faster and then faster on the water's surface.

Ben watched his sister from his perch on a white seat at the back of the boat, saw her gleeful, enormous smile, watched as she blinked repeatedly when droplets of water splashed into her eyes. She began to scream joyfully as their father turned a corner and the tube was launched to the side, sending Hannah over waves formulated from the boat's propellers.

Hannah managed to hold onto her position on the tube—Ben knew how much she hated to be launched off, plummeting into the water—and when her ride was through, Ben reeled her in by the rope.

Hannah stepped onto the back of the boat, soaking, water pouring from her wet body to puddle on the deck. Their father handed her a dry towel, and she wrapped it around her waist and sat down at the front of the boat, smiling.

"Ready?" Sam looked at Ben with a sly grin. Ben knew he was in for it; his father wasn't going to go easy on him this time.

Ben welcomed the challenge.

"Ready," Ben replied. He jumped into the water, the drop in temperature a foot below the surface shocking him momentarily until he resurfaced in his life jacket and his body acclimated. His dad dropped the skis into the water beside him, and when Ben had successfully placed them on his feet, awkward though the task always was, he grabbed onto the handle at the end of the rope his father had thrown into the water to land close by.

Ben lifted his knees so his feet were pointing skyward and the tips of the cumbersome, heavy skis were bobbing out of the water. He positioned the rope between the skis and held on tightly to the handle.

"You good?" his father yelled.

"All set," Ben called back.

A roar of the engine, a jerk, then Ben leaned his body back in the water, tightened his thighs, and stood on the skis.

Waterskiing had come naturally to him. His parents had warned him at the age of ten when he had first attempted to ski that he probably wouldn't stand straightaway, if at all. His mom had told him that she had tried on several occasions and had never succeeded, so when he held onto that handle and stood on his first try, he was surprised at the ease of his transition.

Now, here he was at fifteen, and his transition had been no less simple. It just was. He stood and maintained his balance.

His father sped up; Ben countered with a tighter grip on the handle, the muscles of his body rigid and ready.

His dad turned a corner. Fast.

Ben's skis flew through the wake and his body shot to the side of the boat, yet he didn't falter. His arms, his legs, his torso—they all adapted to the pull, to the waves, to the change in the boat's speed.

He found he was grinning ridiculously.

When his father shot over a wave and Ben leaped out of the water in a jump, he almost lost his balance upon return, but he caught himself. His father slowed down, and Ben had to brace himself as he knew what was coming.

His dad quickly sped up, pitching Ben's body forward. He leaned back, then back farther still.

And caught his balance!

His father was looking over his shoulder, wind tussling his hair. The grin on his face was palpable. Infectious.

Ben laughed.

His father sped up a bit more, then whipped the boat to the side.

Ben was hurled over the wake, his skis leaping into the air once more, but this time there was no catching his balance. When his skis landed on the water's surface, his right foot found purchase before his left and his body lurched to the side. Ben plummeted into the water. Hard.

He resurfaced, shook his head. Breathed deeply.

Then laughed again as he shot his fists into the warm air.

His dad turned the boat around to retrieve him. Ben swam to grab his skis, handed them off to his father in the boat, then climbed the ladder. "That was friggin' awesome," he said.

"Glad you liked it," his dad laughed.

Hannah was giggling at the front of the boat. "He got you good," she said.

"He did," Ben conceded as he looked playfully at his father.

Hannah boarded the tube once again and was sent on another ride. Ben, though beaten up a bit from his fall and the sheer demanding force placed on his muscles from his last go, still opted for one more turn around the lake. His father was a bit more forgiving this second time.

When through, they made their way back to the dock and Sam tethered the boat. They left the thick blue protective covering off in case they wanted to take advantage of the boat's offerings later that day.

The rest of the afternoon progressed splendidly into the evening. There was more swimming, more splashing. Music poured from the outdoor speakers, and several games of cornhole were played in the backyard.

Ben grabbed a snack from inside, then headed back to the beach, where Hannah and their grandmother were sitting in the Adirondack chairs holding hands. No words. They were both gazing over the lake, the music playing in the background.

"We should probably think about dinner," Ben's gram said.

"I suppose we should," his dad agreed. "But I really don't feel like cooking tonight."

"Pizza." Just one word from their mother, but it made them all laugh. Pizza. She had it right tonight.

"Great idea, Annie," his dad said. "Pizza it is. I'll order now."

The pizza arrived forty-five minutes later and they dug in. His dad had to take most of the cheese off the slice he handed to Ben's mom. It was a choking hazard for her now, Ben knew. But she didn't seem to mind, didn't protest at all anyway. She just took the slice and placed the corner in her mouth, tried to bite it off. It took her a while, but eventually she ate the entire slice and reached in the box for another. His dad removed the cheese stealthily even as she was bringing the piece to her mouth.

Dinner ended, and the sun was setting on the horizon, bright and beautiful in its orange and pink hues. Ben sat in the sand of the beach, now dressed in shorts and a sweatshirt, and gazed before him, watched the colors slowly change, then dwindle.

When the stars emerged and the darkness of the night sky began to descend upon them, Ben and his family walked indoors.

"I'm exhausted," Caroline confessed. "Sam, if you don't mind, I'd like to head to bed now."

"Of course not," his dad answered.

"What a beautiful day," his gram said. "A beautiful, wonderful day."

His dad smiled, a bit dispirited now.

Ben could intuit that he was thinking of today's completion and, thus, the dawn of the day in which his wife would no longer be with them at home.

"Good night, everyone," Caroline said.

"Night, Grammie," Hannah answered as she hugged her grandmother.

"Night," Ben said. He allowed his grandmother to embrace him as well, though his reciprocation was a bit more awkward than his sister's.

His gram said good night to their father, and then she walked over to Ben's mom. "I love you, my darling girl," she said.

Ben's mom looked at his grandmother, Ben would give her that, but her face was expressionless. His gram cupped her cheek with the palm of her hand, looked at her daughter wistfully, then leaned in and kissed her on the forehead before turning and walking into her bedroom.

Hannah showered in the upstairs bathroom that she and Ben shared, while their father bathed their mom in the master bath. When Hannah was through, Ben showered as well, then joined his sister on the couch to watch television. When their dad appeared with their mother in tow, he pilfered the TV so he could place a show on that would capture their mother's attention. Ben and Hannah chose to head to their bedrooms for the remainder of the evening.

Ben had been in his room listening to music on his Spotify playlist and drawing with colored pencils and a pad of paper when he heard the melody rising up the stairs.

Ben Folds's "*The Luckiest.*"

He'd heard it before. This was his parents' wedding song. They played it each year on the day of their anniversary.

Why was it so loud? And why was it playing now?

Ben crept down the stairs, turned the corner. His grandmother stood by the wall next to the living room, bending forward slightly and peering surreptitiously beyond the wall. Ben joined her.

His dad held his mother in a loose embrace. His eyes were closed and his chin rested upon the top of her head. His mother's arms were by her side in her pajamas, and her face again held an apathetic expression, but her legs shifted in time with his slow movements as he danced her around in a circle between the couches in the living room.

Ben stood there with his gram as they watched his parents dance. His father's hands on his mom's waist, his chin on her head. His closed eyes that didn't stop the tears from falling down his cheeks to pool with the bathwater still dampening his mother's blond hair.

The song ended, and his father's hands left his mom's waist, traveled to her shoulders, where he held her tighter as they stood together in the middle of the room. His eyes opened and he wept candidly.

His mom extricated herself from his grasp, walked toward the back door that she could (luckily) no longer open on her own, leaving her husband in her wake to stand with his arms crossed over his chest, tears streaming down his face. Shoulders quaking as he lost control of his emotions.

Ben and his gram slowly stepped back. Ben looked worriedly at his grandmother, who wore much the same expression on her own face.

"I'll stay," she whispered. "Just in case your dad needs help. You head back upstairs, Ben." Her words were soft.

Ben nodded and headed for the stairs. He paused, turned back.

"You think he'll be okay?" he asked his grandmother.

"He needs to grieve," she answered. "We'll let him."

Ben turned back, walked to his room. Closed the door behind him. He crawled into bed, rested his head on his pillow, and pulled his light comforter over his body and up to his chin.

He felt cold tonight.

He couldn't process the emotions within.

His father.

His gram.

His sister.

His mother. Gone tomorrow.

He closed his eyes and allowed exhaustion to envelop him, to lull him into a fitful sleep.

CHAPTER NINETEEN

Sam

"Knock knock." Sam poked his head into Annie's room. He saw her sitting in a cushioned chair facing the only window, gazing into the assisted living facility's garden.

He stepped over the door's threshold, walked toward his wife. "How are you today, babe?" he asked. Annie looked up at him, but no emotion registered on her face. Was she trying to figure out who he was?

Over a year had transpired since they had admitted Annie into this home. Her disease had taken its frightful, impenetrable hold, and she had declined tremendously. There were days he felt she was lucid, gave a slight smile when she saw him even. Other days he wasn't so lucky.

"September, huh?" Sam said. "The kids are back in school now." He sat on the edge of Annie's bed. "I know you haven't seen them in a while, Annie, and I'm so sorry for that. I always thought Hannah was pulling through so well, but lately . . . well, lately I've realized that she isn't. She's twelve now, you know? And growing like a weed. She's hit puberty, though your mom had to talk to her about those changes because as soon as I tried to have that conversation, she buckled up and turned bright red." Sam chuckled at the memory, shook his head.

"Speaking of your mom," he continued, "she's doing well. Still living with us, and I still don't know what I'd do without her, really. Steve, my asshole boss, has me working ridiculous hours at work, but I still need this job. It pays well, and although I've looked elsewhere, there's just nothing out there right now with equal pay that I wouldn't have to travel into Boston for. I'm already gone long enough. The kids don't need me commuting to Boston."

Annie looked at him. Her hands were in her lap, and her back was against the wooden backrest of the chair. Her blond hair had become stringy, though it had been cut recently as it rested just below her chin now. Her flower-patterned dress was large, too large for her frame. She had lost weight now that she was having increasing difficulty with the mechanics of chewing and swallowing. Her feet were bare and resting flat on the hard surface of the floor, though Sam was reminded that Annie had always felt most comfortable when her legs were crossed while in a sitting position. She probably didn't know how to do that now.

It was the little things.

Taken away day by day until all those seemingly little things amassed into one enormous plummeting whole that was the remnant of his wife.

Annie said nothing, just continued to stare at her husband.

"Hannah's being twelve still shocks me every day. I wish you knew her, Annie. I mean, really knew her. I know she misses you. I miss you." He paused, searched longingly for a reaction, but when Annie didn't oblige him with one, he continued the one-way conversation.

"I think Caroline's presence in the house has helped tremendously with Hannah. There's only so much I think I can do for a pubescent preteen right now. I'm just so thankful that Caroline and I have an open relationship, that we seem to co-parent well together in your absence. And she's so much like you, Annie. Or I guess I should really say that you were so much like your mom. I see where you got a lot of your mannerisms."

Annie turned her head back to the window and gazed outside. Sam continued to speak. He knew his visits weren't for Annie as much as they were for himself. There was the guilt, of course: the guilt he felt when it had been a little while between visits. But beyond that guilt, he knew he'd take Annie any way she was. This was his wife, and although she often didn't know who he was any longer, he loved her still. Ached for her.

"And it's crazy, Annie," Sam said. "Ben has gotten so damn big! He's sixteen and a half. He's even driving! I can't afford to get a used car for him at all, even though it would be so much easier for him to cart himself around to all those soccer games and practices, but he uses mine if I'm home on a weekend, or he even uses your mother's car. He's still such good friends with Tyler Bower. I see Bitsy a lot. She asks after you. I know she still cares for you, Annie. Very much." He inhaled, smiled dolefully.

"Sixteen. I mean, can you believe that? I know I've told you many times that our son is now sixteen and driving and a junior in high school, but some days I just shake my head, can't believe it.

"And he's good, Annie. He's such a good kid. And he's such a good soccer player. He's had a couple of colleges scouting him and I selfishly hope he gets a scholarship to college. I really do. It would help so much financially. Even a partial scholarship would make me really happy." Sam chuckled.

"Scholarship or not, I hope he goes to college. I know you and I both just kind of assumed our kids would go to college, that it was a natural progression through life for them, at least. I guess maybe because that's what we did? But Ben's been struggling. I really think he's trying to figure life out, you know? He doesn't put much effort into his studies, still says he hates school. He doesn't really put much effort into anything but soccer these days. And his friendship with Tyler. I think Tyler's the glue that holds our son together. I wish I could say I was the one that was able to help Ben through this all, but for some reason, that's not how it's been." Sam paused again, contemplated this.

"I'm just really glad he has Tyler. Maybe when he's with Tyler, he doesn't think about the shitty things in life?

"Anyway," Sam continued, "everyone at support group says hello. I know you don't know these people, but they've become an extended family to me. Dotty still goes, and I'm glad for it. She's a character for sure. Livens things up. Hector's wife seems to be doing well at the home he found for her. She was just admitted and I know it was really hard on him. I don't think he's got anyone other than Doris. He goes home to an empty house in the boonies up north at the end of the day. Definitely makes me appreciate the kids and Caroline. Nan's doing well. Now that her dad's been in that home for a while, she's in school. Wants to work with kids, and I think she'll be good at it. Like you were." Sam sighed, smiling wistfully.

"I don't think Grace's daughter is doing well. It's crazy to me sometimes, you know? To think about the fact that Grace's daughter is so much older than you are. It just puts everything into perspective a bit. Dementia doesn't discriminate. We still end each session with 'Fuck dementia.'" Sam laughed. "I love it!" Sam paused his speech and looked at his wife, at the wrinkles that were increasingly appearing on her forehead and at the corners of her eyes, at her small, dry lips. He studied her, drank her in. He attempted to do so at each visit. He wasn't in denial; he knew their visits were limited.

"Oh, hey, Sam." Bethany was a nurse in her mid-fifties with long graying black hair that she often wore in a bun at the nape of her neck. Sam had gotten to know Bethany quite well as she was often working when he came to visit Annie. Just now she stood in the doorway holding a tray topped with a pudding cup and a chocolate milk box. "I didn't know you were here. Good to see you."

"Yeah," Sam said. "I missed her." He turned back to his wife, who was now looking at the tray in Bethany's arms as the nurse moved farther into the small room.

Bethany smiled brightly. "That I can understand," she said. "I was just about to offer Annie a snack, but would you like to instead?"

"Sure," Sam said. He took the tray from Bethany and sat it next to him on the made-up bed.

"She's been eating really well this week," Bethany informed him. "No coughing, no swallowing issues. It's been really reassuring and so nice to see. I just love Annie."

Sam looked at the bright smile on Bethany's face. She always wore it. Bethany was honestly the most helpful presence in this entire home. She was optimistic and had a loving, caring demeanor. He knew Annie was in good hands when Bethany was working. He also had to chuckle at the fact that Bethany probably took to Annie so well now because for the time the nurse had known his wife, Annie hadn't had emotional outbursts like the time she told a perfect stranger that they were fat, or when she told a new mother that her baby looked like he was about to "blow a big load out of his little asshole." Annie barely said anything anymore and was pretty obliging when asked to do something. In a way, her brain's deterioration had made her care much less hectic, sadly.

"I know you do, Bethany, and I'm so glad for it." Sam said. "We love her, too." He leaned over and grasped his wife's hand, squeezing it gently before letting go.

"Okay," Bethany said. "I'll leave you to it. But you just holler if you need anything and I'll come back soon to check in."

"Thanks, Bethany," Sam said sincerely.

Bethany left the room, and Sam picked up the small plastic cup of chocolate and vanilla pudding. He peeled back the lid and discarded it onto the hard tan tray. Lifting the metal spoon, he scooped a small amount of pudding and brought it toward his wife.

"I know you really like pudding, Annie. I'm glad that's what Bethany brought today. Open up, babe," he instructed softly, kindly.

Annie looked into his eyes. He wasn't sure what thoughts lay beyond that gaze, or even if there were any thoughts, but the simple fact that it was his wife's beautiful brown eyes that were looking at him was enough for today.

He had learned quickly to accept and appreciate the simple pleasures, the simple everyday miracles.

The little things.

Annie opened her mouth slightly, and Sam placed the spoon within. Annie very slowly closed her lips over the metal utensil, and Sam slid it out and back to the plastic container as Annie laboriously swallowed. Sam gave her ample time to do so, and when it appeared she was through, he brought the spoon to her mouth once more, a small amount of pudding resting on top.

After a few bites of pudding, Sam opened the milk container and placed a straw inside. He brought the container to his wife's mouth. She closed her lips over it and took a small sip. The home had found that Annie did well with straws, and although she had to eat slowly, she was still able to chew and swallow her food well as long as it was mashed or soft. Anything with more substance she lacked the capacity to chew well enough.

"Great job, Annie," Sam said. "I'm glad I came today. I

just needed to see you. Sometimes it's a struggle to come, I have to admit. Sometimes I just feel I can't do it, can't see you like this. But other days . . . other days I just need to. I'll try my best to get the kids to visit, I promise, but I know they have a really hard time with it all. I think they're just trying to hold onto the memories of how you used to be. Your mom should be here tomorrow, though."

Annie looked at him blankly, then turned her gaze to the pudding cup in Sam's hand.

"Okay," Sam chuckled. "I can take a clue."

Annie finished her pudding and milk, and Bethany came to check on her.

"She's doing well," Sam said. "But I need to go. I think Caroline's coming tomorrow, and I'll come as soon as I can get back."

"Of course," Bethany said, a smile on her face.

Sam stood from the edge of Annie's bed as Bethany took up the tray. "I have to go, babe," he said to Annie. "I love you so much." He took a step toward his wife and leaned over. He kissed her gently on the forehead, lingering for a moment. He then turned and walked out the door.

Ben was nine and Hannah almost five when the family took a vacation to Acadia National Park in Maine. To save on cost they had decided to camp instead of procuring a hotel room. Even with Airbnb and various other rentals, the cost was a bit high, so they packed the inside of the Odyssey to the roof with a large tent and camping gear as well as food and piled in for the long four-and-a-half-hour drive.

And long it turned out to be. Hannah was not a fan of car rides any longer in duration than twenty minutes, so when the half-hour mark hit the clock on the car's dashboard, she was already asking how much longer it would be.

"A lot longer, Hannah Scrumptious," Annie announced. "And don't

ask again!" She had packed various activity books and music, as well as an audiotape checked out from the library, but these distractions didn't often appease Hannah for long.

They ended up veering off the highway after about two hours and stopping in Freeport, Maine. They exited the car and stretched their legs, ate lunch at a local café where the kids were quite pleased to order grilled cheese sandwiches, and perused the L.L.Bean store. After a bit of shopping, they got large ice cream cones and ate them merrily on a bench on the side of the quaint road in the early-afternoon sunlight. An hour later they piled back into the van to complete the last half of their journey north.

"We're here!" Annie announced from the driver's seat as they found the campground's entrance and drove to their site. A small site, yes, but with a view of the ocean water.

"Oh, this is so wonderful," Annie breathed as she walked to the edge of the campsite and took in the breathtaking view of the glistening water in the distance.

They unpacked the car and spent the rest of the afternoon pitching the large brown tent, hanging a line for wet clothes, and building a fire in the small stone pit where they roasted hot dogs for dinner accompanied by apple slices and potato salad that Annie had prepared at home and packed into the family's large cooler. They'd have to purchase more ice at the office soon to maintain the contents' freshness.

After dinner they decided to walk the campground; they knew somewhere down the narrow one-lane dirt road was a dock with canoes and kayaks. Annie had been eager to explore this area, and there were no complaints from her family.

Hannah took her mother's hand as they began to walk in their shorts and sandals. Annie and Hannah wore sweatshirts, as the sun was descending in the blue summer sky, but Sam and Ben remained comfortable in short sleeves.

After about a quarter of a mile, they saw a small path to their right that led to the water's edge. A rectangular wooden sign with white painted letters that read "To the Dock" with an arrow pointing the direction was staked on a wooden pole before them.

"It's over here," Sam announced, and his family followed him to a set of rickety wooden stairs nestled between large rocks. They descended and came upon the long metal dock, kayaks and canoes tethered to its side. The family knew you could rent paddles from the office if you chose to do so. Since they were fortunate enough to reside in a home on the lake, they chose not to spend money on such an excursion.

Hannah ran down the length of the dock, with Annie calling behind, "Don't run, Hannah! You'll trip and fall into the water, for goodness' sakes!"

Hannah threw her small right hand in the air, her back still facing her parents as if to say, "I've got this, Ma," but she did halt her running steps and smartly chose to walk instead.

Ben followed in his sister's footsteps as Annie held back to take in the view, the ocean water before her, though it was more a bay than the ocean itself, water nestled between the surrounding hills and forestry.

While Annie's gaze was set upon the beauty of her natural surroundings, Sam's gaze was on his wife, on the orange glow the setting sun projected on her hair, on her crossed arms and the fingers that were gently touching her lips. On the smooth, pale skin of her cheek in profile.

He didn't believe he'd ever stop loving this woman.

"Holy crap!" Ben shouted. "Mom, Dad, come look at this. So cool!"

Ben and Annie rushed to their son's side, Hannah peering from behind. In the water swam three jellyfish.

"Oh, my gosh!" Annie exclaimed. "Do you know I have never, ever seen a jellyfish in the wild? Only at the aquarium over in Boston when I was a kid and when we took you two there last year. This is so neat!"

Hannah leaned over, and Annie quickly grabbed onto the back of her sweatshirt and pulled. "Easy, Hannah," she said. "You don't know how to swim well." She laughed.

"Oh, but how neat are they?" Annie kept her hold on her daughter's sweatshirt as she bent her knees further so her bottom rested on her heels. "Sam, do you see these things? Look at how they just float in the water like little blobs. Amazing."

"They are," Sam agreed, but he was still looking at his wife, enjoying her gleeful reaction.

Ben lost interest after a few glances and decided instead to walk the dock.

The family explored a bit longer, then headed back in the direction of their campsite, stopping off at the bathroom across the way from their site. By the time they returned, the sun had almost fully set, it had chilled considerably, and the mosquitos had come out in swarms to feed.

Sam ignited another fire in the pit, and the foursome roasted marsh-mallows on sticks they found in the small portion of woods between their site and their neighbors'.

With the warm, gooey marshmallows settling in satiated stomachs, the family set off to the bathrooms once again. Annie and Hannah headed to the women's side, Sam and Ben to the men's.

"I hope you're having a good time," Sam said to his son as he unzipped his green toiletry case.

"Yeah," Ben replied.

"'Yeah'? That doesn't seem entirely too convincing." Sam chuckled and squirted a small amount of paste onto his toothbrush.

"I don't think camping will be my thing," Ben said. "And I don't like to hike like you and Mom do."

"I know it's not something you enjoy as much as your mom and me," Sam said. "But I really do think we'll have a great vacation. We'll hike tomorrow, but it's not a hard hike at all, and it looks like the views will be great. Again, I get it's not your thing. But we'll spend an entire day in Bar Harbor and I know you'll like that. You like going from shop to shop, especially if it's a trinkety sort of store, right? And ice cream. And I bet there's a candy store somewhere there, too. And who knows? Maybe there'll be a soccer store." Sam lifted his eyebrows and smirked foolishly as he placed his toothbrush in his mouth.

Ben couldn't help but smile himself.

Sam and Ben finished in the bathrooms first and met Annie and Hannah back at the campsite, where they all climbed into the tent.

"Why do I have to go to bed now? It's so early. And I'm older than Hannah," Ben frowned.

"You sure are," Annie agreed. "But it's vacation and it's already past your bedtime, young man." She touched her fingertip to Ben's nose in jest.

"*I love you,*" Annie said to her son. She tucked him tightly underneath his sleeping bag that rested on top of a camping cot. She brought her lips to his cheek and held them there, lingering, and pressed harder to kiss him. "*Mmmwwaaa!*" she said animatedly as she retreated.

"*Yuck, Mom. I'm too old for those kisses.*"

"*What!*" Annie feigned surprise. "*You're never too old for your mother's kisses!*" She held his arms down firmly inside his sleeping bag and kissed his cheek quickly, moved to the other cheek and kissed that. She didn't let up when Ben laughed and writhed beneath her, but continued to kiss him fervently until even she was laughing hysterically.

Ben extricated an arm from his sleeping bag and wiped off his cheeks, looking directly into his mother's eyes as he did so with a smirk on his face.

"*You little—*" Annie held him down once more, kissed him several times on both cheeks, his nose, his forehead.

"*I love you, Ben,*" Annie said.

"*Okay.*"

"*Okay?*"

"*Yeah, I love you, too,*" Ben replied begrudgingly.

Sam leaned over his son when Annie turned to Hannah. "*Love you, buddy,*" he said.

Ben nodded.

"*You sleep well, I hope. Big day tomorrow. Try to have fun, okay? Your mother has really been looking forward to this vacation and most especially to spending time with you kids. We're not able to take vacations often, so this is a really special time. She wants to remember these days when we're old and gray. Let's make the most of it while we can. Before your mother and I know it, you'll be eighteen and headed to college!*"

Ben smiled. He couldn't think that far in advance, but he liked the look in his dad's green eyes, the smile on his lips.

"*Making memories here, kiddo,*" Sam said. "*Let's make some good ones.*"

"*'Kay,*" Ben said.

"*Okay,*" Sam agreed with a nod of his head. "*Love you, bud.*"

"*Love you, too.*"

"*Good night.*"

"*Night.*"

Sam said good night to Hannah, then followed Annie out to the dwindling fire. They sat. No conversation was had. They just looked at the orange flames, listened to the crackling of the embers. After a time, Sam placed one last log into the pit, sat back down, and reached for his wife's hand.

Sam continued to gaze into the hot flames, watched as the logs sparked, the smoke wafted into the cool night air. After a time he turned to his wife.

"*I love you so much, Annie.*"

Annie turned to him, smiled genuinely. "*Where did that come from?*" *she asked.*

Sam shrugged his shoulders. "*I don't know. I just love you.*"

Annie chuckled. "*Well,*" *she said,* "*I love you, too.*"

Sam squeezed her hand, then gently let it go to bring his palm to rest on the side of his camping chair, his gaze trained back on the burning fire before him soaring higher into the sky.

CHAPTER TWENTY

Ben

*H*e was done.

Ben hit the submit button for his college application to UNH. He had written several essays to various colleges and universities as one of the components of the application process, but this was the one he was most proud of. Last year he had dicked around with his studies; had been doing so for several years now, if he was being honest with himself. He hadn't the motivation, the drive to care about an uncertain future, a future in which his mother wouldn't be by his side.

This past summer, the summer before his senior year, Ben's personal epiphany suddenly emerged. It was the summer of self-realization, of letting go, of acceptance. And it was the summer, too, of beginning to give a shit about a future he recognized he wanted to embrace wholeheartedly.

He pushed the chair out from under his computer desk in his bedroom and stood. He stretched and then looked out of the window at his sister making a snowman with her friend Grace. Even at thirteen, Hannah still enjoyed doing such things. Ben thought it was childish, silly, though he could admit to himself that he also found it an endearing trait, one that he had learned to appreciate in Hannah.

Ben walked downstairs and found his father and grandmother at the kitchen table, both cradling mugs of coffee in their hands.

"Hey, there," his dad said. "What were you up to?"

"Finished my essay," Ben said, a proud grin on his face.

"Ah, no way!" Sam said, delight evident on his face. "Way to go!"

"Honey, that's really wonderful," his grandmother chimed in.

"Thanks, Gram."

"So?" his dad said, placing his mug on the table.

"So, what?" Ben asked.

"So, can I have a look?"

"Yeah, I guess so," Ben said. He knew some of the thoughts portrayed in this essay were private, some he had never shared with another soul.

"I see a hesitation," his father said. "It's your essay, Ben. You know you don't have to share it if you don't want to."

"Yeah," Ben said. "I know." He paused, then said, "But I want you to read it." He looked his father directly in the eye. "And you, too, Gram," he said as he turned toward Caroline. "Dad, you said I should find my voice, and that's what I've done. No fancy words, no fancy writing. But it's me in there."

Sam understood how large this offering was from his son. "I'd love to read it right now," he said. "How about I make you some hot chocolate before I head to your room? You're never too old for hot chocolate, you know. Especially with whipped cream and sprinkles."

Ben laughed. It had been a while since he'd had hot chocolate with whipped cream and sprinkles. "Nah," he said. "I'm good. I'm gonna head to Tyler's, though, if that's okay and you don't need the car?"

"Perfectly okay," his father said. "I'm surprised that you were working on your essay during Christmas break. Go out and have some fun! Text me when you're on your way home, though."

"You sound like Mom." Ben smiled.

"I take that as a compliment," his father replied with a large grin.

Ben said goodbye to his father and grandmother, took the car keys from the kitchen counter, and put his coat on. He turned back and waved before heading down the hallway to the garage door.

When Sam heard the door close, he abruptly stood from the table. "I've got to read this," he told Caroline. "I'll be back."

"Of course," his mother-in-law said before taking another sip of her coffee. "I'd love to read it after you."

"Yes," Sam said. "I'll be back." He directed himself with hastened steps to the stairs and eagerly climbed. Ben's laptop was still on, and Sam could discern from the doorway that the essay was illuminated on the small screen. He sat on Ben's chair and began to read.

Benjamin Carson
Application Essay

In reply to your question of which person I would want to spend a day with, either deceased or living, and why, I had no need to ponder.

My answer: my mother.

Yeah, I imagine you're now wondering: What do you mean? Does he not know his own mother?

We need to back up here. I knew my mother.

I know her still.

JoAnna (Annie) Catherine Bailey, my mom, was born in

August of 1979. I'm led to believe she lived a happy childhood in southern NH and had quite the spunk for life when she met Samuel Joseph Carson in college. Regrettably condensing this childhood and courtship for the purposes of this essay, Annie and Sam married in the summer of 2002. Then I was born, followed by my sister as many typical lives fold out through the years.

One of my earliest memories of my mother is her taking me and my baby sister to the beach. I remember the feeling of the sand scratching my skin when she applied sunscreen lotion. I remember eating ice cream. And I remember her smile, can even hear her laugh now if I close my eyes.

I remember her holding the back of my bike when my father had taken my training wheels off. I couldn't tell you how old I was, but I can tell you how I felt when she let go and I didn't fall. When I continued to pump those pedals and could hear her cheering me on from behind. I remember the hug she gave me as she ran to my side after I lost balance and caught myself before falling to the ground. And that smile of hers. Big and genuine. And those eyes. Large and brown.

I remember her singing Wiggles songs to me in our minivan when I was young, maybe five or six. She'd hold the steering wheel with one hand while mimicking the songs' motions with the other and occasionally turning around to look at me in my booster seat, my sister in her car seat beside me. She'd have that smile, and I wonder even now if she sang those songs to me to keep me awake and entertained like she always claimed she did or if she just enjoyed the silliness of acting like a kid herself and this gave her a good excuse because . . . well . . . why not, right?

I remember her on the sidelines of my soccer games. Every single one. I'm honestly not sure she missed a game. She'd always greet me afterward, win or lose, with a huge smile and ask me if I had a good time. And she'd always, always say she loved watching me play. I never doubted her.

I remember my tenth birthday party. We played laser tag and she made my cake. There must have been eight or nine other boys there that day, all geared up and ready to shoot. My grandmother was watching my sister in the arcade portion of this particular venue while we played. My dad was geared up. This I expected. And there was my mom. Hefty bundle on her narrow shoulders, a huge grin on her face. And would you know that when the scores were presented after the game, my mother came out on top? All my friends were surprised at how involved she was, marveled over the fact that my mother actually wanted to play. I wasn't surprised at all. But I was proud.

There's a reason as a society we say the phrase "the sparkle in her eye." My mother had that sparkle. Her eyes would dance. You could just look right into them and see into her soul, see how happy she was, how much she appreciated and loved the life she was given.

She had that sparkle.

Until . . . well, until she didn't.

The first symptoms were seen when I was about thirteen. Just little things here and there. She'd forget the date, or she'd forget to put sugar in her coffee and would spit it out in the sink. Her personality began to change. That smile would waver, and she'd pull a Mr. Hyde (yes, I know of the characters Dr. Jekyll and Mr. Hyde thanks to my mom, who had an insatiable appetite for reading when I was younger even when I did not).

Mom began to act childlike on the soccer sidelines at my games. She'd dance, goof off. She'd yell "Go, Benny Boo!" as if I were a toddler still.

She embarrassed me.

Slowly she stopped telling me she loved me. She stopped hugging me, stopped giving me the kisses on my cheek that I so detested as a young teenager.

Only when that affection ceased did I realize I needed it, needed her.

Depression. That's what her doctor said.

Bipolar?

Hormones?

Midlife crisis?

They put her on antidepressants that didn't help. She continued to decline.

She claimed nothing was wrong with her. But I saw it. One day happy and acting like a kid, the other day mopey with outbursts of anger and inappropriate comments and behavior.

I saw it. The mother I had known, had taken for granted, was slipping away.

Eventually, after lots of struggle, after losing her job, after losing the ability to drive safely, after she'd wander around the neighborhood without telling us where she was going, my father and grandmother took her to see a neurologist in Boston who finally gave her a true diagnosis.

Frontotemporal degeneration.

My mother had dementia and she'd only get worse.

My grandmother moved in with us to help care for me and my sister so my father didn't lose his job. She cared for my mother during the day and took me and my sister to our after-school activities. I honestly think she saved us as a family in a way.

I watched my mother slip day by day. Her motor abilities worsened, and she'd bump into furniture and need help ascending and descending the stairs in our home. She never hugged me, never told me she loved me.

Her eyes would never sparkle again.

Eventually, my mother was admitted to an assisted living facility where she continued to lose herself. I didn't know how to handle these changes, so I made the choice not to see her. I couldn't watch her look at me as I'd enter the room with a blank expression on her face. I couldn't watch as my father would spoon-feed her.

I couldn't watch as she lost the ability to chew and swallow entirely.

I regret that choice every day.

See, even though she wasn't the mother I remembered, she was still my mother. She may not have known who I was at the end, but I knew her. She may not have held any of the memories she was so adamant and wholeheartedly orchestrating for her family, but I remembered them. She did, after all, do these things for me, for my sister. This is something I know now.

My father, though, my father was with her to the end. My father held her head in his lap as she breathed her last breath. My father, who was suffering immensely, never gave up on her.

My mother, JoAnna (Annie) Catherine Bailey, passed on June 22nd of this year. It was only after her passing that I was able to begin to grieve, and, in grieving, begin to heal.

I'm still angry. I'm still confused. I'm still wracked with guilt. And through it all, I miss my mom every single day.

So who would I want to spend a day with?

My mother.

Even for one moment in a day, I'd like to see my mother. I'd like to feel her cheek against mine. I'd like to hear her tell me she loves me. I'd like to hear her laugh.

I'd like the little things back. The little things we take for granted every day.

And I'd like to see the sparkle of life in her big, beautiful brown eyes.

CHAPTER TWENTY-ONE

Sam and Caroline

*S*am, grayer and more wrinkled now in his mid-fifties, turned in his white chair beneath the large erected wedding tent under the stars of a warm summer's evening. The band had announced it was time for his son to dance his first dance with his new wife, a lovely woman by the name of Paige.

Annie would have loved her.

An elderly Caroline sat beside him at the table, dashing with her short white hair curled, and wearing an ankle-length blue dress that complemented her pale skin. Hannah sat beside her grandmother, Hannah who had just received her bachelor's degree and had developed into a woman who reminded him every day of her mother.

Sam watched his son lead his new wife to the wooden dance floor that rested on top of the grass in between the circle of tables.

Ben had met his wife at UNH, where he played soccer under a partial scholarship and began his studies in the field of neurology. He still had schooling to complete. Sam was amazed daily at the transformation he'd seen. Ben, the confused and hurt teenager, morphing into Ben, the studious, driven, loving man.

He twirled Paige in her sleek, white dress. Their smiles were enormous, carefree, delighted. Ben grasped his wife's waist, and the band began to play. Sam recognized the melody instantaneously. He had played it every year on his wedding anniversary with Annie, even after she had passed.

Ben Folds's "*The Luckiest.*"

The tears pooled. They couldn't be helped or hindered. Nor did he want them to be.

Ben turned his head, his gaze finding his father's eyes.

He nodded.

Sam nodded back, the tears falling freely.

"Thank you," he mouthed to his son.

Ben smiled and turned back to his wife, smiled at her.

Sam swiveled to look at Caroline and Hannah. Both were weeping.

Sam then turned toward a small table that had been erected by his side. A framed picture of his wife rested on the white linen draping. Nothing more. Just his wife, her face smooth and pale, her blond hair cut into the bob he had known so well.

He remembered this photo, remembered the day he had taken it. Hannah was just a small baby at the time, Ben just a little boy. They had headed outside to dip in the lake, and Annie had grabbed the camera. She left it on the small table resting between two Adirondack chairs on the beach in their backyard. Sam had snatched it up, walked toward his wife, and called her name. He was close to her now. She turned. He framed her face in the viewfinder, near, intimate. She had turned her head, a ginormous smile on her face as she did so. And that's when he clicked the shutter.

It was that smile he'd never forget. Never. It was her appreciation for the everyday he'd never forget and had attempted to emulate through the passing years. He knew she was happy as she looked down upon her family now. Knew she was content with the lives they had led.

And through it all, even after all these years, all he had to do was close his eyes to see her smile, hear her laugh, and see the look of pure and unadulterated love in her eyes.

The wedding was through. Ben and Paige had gone home. Hannah, too. Caroline still lived with Sam in the lake house he and Annie had bought together so many years ago. They were alone now, but happy together.

It was late. Much later than Caroline typically stayed up at night. But she wasn't tired. Not tonight.

She sat in an Adirondack chair, her bare feet burrowing into the sand. They were cold, but she didn't mind.

She wrapped her jacket tighter over her torso, crossed her thin, weathered arms over her sagging chest, and looked at the moon's reflection on the surface of the water.

Still, calm, comforting.

An owl hooted in the distance, and footsteps sounded their slow advance toward her.

Sam sat down in the unoccupied chair.

"What a night," he sighed.

"Yes, it was a wonderful night," she agreed.

They sat in companionable silence for a time until Sam turned to his mother-in-law once more.

"Caroline?"

"Hmm?"

"Annie was there with us tonight," Sam said wistfully.

Caroline turned to look at him. "She sure was, Sam," she said. "She sure was."

She extended her wrinkly hand to the side, and Sam

gently squeezed her palm, feeling her soft, smooth skin, the pronounced veins.

Together they sat, enjoyed the coolness of the night.

And under the starlit sky with a full moon illuminating the still waters of the lake, Annie enveloped them, embraced them.

Not even the owl perched on a nearby tree could miss their contented, tranquil expressions as two people who had lived through love and heartache, who had survived and persevered, held hands through the early-morning hours of a dawning summer's day.

THANK YOU

With millions of books to choose from, I am humbled by the fact that you have chosen *Little Things* to read. I hope that the story of Annie, Sam, Caroline and Ben has touched you in even the smallest way. If it has done so then I have succeeded as a writer.

Please consider leaving a review of *Little Things* on Amazon (https://www.amazon.com/review/create-review/?ie=UTF8&channel=glance-detail&asin=1734244518) and/or Goodreads. Ratings and reviews help get *Little Things* in the hands of new readers and are immensely appreciated.

Thank you!

AUTHOR'S NOTE

I've yearned for a while now to write a story about dementia in a woman my age—that is, a woman in her forties. I am incredibly close to my mother, and having dealt with Alzheimer's in my family, and seen friends struggle with dementia within their own families as well, it's heartbreaking. Alzheimer's, especially in the elderly population, isn't uncommon, sadly. Yet dementia in the younger population carries so many different struggles—in addition to the heartache inspired by an elderly loved one's diagnosis and decline—that we may simply not even think about: struggles involving finances, possible contemplations of divorce due to the changing nature of the marital relationship (specifically before diagnosis, when one isn't aware of the reason for the loved one's behavioral changes), running of the household, young children. The hardships one must overcome have to seem insurmountable at times.

Initially I thought I'd write a tale of a woman struggling with early-onset Alzheimer's, but in my research, I came upon frontotemporal degeneration, and I just knew. I knew without a doubt in my mind that this was the diagnosis my character, my Annie, would have.

I placed myself in Annie's position while writing, which induced a plethora of emotions as I typed. I thought of my mother and how this diagnosis would affect her. I thought of my incredibly supportive husband and how it would affect him—not only emotionally but financially. And I thought of my three boys, who are used to a mother who showers them with affection. How would they react, how would it affect them, if I came across (especially before diagnosis) as just simply not caring for them any longer? And then I thought of myself if it was my husband who was diagnosed with FTD. How could I possibly live this life without him? How could our boys be expected to come of age without their father? My family isn't currently in this predicament, and yet my heart aches.

I knew then that I didn't want to write about Annie's personal experience, but the experiences of those who love her the most, those she leaves behind.

Thus was born *Little Things*.

I extend my heart to those individuals who are living day by day with a loved one with FTD. This is an agonizing diagnosis. I can only hope my tale of Annie, Sam, Caroline, and Ben has done your struggles justice.

For those that would like to learn more about FTD, I found the following sites integral in my research.

Alzheimer's Association (alz.org)

Penn Frontotemporal Degeneration Center (ftd.med.upenn.edu)

Association for Frontotemporal Degeneration (theaftd.org)

Family Caregiver Alliance (caregiver.org)

"Frontotemporal Dementia: Devastating, Prevalent, and Little Understood," reported by Bill Whitaker, *60 Minutes*, CBS News, February 2, 2020 (cbsnews.com/news/frontotemporal-dementia-devastating-prevalent-and-little-understood-60-minutes-2020-02-02)

On YouTube:

"Frontotemporal Dementia," Mayo Clinic (youtu.be/EHSdNjhkvE8)

"Frontotemporal Dementia," MassGeneralHospital (youtu.be/7l4f9nGvmF4)

"Frontotemporal Dementia (FTD) from a Caregiver," Alzheimer's Support Network (four-part series; Part 1 at youtu.be/wxCBNPq0k_0)

"It Is What It Is - Frontotemporal Degeneration: Tragic Loss, Abiding Hope," TheAFTD (youtu.be/drgzhKe_YWI)

"Prime of Life: A Family's Story (FTD)," CurePSP (youtu.be/14bWXgIvshc)

"FTD - Planning for Hope: Living with Frontotemporal Disease, a 1-hr Documentary Film," FTDPlanningFor-Hope.com (youtu.be/_frvVBgRHYI)

ACKNOWLEDGMENTS

The writing of a book is quite the process, and *Little Things* was no exception. The finished product you hold in your hands now came to fruition because of the time and efforts of many individuals, and words just seem inadequate in portraying my heartfelt thanks to those who aided me through this journey. Yet, I'll try.

First, and foremost, I thank my husband. He is not a reader. This is not a passion we share, and yet I feel his love for me each and every day. His support through the writing of *Little Things* never wavered, and for this I am truly thankful.

Huge thanks to my mother. She is one of my biggest cheerleaders, from offering verbal support, to reading my unfinished manuscripts. I love you!

Lila Wall and Heather Elmer, thanks again for being beta readers. A novel is always more polished when a writer can accept constructive criticism.

My thanks to my book cover designer, Danna Mathias. You've done it again! Your artistic expertise is immensely appreciated. The cover of *Little Things* is perfect!

Mary Beth Constant is my copy editor. Mary Beth, thank you! *Little Things* would not be the book it is without you. You never cease to amaze me.

I can never launch a book without thanking my boys. This book was especially difficult for me to write when I was thinking of them and how a disease such as Annie's would affect our family. Boys, I love you all so very much. I hope all the times you saw me writing, all the love and enthusiasm I've placed into this novel, will help you chase your own dreams, whatever they may be.

And finally, to my readers. I thank you for your support. I hope *Little Things* will touch your heart.

ABOUT THE AUTHOR

An author of both adult and children's fiction, Amy Fillion graduated from the University of New Hampshire with a degree in psychology. She worked in the field of early intervention before making the decision to leave and stay home with her growing children. Amy has an insatiable appetite for reading, and you can easily find her juggling between three books at any given time (paperback, ebook, audiobook.) When she's not reading or writing, she loves to walk and cycle outdoors. She lives in New Hampshire with her husband, three boys, one rescue dog (best office companion ever!), and three crazy rescue cats.

Never miss a book release or important news! Sign up here to stay informed and get a free copy of Amy's short story *Hold On* : http://eepurl.com/gPCU1X

ALSO BY AMY FILLION

Adult Novels

Grace and Ally

Secrets of Spaulding Lane: Nancy

Secrets of Spaulding Lane: Marni

Secrets of Spaulding Lane: Rose

Broken and Breaking Free

Children's Books

Fairville: Room of Reveries Book 1

FenneGig: Room of Reveries Book 2

Esmerelda and the Courageous Knight: Room of Reveries Book 3

Wonderwell: Room of Reveries Book 4

SkyTopia: Room of Reveries Book 5

The Ancient Curse: Room of Reveries Book 6

A Magical Farewell: Room of Reveries Book 7

Made in United States
North Haven, CT
15 August 2024

56092942R00178